Bound by Shadows

Mafia's Children, Volume 3

Amara Holt

Published by Amara Holt, 2024.

Copyright © 2024 by Amara Holt

All rights reserved.

No part of this book may be reproduced, distributed, or transmitted in any form or by any means, including photocopying, recording, or other electronic or mechanical methods, without the prior written permission of the author, except in the case of brief quotations in book reviews.

This is a work of fiction. Names, characters, places, and incidents are the product of the author's imagination or are used fictitiously. Any resemblance to actual events, organizations, locales, or persons, living or dead is coincidental and is not intended by the authors.

PROLOGUE

Valentino

I stopped in front of my father's office, staring at the dark mahogany door, slipping my hand into my pants pocket, pressing it discreetly so no one would see my brief tremor. I couldn't show vulnerability; I had to project an image of unbreakability. I was being trained for this, and I failed, miserably. That's why I was here. For that reason, Don called me—or should I call him Dad?

A long sigh escaped my lips as I withdrew my hand from my pocket and knocked on the door, trying to ignore the bloodstain under the folds of my fingers.

"Come in," the Don's deep voice approved my entrance.

I turned the doorknob, stepping inside one step at a time, determined, knowing I deserved the reprimand I was about to receive. I was the one at fault; I had put my men's lives in danger by leading them into that ambush. It was all my fault. *I needed to be the best.*

"Sit down, Valentino." Dad, who had his hands resting on his desk, kept his eyes fixed on my actions.

He gestured to the chair in front of his desk, maintaining that judging expression over my presence as if he were choosing the words for his successor.

I gripped the back of the chair, pulling it subtly back, and sat down, placing my hands on my knees, leaning slightly forward, and looking at my father, waiting for the reprimand.

"What happened to your hand?" he asked before starting the lecture.

"Nothing." I made a brief motion with my head.

"What were you punching?" he asked again, unable to hide anything from the man who knew all my flaws.

"I failed. I deserved this pain. I deserve worse pain." Dad shifted his gaze from my hand to me.

"You know that no one is perfect; we all have our faults..."

"No! I don't want you to pat me on the back. I made a mistake, Dad. I put five men, with wives, children, a *famiglia* to feed and care for, into that warehouse, into an ambush. There was a damn little shit of a cop there. Even though I killed him, it could have been our men in jail. How did I not foresee that it was packed with cops?" I ran my hand through my hair, irritated by my reckless actions.

"Valentino, anyone would have gone in there. I would have gone in myself. You did what I would have done. You handled the situation, kept your cool, ordered your men into action, and they all shot. You're 20 years old and one of the best we have here. Even though the mission was a failure in your eyes, even though we gained nothing from it, you brought your five men back alive. And you know what? I just got a call from the governor saying that, in his eyes, the mission was a success." He shrugged.

"What do you mean? I thought we had failed," I was confused at that moment.

"Son, it was a test for you too." Tommaso tilted his face to the side, looking for my reaction. "That cop was trying to hunt our *famiglia*, and you know we have the governor on our side. Just as the cop was investigating the governor secretly, it was ordered that we kill the cop. Governor Adelmo requested that I take out Luiz, and that's exactly what you did."

"And why didn't I know about any of this?" I asked, bewildered by the confusion.

"Simple. I wanted to see your reaction to federal agents. And as I predicted, you were the best, maintaining a calm that I wouldn't even have. You need to stop being so hard on yourself, son." Dad removed his hands from the desk.

Damn, so this was another one of his tests? How did I not realize it? At first, I used to get frustrated with the tests Don gave me, without even warning me. He put me through endless trials, but it had been over a year since the last one. I thought they were over, but another one came, and in his eyes, I was perfect.

"I thought your tests were over," I said.

"Yes, they were. But this opportunity came up, and I wanted to put you there. I wanted to see how my son would react to a real ambush," he said with such calmness.

"But what if I really had failed? There was no Plan B, no other men to rescue us."

"I trusted you. I knew my son would find a way. I just didn't expect him to handle the situation with such calm. I don't even have that. I'm known for being impulsive, and you handle everything. You were clearly born for this." I didn't show any smile, even though Tommaso's eyes were shining in my direction.

I should have been proud, but it only made me push myself harder. No one knew the hell my thoughts were, the way I mutilated myself when I felt like a failure. I needed to be the best, and when I made a mistake, the right thing was to be punished for it, to learn from my pain and not repeat it.

Sometimes I found myself looking at my twin brother. Santino was always so relaxed, always looked at everything around him with extreme calmness, even though he inherited Dad's impulsive nature, San didn't have the burden of carrying a clan like ours on his shoulders.

In many moments, I envied him for that. It was as if someone was always watching me, studying me, or even waiting for my failure.

But I needed to be perfect. I was perfect, even if it meant feeling suffocated, anxious, and extremely pressured.

Tommaso stood up from his chair and made a gesture with his hand for me to do the same and rise from mine.

"Come here, Valentino." I moved toward him as Dad pushed his chair back. "Sit down!"

He ordered me to sit in his chair, and I did, feeling the softness of the leather seat, looking at the mahogany desk, his glass of whiskey next to it, as if I could sense the moment I would be in that position.

"Do you see all this? Do you feel what it's like to sit in the Don's chair?" I could feel my father's breath near my face, knowing he was tormenting me with the responsibility I held.

"Yes, I do," I whispered.

"All this, Valentino Vacchiano, will one day be yours, and I know you'll be the best Don the Cosa Nostra has ever had," he declared in a normal voice, walking in front of his desk.

Looking at me with pride, knowing that I was his perfect offspring, and confident that I would always do my best for our *famiglia*.

I closed my eyes, clenching my fist, feeling the pain in the folds of my fingers, knowing that this was what I wanted—to be the ruthless Don of the Cosa Nostra, cold, calculating, acting only with my mind. My heart would be reserved only for my family, except for one person, *her*, the girl who would be my wife. She would never have anything of me, would never possess my heart. A woman could be the ruin of a man.

Even though I had chosen to be the Don, knowing that Yulia Aragón would be my wife according to the agreement with the Colombian Cartel, I would feel nothing for that *Colombian girl*.

CHAPTER ONE

Yulia

4 years later...

I let out a long sigh as I looked at the pile of open books on my bed, cursing Professor Derek from Anthropology again for assigning so much work for a single weekend.

I heard the door to my room open and saw Billie come in with a cup of hot chocolate. I wet my lips, as it looked really good, steam rising from the cup indicating it was hot.

"A cup of hot chocolate, since that's all we can have today." She shrugged her shoulders, coming over to me and placing the cup on the bedside table.

"Have I mentioned how much I hate the professor today?" I grumbled, twirling the pen in my hand.

"Not yet today, but feel free to vent. I'm listening." Billie said with a teasing tone, sitting at the foot of my bed.

We shared a room in the Zeta sorority, took the same courses, and shared everything with each other—our crazy, completely dysfunctional families, or ridiculous habits.

We were like two peas in a pod, inseparable.

The best person Stanford had brought me.

"Not to discourage you, but from the lights, it looks like there's a party at Theta. It seems pretty lively..." Billie bit her lip suggestively. "A little getaway might not hurt, right?"

"We're here all Saturday, it's not like we're missing much." I grimaced, knowing how much I loved weekend parties.

"Sunday is a new day, isn't it?" Billie hopped off the bed.

"But I haven't even had my hot chocolate yet." I pouted, getting off my bed and leaving everything as it was, including the scattered books.

"Girl, I made it, it's probably terrible. Come on, let's have some tequila instead. It'll be better than this chocolate." Billie jumped, struggling to get out of her pajamas.

I looked at my cup, that steaming liquid, or a night out as usual, coming back to the sorority house so crazy that I didn't even remember how I ended up in my room.

The second option was always the wiser one. After all, there were two more years of freedom left, so I needed to enjoy every second of it.

Yes, I was counting down the days until the end of my freedom, the day I would join the Sicilian Mafia Don, a stupid deal my brother made and dragged me into.

I took off my sweatpants and my light jacket.

"Wear these pants." Billie threw a pair of black leather pants at me, and I caught them before they hit the ground.

"Great choice." I smiled as I put on the pants.

I had to do a little shimmy to get the pants over my hips. I used to share clothes with Billie, the only difference being that her clothes were always a bit tighter on my hips because I had a bit more curves.

"This crop top will make your boobs look great." She tossed me another piece of fabric.

"Big boobs, I love it," I teased, taking off my bra, knowing that the top was meant to be worn without one.

My stomach was exposed, the piercing in my navel shining on a delicate chain.

A girl in college needed to do a few things, and I had my list.

Among them, getting a piercing, *I had one in my navel*, getting a tattoo, *I had a blue butterfly just above my butt*, and of course, having sex, something I didn't realize would be so difficult, as if something was blocking me.

I was even seeing the campus therapist. There was a block, I couldn't be touched, not in the way a man and a woman should touch each other. I even considered that I might be a lesbian, but I couldn't even look at a woman with desire.

I knew something was wrong. My therapist suggested talking to my brother or a family member, but how could they help me?

How was I supposed to bring up the subject? *"Hey, bro, do you know why I can't have sex?"* Of course, Ferney would think I was throwing myself at every guy in college.

But it was this damn block, my body judging me, making me feel dirty, and it wasn't because of my idiotic fiancé. At the boarding school where I studied, a guy kissed me, and when his hand became inappropriate, moving down to my butt, I went into alert mode.

My body would tense up, I'd start sweating, panic would overtake me, as if they were violating something that was solely mine, my body, and no one could touch it!

It was always the same reaction, not to mention when I'd start screaming as if walls were closing in on me.

Billie dressed in a denim skirt and a leather bikini top. I put on my black heels along with my outfit, letting my long hair hang loose, and stood in front of the vanity, doing a quick makeup job. After all, we were eager to go wild that night.

"Am I approved?" Billie asked as she stood up from her vanity. I glanced at her reflection in my mirror—her legs on display, the short denim skirt, and high boots making her tall, just like me. Two short girls who needed heels.

"Clean enough that your mom would never approve of that outfit," I teased, knowing her mother would never accept that clothing.

"At this moment, I'm feeling like a cat," Billie said, tossing her light brown hair back and winking her green eyes.

"Shall we, my diva?" I stood up from my stool, rubbing one lip against the other to spread my lip gloss.

"Hopefully, Connor will be there for you to get some action." Billie rolled her eyes, knowing I had been stringing poor Connor along.

It wasn't my fault. I had told him to move on several times. After all, there were beautiful girls at college, and I was more like a defective toy; we couldn't move beyond kissing.

All I wanted was to lose my virginity before my wedding, but time was passing, and I was still a virgin. I hadn't even seen a cock up close.

Damn, Valentino Vacchiano couldn't have what he always wanted from me. I couldn't marry pure to that scoundrel, who by now must have slept with the whole of Sicily.

I took my friend's hand, and we left our room, just nudging the door closed. After all, we trusted each other there; there was no chance of anyone entering my room.

CHAPTER TWO

Valentino

I parked the motorcycle in front of those sororities, taking off my helmet and looking around, observing the party happening in one of the houses whose name I couldn't distinguish. I was just wondering if my fiancée would be there.

But I knew she lived in Zeta. I discovered this through her social media, of course, through a fake profile. That little Colombian blocked me on Instagram when I forced her to delete all the photos revealing her curves. Damn it! She was the future wife of the Don of the Cosa Nostra. She should at least post some more decent photos. Yulia was 17 when she blocked me; she must be 20 by now.

I knew she continued to post bikini photos; I saw each one on my phone, wondering how I'd exact my revenge when I had her in my arms. The Colombian thought she could outsmart me, little did she know that I had been watching her every move.

Damn the girl chosen to be my wife.

I dismounted the bike, feeling the jeans tight against my groin as the fabric rode up. I removed my leather jacket, leaving it on the bike.

This bike wasn't mine; I rented it when I came to California, taking advantage of being in the United States and stopping in New York to visit my cousins who had settled there. Of course, I couldn't ride a bike all the way, so I rented this one to feel the wind on my face and clear my thoughts.

I walked toward the quiet sorority house where my fiancée lived, cursing the damn *Stories* that made me come after Yulia. A photo of a man with his hand on her waist, looking too intimate, made me speculate on millions of theories about someone else taking the damn virginity that was supposed to be mine!

I stopped in front of the door. The house was white, as was the door. I rang the bell, looking down at my combat boots and then lifting my eyes as the door opened, revealing a girl with blonde hair in a messy bun and glasses as large as her face.

"Where's Yulia?" My approach must have startled the useless girl, making her take a step back.

"Wh... who's asking?" she stammered, her voice trembling.

"Her fiancé. Where is she? Call her now." I looked over her shoulder, noting that the place seemed to be outdoors.

"Y... Yulia doesn't have a boyfriend..."

"Damn it, girl, tell me where the hell Yulia is." I was almost pushing her aside, my patience with scared little girls wearing thin.

"U... she went... went to the party." She pointed to the house where the chaos was happening.

Great, just what I expected: arriving at my fiancée's college and finding out she was at a student party.

This is what happens when you show up unannounced; it's how you catch someone red-handed. I didn't even say goodbye to the girl, heading toward the ruckus, curling my lip in disgust. I hated this kind of mess; I liked everything organized, parties with decent music, not this racket, drunk women, and guys with the stench of cheap liquor.

Maybe what I preferred was something depraved, specifically the BDSM club I frequented.

Damn, was I at this hellhole out of jealousy? Out of possessiveness? For fuck's sake, just because I saw a man with his hand on my girl's waist?

I pushed through the students, avoiding the drunk ones who barely made sense, passed through the door, and felt a hand slide over my shoulder. I turned to see a blonde with her breasts popping out of her low-cut top, the sight of her shouting "fuck me" pleasing my eyes.

I was crazy for sex, a fucked-up guy who loved to fuck. Maybe sorority parties weren't so bad after all if they came with young hotties.

"Hi, cutie, new around here?" Her finger grazed my neck.

"I'm looking for someone," I declared, being direct, trying to keep my focus on my fiancée and not on those breasts.

"Can I help you?" She bit the corner of her lip.

"Yulia, Yulia Aragón," I said her name, needing to use English, a language I hadn't spoken in a long time.

"Oh, Yulia." The girl's shoulders drooped when she realized I was asking for another girl. "She's in the room with her friend and her little boyfriend..."

My growl made the blonde smirk with malice, not even flinching. But at that moment, even her breasts didn't capture my attention. All I wanted was to kill the bastard who called himself my fiancée's little boyfriend.

There might be two years until our wedding, but Yulia Aragón was the damn woman who was designated to be mine. I chose her, so she'd better keep her pussy for me.

I shoved the blonde aside, bumping into several people, and entered the room, searching for the girl I had only seen in photos on my phone. Even the damned brother hadn't introduced us, all to keep his sister from being in my presence prematurely. He knew how things worked since he practiced the same with my cousin.

The scene I witnessed next drove me mad, enraged. All I wanted to do was act like a caveman, grab Yulia by her hair, and drag her away from that wimp. To make matters worse, my fiancée's tongue was in the playboy's mouth.

Acting on instinct, I approached her. My steps made her break the kiss with the idiot, as people I had shoved let out shrieks. Yulia lifted her eyes, which had been closed seconds before as if focusing on something. She recognized me, her eyes widening as she jumped off the man's lap.

I tilted my head to the side, clenching my fists so tightly I could feel the pain my nails caused in my palms.

"Valentino, what are you doing here?" Yulia started speaking, but my damn focus was on just one thing: grabbing that bastard by the neck, squeezing hard enough to make him scared enough never to touch my girl again.

Avoiding Yulia, I leaned over the man still seated, my hand going straight to his neck, squeezing it with all my strength, seeing his eyes widen.

"Never dare to touch my fiancée again," I growled through clenched teeth. Even the music in the place stopped, everyone watching the situation.

"Valentino, you're crazy. Let him go now." I felt the small hand gripping my shirt.

"Did you understand what I said?" Ignoring the girl next to me, I continued intimidating the student.

"Y... yes," he stammered.

"Yulia Aragón is my fiancée, and I'm crazy enough to kill anyone who dares to touch her," I roared, tightening his neck even more, just to push him to the limit, smiling ruthlessly as I released him, shoving him backward and hearing his coughs.

I straightened up, looking at everyone who was watching the situation, seeming like a bunch of frightened rabbits.

"If I find out that a damn idiot touched this girl..." I pointed a finger at the terrified girl. "I'll come out of my country and come specifically to kill the bastard. Yulia Aragón has a fiancé, a fiancé crazy enough to kill anyone who touches what is his!"

I left it implied without revealing myself as the fiancé, but also making it clear that I was her fiancé. They could fuck themselves and interpret it as they wished.

Gathering all the remaining patience I had, I turned my body, circling my hand around the little Colombian's wrist, pulling her with me as I left that place.

CHAPTER THREE

Valentino

"Hey." The girl tried to pull her arm away, but I stopped her movements by pulling her with me. Her strength couldn't be compared to mine.

All the idiots around us cleared a path as we walked by, probably making them remember my face well. I wanted no fucking student near what was mine, keeping away from my fiancée.

I passed through the door and headed towards the grassy area. Yulia kept trying to pull her arm away, doing everything she could to make herself noticed, as if I wasn't seeing her there.

I turned my body when I finally found a calmer spot, still not releasing her wrist, and looked down at her face. I lowered my gaze, thinking she was wearing sneakers, only to be surprised by how short she was even in heels.

But what infuriated me the most was the damn cleavage, so loud, like those other girls', saying "fuck me." Who did she think she was to wear such a vulgar shirt?

"Who do you think you are to come to my college and cause all this commotion?" The little Colombian tried to pull her arm away for the umpteenth time.

I moved my body closer to hers, tightening my grip on her wrist, feeling the rage taking over every part of my body, as if small fragments of anger were coursing through my bloodstream, making me feel control slipping from my hands.

"Do you want me to actually say who I am? We both know you know," I growled, lowering my face toward hers.

"The agreement clearly states that we have nothing until the wedding date." The little girl raised her face, unafraid of my gaze.

Her delicate skin right in front of me, her full lips, rosy cheeks, eyes so dark I couldn't even see her pupils properly, her pale skin contrasting with her black hair. Damn, if she were less attractive, I wouldn't be so pissed off. I knew Yulia Aragón was one hot woman that any man would want to have without much fuss.

"And you know better than anyone that nothing explicitly says I can't have fun without you. So know that what you're doing is a massive breach of contract," the Colombian continued her defiance.

"I'm the one in charge, with or without a contract. In the end, it's in my arms that your life will end," I mocked, tilting my head to the side, watching her moisten her lips in her desperation.

"My life ended when my brother thought that to get what he wanted, he needed this stupid ring." Yulia raised her free hand to grip my shirt. "You won't get anything from me. Go away, get out of my life!"

I felt her nails scratching my chest. With a brief step back, I got a clearer view of her breasts—perky, well-shaped, clear teenage breasts that had never been touched. Maybe there was a possibility she was still a virgin.

"Look at my face, you idiot." I felt her fingertips brush against my beard along my chin. She saw my eyes on her breasts.

"Just assessing what will be mine completely in two years," I declared mockingly.

"If I could choose, I would never want to be yours." Yulia pulled her hand from my chin as if I had burning coals on it.

"Anyone would give their life to be my first lady..."

"My life has much more significance than serving a dumb Don like you," I growled at her words.

Yulia realized she had gone too far, making me release her wrist, holding onto her neck tightly with both hands, watching the light in her eyes fade away.

I wasn't the Don of the Cosa Nostra yet, but I knew my moment was coming, and when I returned, my father's seat would be waiting for me.

"Repeat what you said," I grunted in my anger.

"Never!" Even in her desperation, she didn't give in.

"You will repeat what I say now, and say, 'Sorry, master,'" I snarled the word *"master"* that I was always called when I was in my apartment or at the BDSM club.

"Never!" I smiled crookedly, tightening her neck even more.

If Yulia wanted to play, she needed to know I would push her to her limits, until she thought she couldn't breathe and had no choice but to apologize.

"Come on, little fiancée," I provoked, scaring her. Yulia slowly closed her eyes but didn't say the damn two words.

The air was beginning to fail her body, her delicate pupils closing completely in front of me. She wasn't going to speak. Her body becoming limp made me release her neck, acting quickly to hold her waist as she started coughing, gasping for air.

"Are you crazy, damn it?" I grunted as she coughed, pulling in air forcefully, as if filling her body with the missing air.

"Never..." Yulia slowly lifted her eyes towards me. "You will never get anything from me using aggression. Know that I'm not afraid of what you represent, Valentino Vacchiano!"

I tightened my grip on her waist a bit more, feeling how perfectly she fit into my fingers. Even though she was small, I could do whatever I wanted with that tiny body.

"So we have a big impasse. I can get everything with aggression, and nothing will make me want to do less with you." I smiled in a wicked manner.

"Get lost, Valentino. I don't want anything from you—I don't want your kisses, I don't want your touches, let alone be yours. I feel dirty every time I think I'll have to give myself to a disgusting person like you." The Colombian thought her words affected me.

Actually, they did affect me, but in a way that was negative for her, increasing my desire to have her.

"When you were sticking your tongue in that idiot's mouth, you seemed pretty happy..."

"That's because I feel nothing for you. Anyone is better than you, even a rock on the ground has more value than your presence in my life," the little one spoke firmly, making my anger grow with every moment.

"Maybe what I came here to do has already been accomplished," I whispered amid my wicked smile.

In front of all those students, I knew none of them would approach her for the next two years. Those who didn't know would be informed by those present. Yulia wouldn't be touched by anyone else.

Of course, I wanted to taste her lips, but maybe that would wait for two years. This little Colombian would still be in my arms, moaning while I fucked her hard.

"What are you talking about?" Yulia still hadn't realized the shit I had caused in her life.

"You'll find out soon enough, amore mio," I mocked, releasing her waist and gently tapping the tip of her nose with my finger.

I turned my body, knowing the scared little girl turned back to the party. At that moment, all I needed was to get out of there, grab my bike, and escape from that place—escape from the enticing sight of my fiancée, her curves, her sharp tongue, her sweet and unfiltered voice.

Damn, I wanted Yulia Aragón. Seeing her in front of me for the first time only increased my desire for her.

I stopped by my bike, reaching into my pocket for the keys when I felt a hand on my shoulder, knowing it wasn't who I wanted it to be.

"Hi, handsome, looking for some fun?" I turned my face to see about four students there.

Breasts, so many breasts, all bouncing from those low-cut tops, loose hair, perfect for grabbing with my hand.

"Let's have a private party, and we need a man like you," another said, and at that moment, maybe I wasn't thinking with my brain but with my balls.

The anger I felt from being practically rejected by my fiancée, tormenting me, wanting revenge, wanting her to know that you should never mess with a Vacchiano and think we'd stay silent.

"What exactly are we talking about?" My eyes roamed, coveting each of those bodies.

Maybe coming here had been a great idea. After all, I had never fucked any college girls before.

CHAPTER FOUR

Yulia

I spent Sunday in my room, focusing on my studies; I needed to finish that paper. After Valentino showed up at the party, he ruined my night, making me go back to my sorority and leaving Billie alone there. My friend even wanted to come with me, but I knew she had her own family issues, just like I did, so I let her stay there, drowning her sorrows over the fact that her parents had forgotten her birthday that week for another year.

Billie was the daughter of two famous Hollywood actors. Her mother constantly competed with her in terms of beauty, while her father, when he wasn't in some sensationalist news story, was looking for something to put in the spotlight. Billie abhorred the celebrity world, which was why she always stayed away from her parents.

Not that it was much of a sacrifice, as her parents only remembered they had a daughter when they wanted to present themselves as the perfect family.

Since I had slept more during the night, I let my friend sleep in the morning and finished most of our work alone. In the afternoon, she helped me get everything ready to turn in the next day.

I didn't even get the pleasure of feeling hungover; my damn fiancé even disrupted my drinking.

Luckily, I hadn't heard anything more from him, as I spent most of my time in my room.

I went down the stairs with Billie, both of us subdued in our conversation. It was Monday morning, the worst day of the week when everything started over: studies, teachers, exams, assignments...

We entered the kitchen, noticing Jenny with her giant glasses making breakfast. She was one of the few who actually made coffee here; the rest of us took advantage of the coffee she made.

"Do you girls want coffee?" she offered with her usual smile.

"Yes, I need it," Billie went over to her.

"Did that man find you?" Jenny asked, looking in my direction.

"What man?" I asked, not understanding what she was talking about.

"A tall, handsome guy, looking like a bad boy with those boots. I wondered if he came out of some movie with all that macho attitude." I noticed when the girl let out a sigh.

"Are you talking about Valentino?" I rolled my eyes, grabbing a cup to serve myself coffee from the electric pot Jenny had made.

"I don't know his name. I only know he called you his fiancée. I didn't know you had a boyfriend, let alone a fiancé." She adjusted the rim of her glasses, looking at me with curiosity.

"Yeah, it's complicated, and yes, he found me, unfortunately," I finished the sentence in a whisper.

I could still feel his hand on my neck, the way he tightened it, how he made the air leave my lungs, wanting me to say "sorry, master." He must be crazy if he thought I would ever call him master.

This was all such nonsense, it felt like that movie Fifty Shades of Grey, sometimes I even felt like I was living in the film 365 DNI, where I was marrying a mobster who seemed to be a sadist. Did I need to learn about this?

Was Valentino the type who liked to tie up women?

Damn, I couldn't even give myself to a man, let alone one who liked BDSM. Of course, these were all just theories in my crazy head, but that's what I perceived: his hand on my neck, the smile when he wanted me to call him master, as if Valentino wished for me to be his submissive.

Luckily, Billie changed the subject, leading us into a conversation about professors. Jenny was one of the nicest girls at the college, doing everything for everyone.

I finished my coffee, and Jenny decided to come with us to campus, carrying all my books. I noticed strange looks directed at me, and I smiled when I saw Connor standing by a tree. He didn't show any smile, which was expected after what that crazy Valentino had done to him.

I approached him, wanting to apologize in person since he hadn't responded to my messages.

"Connor," I called his name, trying to soften the situation.

He looked at me over his shoulder as if he were being watched.

"Is there a problem?" I looked back as well.

"Yulia," he whispered my name, yes, he whispered it in fear. "Everyone's talking about that crazy man who called himself your fiancé. Why didn't you ever tell me you had a fiancé?"

"Yeah, well, I'm sorry." At that moment, I felt very guilty, beating myself up over the shitty life I had.

"I want you to stay away from me. We're done. I don't want to risk having a body part cut off. That lunatic choked me, threatened me. I never want to go through that again." He turned away from me, and I quickly turned my face, realizing that Connor practically ran away from me.

"Friend," Billie called me, standing next to her was Beth, one of the freshmen who loved group sex. *How did I know that?* She made it a point to spread it around the whole campus.

"Tell your fiancé that he can join our orgy anytime he wants." I opened my mouth, but what was she talking about?

"What are you talking about?" Billie was the one who asked.

"Oh, you don't know yet? On Saturday, we found the lost kitten and dragged him to our lair. There were only three men, but it didn't matter to the ten girls, as that Italian took care of almost all of us alone. If he really is your fiancé, you can consider yourself a lucky woman because what an Italian hottie, and he made us all blush from how he whipped us with his belt. We even asked for his number, but he said to ask you and tell him how his night was." Beth smiled as if she expected me to pass on the number.

"Beth, she doesn't have his number, and that crazy guy isn't even her fiancé. It's all in his head," Billie defended me.

"What a shame." She pouted and walked away from us.

"I want to kill that damn Italian," I whispered through clenched teeth, feeling a never-before-felt rage take over me.

"Friend, he did this on purpose, for you to know what he did," Billie said, even more scared than I was.

"Now you still have doubts about the idiot I'm going to marry?"

We both continued walking towards our first class, still with everyone staring at me. It seemed that the topic had spread, and I had become what I feared most—a subject of gossip, with everyone watching and whispering about what had happened.

Valentino Vacchiano was going to regret ruining my last two years of freedom, even if I had to take revenge when we got married.

CHAPTER FIVE

Yulia

Two Years Later...

"I can't believe you thought I would miss the big day." Billie looked out the car window, admiring the beauty of Sicily.

"Big day? The day I'm giving my life to that damn mobster?" I grumbled.

All Valentino did was ruin my life, showing up at my college two years ago, marking me as his, participating in that orgy and labeling me as the cheated-on wife. Even though I said he wasn't my fiancé, everyone was scared enough to never approach me again.

We were in a Cosa Nostra car, which had picked us up from the airport. One of their drivers, a man in black, didn't even speak to us, which didn't surprise me at all; my brother's men were the same.

Ferney Aragón, my brother, was the head of the Cartel Los Sombríos. It was an agreement made with him.

My sister-in-law Amélia said she was already at the mafia headquarters for my wedding, and of course, I was supposed to be there by now. But I decided to delay my trip to extend my vacation, spending a few more days in the Hollywood resort paradise with Billie.

I relaxed, enjoyed myself, went out, danced, but didn't have sex, which made me feel like a complete idiot, stupid for not being able to let go, for having this block. Who, at 22, was still a virgin? What was wrong with me?

It made me wonder if I would be able to surrender to Valentino. What would our first time be like? Would he abuse me? Just thinking about it made me scared, a fear that even made me tremble.

The car began to slow down as it entered a gated community with only one street but with huge, luxurious houses, heading towards one of them, the largest of all, which could even double the size of the others.

Was this the headquarters? My new residence?

The car stopped in front, and I swallowed hard, trying to stay calm for the moment. But it was time, I would have to face my worst torment, Valentino Vacchiano, my future husband.

"I'll be with you, friend, I'll be right there..."

"Not forever. After the wedding, you'll be going away." I pouted, looking like a spoiled child.

"But I'll always have my phone ready to answer your calls." She winked her green eye.

My door was opened at that moment, I took the outstretched hand, my blue heel touching the ground, the pleated skirt swaying with the gentle sea breeze I could see from the side of the house.

"Friend, with all due respect, this place is gorgeous," Billie murmured beside me.

"That's what Ammie told me," I recalled what my sister-in-law had mentioned.

"Is it time to switch our language now?" Billie murmured, knowing they spoke Italian here.

"Unfortunately." I rolled my eyes, following her towards the door, knowing my suitcase would be taken by the driver.

I had let them know I was bringing my friend with me. Billie was like a sister; I couldn't go through this alone, even though my sister-in-law, whom I considered a sister, was also by my side.

Amélia was the best thing in Ferney's life; they complemented each other so intensely that it was as if they communicated with just a look. That's what I called love and devotion. Amélia snapped her fingers, and my brother would run to do what she wanted. Just as she did everything for him, a two-way street, they completed each other.

I stopped in front of the door, and before I had time to knock, someone opened it, making me take a small step back.

"Hello." A lady with blonde hair, like mine, short, smiled, making her blue eyes sparkle. "I'm Verena, I think I scared you because I saw the car through the window. I was eager to finally meet my daughter-in-law."

Was that Valentino's mother? God, I could easily say she was his sister.

What a beautiful woman, I don't think I would ever be on the level of someone like her who had been the first lady of the Cosa Nostra.

"Oh." Was all that escaped my mouth, but Mrs. Verena didn't even seem to notice my shock, or pretended not to.

Opening her arms to give me a hug, the lady had a lovely scent, just like me, wearing heels.

"It's a pleasure to finally meet you, Yulia." Verena stepped back with a smile.

After introducing my friend, the lady escorted us into the house, and all I could do was look around in awe. I knew I grew up in luxury; my brother never let me want for anything, but this was overwhelming. However, my admiration faded from my eyes when I entered the room and saw the number of people there. I didn't recognize anyone from her family; the only people I knew were my brother and his wife.

"Wow" I let out a startled squeal as a little whirlwind attached itself to my leg.

"Auntie, I missed you." The messy red hair revealed the little Kalinda, unlike Aurora, who always had her hair neatly done.

I smiled, bending down to lift the 3-year-old girl into my lap.

"My little ray of sunshine, how you've grown." She gave me a wide smile, her blue eyes, different from her mother's, sparkling in my direction.

I already knew Amélia's mother, and the twins Kalinda and Aurora were the spitting image of her, with their red hair, smooth faces without freckles, and blue eyes.

"Auntie, you look so pretty." Kalinda touched my face with her hand.

She soon wriggled free and darted to the ground as quickly as she had appeared. I raised my eyes to all the guests present, and my sister-in-law was the first to stand up, smiling as she approached me.

"Yulia, oh how beautiful and tanned you look." She smiled at my new tan.

"Totally natural," I said casually, knowing I had been out in the sun with Billie to get this tan.

We embraced tightly. Ammie was taller; she must have been almost as tall as my brother.

As soon as my sister-in-law stepped back, she started introducing everyone present. Valentino's sister, Pietra Ferrari, and her husband, Enrico Ferrari, had many Italian features, dark hair, green eyes, and tanned skin, unlike her mother.

When Amélia got to the next person, I was shocked to see the striking resemblance to Valentino.

"Calm down, little sister-in-law, I'm not your future husband." That must have been his brother.

"If it helps, no one told me this, but I'll tell you, they still pass for each other, which always irritates me. Valentino doesn't have a tattoo on his chest, but this copy here does," the blonde next to him said with a mix of affection.

"The copy is him, not me," Santino looked at his wife as if he wanted to tease her.

"Dear, you were born a few minutes later." It seemed like those two had a huge bond. Even though they appeared to be teasing each other, they looked at each other with affection.

My sister-in-law continued with the introductions, arriving at my father-in-law, a tall man with dark eyes, unlike all his children, but with much resemblance.

Tommaso Vacchiano was no longer the Don of the Cosa Nostra. From what I understood, he had passed his position to his son more than a year ago. I searched for the missing person, my future husband, but I couldn't find him until I heard footsteps coming from behind me. It wasn't necessary to turn around to know that it was my obnoxious fiancé.

CHAPTER SIX

Valentino

"It seems there's no more escape." I lifted my eyes from my laptop, giving one last look at the spreadsheet that my cousin and the Don of the Swiss mafia had sent.

Matteo, who had a cigarette in his mouth, declared while inhaling its smoke.

"It looks like she's already arrived." I rolled my eyes and closed the laptop.

"Our days of glory are over," Matteo mocked, putting the cigarette butt in the ashtray and giving me a small, smirking smile.

"The good thing is, if there's nothing for me, there's nothing for you either." I got up from the chair, adjusting the fabric of my dress pants.

Matteo had become my companion since Santino turned into his wife's lapdog. We went everywhere together, frequented the same club, and had a partnership even when we were caporimes of the Cosa Nostra. When I was appointed as the head of our clan, I had to change some positions. I decided to keep most of the caporimes who were my father's, changing only the higher ranks, after all, Aldo, Enrico, and Tommaso deserved their permanent vacations. My brother became my underboss, and Matteo, with whom I already had a friendship and, like me, grew up in the mafia, was initiated early into that world. He never seemed bothered by the fact of speaking to the future Don, which is why I appointed him as the consigliere of the Cosa Nostra.

Matteo was a clever man, a bit older than me, and had lived a hell of a life, making him fit to be my advisor.

I ran my hand over my throat, opening the first button of my shirt, and gestured for Matteo to follow me. It was time to revisit my little Colombian and see the damage I had left in her life without even making much effort.

I left the office, descending one step at a time, seeing from behind the staircase the girl with long, flowing black hair, wearing a skirt mid-thigh, and light blue heels matching the skirt. I passed behind her, my eyes meeting Yulia's brother.

I was waiting for the moment he would make one of his threats, as it seemed the situation had reversed. Now that I was getting married, I would become her owner. When it was his turn with my cousin Amélia, he didn't even show mercy to the poor girl, even though they got along well now.

I stopped next to my father, who had his hands on my mother's shoulders. She was sitting on the sofa holding my brother's little one, my niece Bella, daughter of Santino and Cinzia. I made a face when the little one drooled onto my mother's hand.

"Calm down, brother, have you thought about having a daughter?" I lifted my eyes to Santino's mockery.

"I'm with Enrico on this one." I shrugged, meeting Enrico, who was sitting next to my sister on the same sofa as Ferney and Amélia.

"Only the good ones have sons; the failures have daughters for us to marry," Enrico said with mockery to my father, even though he married his daughter.

"Go fuck yourself, I still regret never putting a bullet between your legs," Tommaso grumbled.

"That's because I gave you the best gift a son-in-law could give," Enrico continued with his taunts.

"Yes, I should have kept my grandson and done away with you..."

"Oh, both of you, enough!" My sister made that face she always did when my father and Enrico recalled their near-fight.

Even though they pretended to have these conflicts, we all knew they couldn't stay apart.

At that moment, I turned my face towards the little Colombian who was going to be my wife. She, who had her eyes on me, was analyzing me without even appearing intimidated. I raised an eyebrow at her, making my displeasure with her scrutiny clear.

But Yulia didn't look away; it was clear that two years hadn't turned my future wife into a beautiful submissive. I'd still have to train her.

"Is it true what your father said, Valentino?" I turned my face when Ferney's voice caught my attention.

"Depends." I furrowed my brows, unsure of what exactly he was referring to.

"About you traveling alone with my sister afterward."

"Oh, that's true," I affirmed what he already knew.

"What's the reason for this trip?" Ferney asked again.

"I thought the honeymoon was for that," I said with a mocking tone, as everyone knew I was taking Yulia away from the estate. After all, anyone who didn't know should buy Verena; my mother would take care of staying here every day, all to keep an eye on how I would handle my wife.

"That's not your case; why are you taking my sister away from the estate?" he insisted.

"What I do or don't do with her is none of your business. Did you report to my uncle when you married Amélia?" I tilted my head to the side, maintaining the mocking expression that everyone hated.

"I'm talking about my sister, and I also know you practice sadism. You won't do that to my sister!" Ferney stood up from the sofa, clenching his fists as if he wanted to hit me.

"Don't worry..." I received a nudge from my father, who knew what I was about to say and wanted to rein me in. "I'll do something worse to her."

Ferney came towards me. I knew he was unarmed; only unarmed people were allowed in there. So, I pulled my weapon from behind my back, raising it towards him.

"A finger of yours on me, and I'll forget we have an alliance to formalize. Your sister was given to me, and I'll do with her as I please. I'm not afraid of starting a war with you; if we pencil it out, who has more to lose?"

The Cartel boss was breathing heavily, standing in front of me.

"That wasn't the agreement we made." He directed his gaze at my father.

"I'm not the Don anymore; I wash my hands of it." Tommaso raised his hands. My father never crossed any boundaries regarding my authority, always making it clear that he was no longer the Don of the Cosa Nostra.

"It's the fucking Don who will do whatever he wants with my sister!" Ferney wasn't lowering his guard easily.

From the corner of my eye, I saw my cousin approaching her husband, and I also felt my mother's delicate hand on my shoulder.

"We can resolve this without hostility," Mom said in her calm voice.

"Oh, really? Then you tell me why your son wants to take my sister away from the estate? Away from everyone who can defend her?" Ferney growled at my mother.

"He wants the opportunity to get to know her better," Mom lied so well that even I believed it.

"And I believe in Easter bunnies." The Cartel boss rolled his eyes.

"Valentino is just taking five days off. Since he took over the Cosa Nostra, he hasn't taken any vacation; it's nothing like you're thinking," Mom defended me.

I knew she just wanted to defuse the situation, and later she would make me promise not to hurt Yulia, not to commit any of my craziness.

"I need to hear it from your mouth." Ferney turned his eyes on me.

"You know I'm not trustworthy; my word means nothing." I shrugged. "I promise whatever you want me to promise, but I don't care about anything regarding your little sister. My only purpose with her is to produce an heir..."

A noise interrupted us, shards of glass shattering on the floor. Everyone turned to see where it was coming from, until my eyes focused on that vast expanse of starless nights. Yulia had picked up a decorative item from the house and thrown it on the floor, drawing everyone's attention to her.

"I'm right here!" Apparently, she got what she wanted.

CHAPTER SEVEN

Yulia

I started to panic seeing that gun pointed at my brother, especially since he was at a disadvantage for not being armed.

Acting on impulse, I grabbed the ornament and threw it on the floor, thus drawing the attention I wanted.

"I'm right here," I said as everyone turned to look at me.

Even Billie was taken by surprise; perhaps she hadn't expected such a reception, and neither had I.

"You wanted this, brother; you gave me to this... this..."

"Watch the word you use." I narrowed my eyes at my future fiancé, who at that moment seemed intent on intimidating me.

"This idiot," I said without hesitation, confronting the Don of that stupid mafia. "Now face the consequences, brother! There's nothing you can do."

I finished the sentence with a long sigh, everyone looking at me as if I had grown an extra head. All of this because I confronted the Don? What could he do to me? Anyway, for Valentino to get what he wanted, his heir, he would have to abuse me, and just thinking about that filled me with dread.

"Deep down, your foolish sister isn't so foolish," Valentino said with a mocking tone, seeming almost natural for him when he wanted to unsettle someone.

"Before my wedding, I promised Amélia's father that I would protect her. I expect you to do the same," my brother continued with his defiance.

"I will protect your sister; I never said I wouldn't. She will be my wife, the First Lady of the Cosa Nostra, and will have all the privileges she desires, but I never said she would be loved." He shrugged at that moment, lowering his weapon.

I slumped my shoulders, wishing my brother would sit his ass on the damn couch and just play his role as a family member. After all, he gave me away for an alliance; it was pointless to try and protect me now, not when all the shit was already done.

A lady asked for permission, and before I knew it, they were cleaning up the broken glass I had shattered.

"Mom, don't cry; I'm sure Daddy won't be offended by the wedding gift your new daughter-in-law just broke." I looked up, startled, noticing Valentino's brother speaking. I realized that although both of them had a certain look of mockery, his was much more blatant.

"Shut up, Santino, it's a lie, dear. Anything he can do to embarrass you, you can be sure he will," Pietra, the twins' sister, came to my defense.

"That's fine; it was an old ornament I wanted to get rid of anyway." Verena smiled warmly at me.

The baby was now in her mother's lap, keeping her entertained.

"Of all the evils, the lesser one. I loved the idiot Valen; it reminded me of you saying that your wife would be submissive," the blonde, Valentino's sister-in-law, mocked him.

It seemed that everyone there felt free to speak openly among themselves, even with the Don, treating him like a family member without the hierarchy that usually separated them.

"Dear, do you want to clean your leg?" I lowered my face to where the lady who was cleaning pointed.

"Oh! I didn't feel it," I murmured, realizing that a shard of glass had flown onto my leg, cutting it.

Blood was running down my skin, touching my heel.

"Come with me; I'll help you." My mother-in-law gestured for me to follow her, and Billie came along.

"Friend, this is better than the soap operas my mom makes; I was almost asking for a bowl of popcorn," Billie mocked in English, thinking that Mrs. Verena didn't understand.

"That's because you've only been here a few hours; imagine me, who has lived this madness for thirty years of marriage," my mother-in-law responded in Italian, understanding what Billie had said.

"Sorry, ma'am." Billie smiled at the moment she was caught in the act.

"It's alright, dear. I'm used to the children I have; after all, I was the one who brought those creatures into the world." She shrugged, leading us into a huge kitchen where two cooks were working.

I sat on one of the stools, and Mrs. Verena appeared with a small first aid kit, placing it on the granite counter.

"Can I ask a question?" I requested, watching the lady rummage through the white bag.

"Yes, dear," she replied with a smile on her lips.

"Is it true? Valentino wants a honeymoon?" I whispered, afraid we might be overheard.

"Yes, my dear, but only two people know, his loyal henchmen, Santino and Matteo. But according to what Cinzia discovered, it's an island, very beautiful, but she didn't find the location. If there's anyone you can always ask for help, it's the women in our family. We will be by your side at all times; it will only be five days. Valentino is a brute, but I'm sure he can be softened." The lady's blue eyes shifted from me to my wound.

She carefully cleaned the wound.

"Yes, but I don't want to soften anyone; I hate him. I hate everything he did to my college, going there, participating in that group sex, ruining my last two years of freedom," I responded to my mother-in-law with honesty.

"I know, and I'm sorry. I should never have approved Tommaso's crazy idea of sending his son; he told us he only wanted to meet you. I should have known there was something behind it. Sometimes even I forget the devilish children I brought into the world." Verena looked at me with sympathy.

I knew at that moment that I would have the support of that woman; she would stay by my side, but that was if her sick son didn't take me away from them.

"But if it's any consolation, the more you step on him, the more he'll feel the sting of pain. I married a Vacchiano, I struggled with him in our early days of marriage. I wanted everything from him, even though he had chosen a different path at first. I knew he would be only mine if I continued to put him second, if I didn't give in easily. Even though it was hard, I loved that big fool." I smiled seeing my mother-in-law cursing her husband, realizing that she truly loved him.

I never knew their story, but it seemed it was also an arranged marriage, and Verena must have had a rough time with her husband.

The wound was superficial, just a cut. Mrs. Verena finished cleaning it for me, not even taking me back to the living room, but leading me up the stairs to my accommodation, since my wedding was the next day.

CHAPTER EIGHT

Yulia

I stopped in front of the mirror, my reflection showing the woman who would be married in less than an hour. The dress I made myself—if this was the only wedding I was going to have, then it should be the one where I crafted my own gown.

A strapless design, accentuating my cleavage, with tiny stones mimicking diamonds on the bodice. A corset cinched my waist, molding it perfectly. Billie was at my back, fastening the small pearl buttons.

The dress flowed in a cascade of tulle, with tiny stones scattered as if they were cascading down from the bodice. At my waist, a small satin ribbon, adorned with a jewel-encrusted embellishment.

Amélia styled my hair into a high bun with a tiara nestled in it. The strands were secured with pins, creating soft waves, while my bangs fell gently on my rosy cheeks. Loose strands framed my ears, accentuating the large diamond earrings that touched the base of my neck.

I was ready. The big moment had arrived.

"Isn't it strange to marry a man I haven't even spoken to since I arrived here yesterday? What if we have nothing to talk about? What if we end up arguing all the time?" I shrugged in front of the mirror, admiring my stunning reflection.

I felt beautiful, like a true princess. The dress fit my body perfectly.

"I'm sure there won't be a shortage of conversation, dear," my sister-in-law said, placing a comforting hand on my shoulder.

"But he doesn't even know how to talk to me. To me, Valentino is a complete stranger who thinks he can ruin anyone's life," I grumbled, recalling my past with that idiot.

"Yulia, you know I can give him a piece of my mind, don't you?" Amélia, being Valentino's cousin, had a freedom with him that I didn't.

Would I ever have any kind of freedom with him? The kind that couples have? To talk about everything, just like my sister-in-law and brother always did, sharing all their experiences? Of course, it wasn't always like that; I witnessed when things went wrong for them.

But in the end, Ferney did everything to have his beloved by his side, something I wasn't sure I would get from my husband, considering he was a self-centered man who only thought of himself.

"It won't help, just as it wouldn't help if Ferney told him to stop. Valentino himself said he can promise things, but his word means nothing. In other words, when it suits him, he'll do whatever he wants. What kind of man is that? He doesn't even honor his own word." I turned my body to face Amélia.

"I grew up in a different clan, but I know enough about the Cosa Nostra to say that they bluff a lot, but in the end, they always honor their word. I know it won't be easy, my dear. I also know you're not a naïve fool like I was, thinking your brother would be a prince in our early days of marriage. But know that I'll do everything within my power for you." Ammie held my hand, her green eyes fixed on mine, her freckles contrasting with her beauty.

A knock at the door interrupted our moment.

"Come in," Amélia said, her expression quickly changing when she saw her husband appear in the doorway. Her eyes lit up, and a shy smile graced her lips.

That's what I wanted: that devotion, that surrender, just with a glance. My brother, who had first sought out his wife, then looked at me.

His smile widened as he took in my dress.

"My dear sister," he said as he entered the room.

I knew that in my early years, he had done everything for me. If it weren't for Ferney, I might not even be alive. My father died in a gang fight while my mother was still pregnant with me. The age difference between Ferney and me was significant—my mother shouldn't have even gotten pregnant with me. She was an addict who died of an overdose. I was never told much about her; all I knew were unexplained facts.

Mom died of an overdose and didn't care for me. My brother provided for us, starting work at a very young age. Mom always had many addicted boyfriends, and I thought that was all there was—nothing concrete, nothing explained.

Ferney used to say that if I didn't remember, there was no need to know.

But it was a part of my life, a painful part that under my brother's protective eyes, I didn't need to know.

Following Father came the triplets, Otto, Kalinda, and Aurora, all dressed up and accompanied by the two nannies. It was the only way to go out with these three little tornadoes, although Aurora was the calmest of them all, she sometimes joined in with the more mischievous ones.

"You look beautiful, my sister," Ferney said, coming towards me.

"It's a shame it's not for an occasion that pleases my eyes." I forced a smile.

Billie took the triplets and Amélia, helping my sister-in-law, leaving me alone with my brother.

"Yulia, if I could turn back time, I wouldn't have given you away." My brother sighed deeply.

"It's okay, brother." I was trying to keep a clear mind.

"You know I'll always be loyal for your sake with our Cartel."

"Brother, for many years, you did everything for me. Now it's my turn to contribute. If I'm alive, it's thanks to you." I didn't want Ferney to blame himself, so I held his hand, gently caressing his fingers.

"Yulia, I love you. I'll tell you what my father-in-law said to Amélia at our wedding. Even though I was a complete jerk with my wife back then, I need to know you're entering this prepared." I nodded, not taking my eyes off his. "Never settle for scraps. Don't beg for his love. You deserve the world, you deserve to be loved, and you deserve him to realize that on his own. Be strong, don't give in easily... okay, maybe I've changed that last part. I can't imagine you being a naïve fool; after all, you're an Aragón."

"Brother, if there's one thing I'm not, it's a naïve fool. That idiot will pay for ruining my two years of college." I shrugged, and Ferney smiled.

"You know my number. Whenever you need me, I'll be ready to help you, my little sister." We both smiled, and he pulled me into a tight hug.

CHAPTER NINE

Valentino

I clenched my hands tightly, shoving them into my pockets to hide the fact that I was nervous. Damn it, it was just a fucking wedding.

My nails dug into my palms, feeling the moment the soothing burn began to take over my body.

It was late afternoon, and my wedding was taking place in the same spot as Santino's, behind the headquarters, with the setting sun in the background. The full suit my father practically forced me to wear was starting to sweat more than I wanted. Damn, I wanted to take this shit off. Fuck, I didn't even want to be here; I hated being in situations I couldn't control.

I never wanted a wedding, but I always knew I'd have one, sooner or later.

And if it had to be with Yulia, the girl with the challenging gaze, rosy cheeks, black lashes, and that little plump mouth… if I had to get married, it might as well be to that hot Colombian.

My thoughts were interrupted when the girl in white appeared on the path of cobblestones made just for the wedding. She was stunning, divine, even looking like a princess—my princess.

Everyone seated stood up. White chairs had been placed on either side of the cobblestone path. Next to Yulia was her brother, who wasn't even wearing a full suit; only I had to wear this damn getup, all because they needed photos of the Don's wedding.

My eyes stayed fixed on the petite girl. Even with heels, she was at her brother's shoulder height. Her eyes didn't focus on me but on something in the distance. Maybe towards the sea to avoid looking at me. Her hair was divinely styled, her makeup soft, delicate, just like her.

Yulia had all the traits of a delicate girl. When she wasn't opening her mouth to speak her bullshit, I still remembered her calling me an idiot in front of everyone.

I saved that for when the time was right to punish her.

Ferney stopped in front of me. I took a step toward them, taking his sister's hand that was extended to me.

"Do you promise to take care of my sister?" he asked, something I had already said I would do.

"Yes, I promise." That promise wasn't hard to keep; after all, I never said I wouldn't take care of and protect that little girl from all harm.

I just didn't promise to protect her from myself. The harm could be inside me.

There were so many things I wanted to do with that Colombian girl. I even had my apartment renovated, a place where only invited guests were allowed, where everything was permitted, and you couldn't leave without getting some special bruise. Damn, I wanted to take Yulia there, fuck her hard, tie her up, gag her, hear her screams of desperation when she couldn't handle the size of her pleasure. There was a part of me that no one knew about, a part I kept hidden, out of shame, simply because I could never stop mutilating myself when I failed at something.

That's why I needed to be perfect in everything I did.

Yulia's small hand was placed on mine, which covered it easily. I felt her cold touch against my warm one, so warm I could feel my palm sweating, sending small waves of shock through my body.

Apparently, she felt it too, as her eyes widened in surprise as she looked up at me.

We turned to face the pastor, who began the ceremony. It was a quick affair, just to seal our union. When it was time for our vows, Yulia began to repeat after the pastor:

"I, Yulia Aragón, promise to be faithful to my husband, respect him, never fail to fulfill my duties as a wife, in health or in sickness, in wealth or in poverty, until death do us part." Yulia repeated with a tremor, as if she hated every one of those words.

It was my turn. The pastor looked at me, expecting me to repeat after him, vows made according to the rules of our clan.

"I, Valentino Vacchiano, promise to protect, care for, and cherish my wife, keep her away from all danger, in health or in sickness, in wealth or in poverty, until death do us part." My vows were different from hers. After all, I didn't need to promise her my fidelity, unlike her.

I saw those big black eyes roll when I didn't promise to be faithful to her. Did she really think that would happen?

The pastor continued with the union, and we exchanged our rings. I placed a delicate ring with a perfect jewel for the bronze skin of the Colombian on her ring finger.

I tried to keep my eyes away from her cleavage, which was so glamorous, as if begging to be touched. One thing couldn't be denied, Yulia Aragón was possibly the most beautiful creature I had ever had my hands on and would give me beautiful children.

"I now declare you husband and wife. The groom may kiss the bride," he said, the moment I had been waiting for, finally to feel my wife's lips.

It was impossible for those sweet lips not to provide a good kiss.

Releasing her hand, I held her waist, pulling her gently closer to me. Yulia lifted her face, and from the movement in her neck, I knew she swallowed hard.

I lowered my face, raising one of my hands to touch her cheek, feeling her skin delicate as a feather. My mouth touched hers, fitting into the cushions that were her lips.

Yulia didn't move, didn't show any sign of wanting to deepen the kiss, but I wanted more. I wanted to feel her tongue touching mine. Was it as velvety as her lips?

I opened my mouth, coaxing my tongue into hers, feeling hers touch mine timidly, without even entering my mouth, just grazing as it invaded her mouth.

Noticing that she wouldn't give more than that, I pulled back, my eyes fixed on hers, which were closed, and slowly opening them. Had she closed her eyes for such a simple kiss?

Without a doubt, she was the best choice for me.

"Your lips are sweeter than I thought," I murmured, taking a step back.

"Pity I can't say the same about yours." I raised an eyebrow, searching for any hint of sarcasm in her words.

And damn, I didn't find it. I quickly withdrew my hand from her waist, shoving it into my pocket, clenching my nails into my palm, wanting to feel the damn pain of not being the best.

"That's something we'll see," I growled through gritted teeth, finally pulling my hand out of my pocket, not realizing I had squeezed it so hard it had made a small cut.

CHAPTER TEN

Yulia

His hand filled mine, covering it with his fingers. Of course, I had obviously lied about his lips not being good. It was a complete sacrifice for me not to give in to that kiss, but there was a part of me that refused to accept that there was anything good about Valentino. I kept guiding myself by that part.

We continued walking to the opposite side, where we were asked to take photos. After all, they needed pictures of the Don at his wedding. If he was the Don, did that make me the First Lady now?

All the guests, who weren't many, went inside the residence where dinner would be served. After that, we would head to our honeymoon, which I didn't even know the destination of. All I knew was that he told me not to unpack my suitcase because we would be gone for five days.

We were accompanied by the photographer and my mother-in-law, at least she was there to save me in case this crazy guy decided to act out.

"You can stop there," the photographer said, making us stop walking, which almost made me thank him because Valentino walked quickly, and the lawn we were walking on was sinking under my heels.

Valentino released my hand. I faced him, doing what the photographer asked, standing next to him, taking a photo with his hand on my waist.

"Oh, dear, did you get hurt?" I looked at my mother-in-law as she came toward me, worried.

"Oh, me?" I was confused because I didn't feel any injury.

"Yes, look at your hand," Verena pointed to my hand.

I opened both hands, looking at them and finding dried blood there, the same hand that had been holding Valentino's. But I knew it wasn't my injury; I would have felt it. I lowered my eyes to his hands, finding them in his pocket, as if he wanted to hide. I raised my gaze to his, and Valentino had his green eyes narrowed at me.

Mrs. Verena took my hand, wanting to see the wound, a wound that didn't exist.

"I think I cut myself when I was putting on the dress and didn't even notice. It was just a tiny cut." I shrugged, not understanding why I was defending my crazy husband, but it was obviously his blood. If anyone had a wounded palm, it was him.

"We'll wash it off later to remove the blood." Verena smiled warmly at me.

We continued with the photos. After the brief incident with the blood, Valentino was more tense than usual. Many photos were taken until the photographer was dismissed, at least the session ended.

Mrs. Verena was called inside, leaving me alone with her son. When we were alone, I seized the moment and spoke:

"That blood isn't mine." I stopped walking, holding onto his arm.

"And what does that have to do with me?" Valentino declared with all his arrogance, lowering his face to mine.

"Everything, it has everything to do with you!" I crossed my arms in the midst of my reprimand. "Show me your hand, that blood is yours."

"You'd better lower your tone. I didn't ask you to lie for me. If you think I'm going to thank you for that, you're very mistaken." I opened my mouth in astonishment, actually, I was shocked.

I lied to save him from an awkward situation with his mother, and this is what I got? A sample of ingratitude? Not even a thank you?

"Asshole," I muttered, stepping away from him and trying to walk quickly, but my heels sinking into the lawn made it difficult.

A low laugh was present next to me. I tried to ignore it, not wanting to look to the side, but it became hard when Valentino held both sides of my waist, easily lifting me into his arms, noticing that I couldn't walk.

In my brief scare, I held onto his jacket, without even looking at his face. By that time, the sun had already set, and the night was taking over.

I didn't want to look at him. I refused to accept that I had a complete idiot for a husband.

We approached the side of the house, where I could walk again. He gently put me down, and I had to hold onto his jacket to maintain my balance.

I lifted my face at that moment, meeting the perfect features of my husband above me. He could at least be uglier, a man with no physical attractions that wouldn't leave me fascinated, but all that was in vain. Valentino was beautiful, his green eyes, bronze skin, the dark brown beard marking his face, and his hair always well-groomed, as if he didn't even need to fix it.

"Aren't you going to thank me for what I did for you?" I asked again.

"No, you did it because you wanted to." He subtly shrugged his shoulders.

"Sometimes it's necessary to admit when you're wrong," I grumbled, turning away.

"But I'm never wrong," he said from behind me, with such conviction that I almost believed those words.

I continued walking toward the entrance door, a step ahead of him, fuming with anger, wanting at that moment to punch Valentino Vacchiano's perfect face because we had been married for less than an hour.

As we entered the residence, I felt his hand cover mine, filling it. I wanted to look down to see if I could find his injury, but I realized he had reversed the position, meaning my bloodied hand was on the other side. He probably did that on purpose.

We were congratulated, receiving many hugs, including from the little ones. I met Valentino's eldest nephew, little Tommaso, who shared the name with his grandfather but was called Tommie by everyone there. He was seven years old, a small copy of both the Vacchianos and the Ferraris, with features from both sides.

Pietra, Valentino's older sister, was very friendly, as was Cinzia, his sister-in-law. Santino carried little Bella in his arms, a beautiful girl who had just turned one, according to Cinzia. They seemed to get along very well, and from what it looked like, Santino always catered to his wife's wishes, with Valentino mocking him for something similar to my conclusion.

My friend Billie was constantly with Amélia, and fortunately, the two got along well, so I could be more at ease.

Dinner was served, and we all sat at the table. Valentino complained about something I didn't even pay attention to, but it must have been something about his jacket, as he quickly removed it, seeming relieved by the act.

With every passing minute of the dinner dragging on, I became more nervous about this damn trip.

CHAPTER ELEVEN

Yulia

I left my wedding dress at the venue, removed with the help of the girls. I said goodbye to everyone, feeling choked up when it was Billie's turn. We had always been very close, and now our separation had come. Of course, Valentino showed no reaction.

We headed to the car waiting for us, heading toward the airport in Catania. From there, we boarded the family jet that was waiting. My bags were placed inside the jet, and I settled into one of the seats. Throughout the journey, Valentino remained silent, and I didn't even make an effort to start a conversation.

Three of his men came with him, and they were as quiet as he was.

The jet was already in the air. I unfastened my seatbelt, feeling the pins in my hairstyle bothering me. I should have removed that absurd amount of bobby pins.

I got up from my seat. Valentino was next to me, working on his laptop, seemingly focused, though maybe not so focused, as his eyes lifted toward me when I stood up.

"Where's the bathroom?" I asked, needing to go.

"At the end of the corridor." He quickly lowered his eyes.

I walked down the corridor, entered the small bathroom, did what I needed to do, and finally washed my hands. I sighed deeply, wondering if the outfit I was wearing was too short for where we were going. After all, I didn't even know where we were headed.

I lowered my white jeans skirt a bit more, leaving the restroom and heading toward my seat. I slowed down when I saw the flight attendant standing next to Valentino's seat. My eyes clearly focused on his hand sliding up her thigh.

I took a deep breath, controlling all my emotions. *Be strong, Yulia, be strong...*

I repeated this in my mind several times as I approached the situation.

"Is it only when the cat turns its back that the rats have a party?" I muttered loud enough for him to hear, changing the popular saying.

I wanted to appear indifferent to the situation, but all that came to mind were his tattooed fingers sliding over that woman's leg. It affected me, it bitterly affected me to see my husband paying attention to another woman and not even bothering to talk to me.

"Do you need something, ma'am?" the flight attendant asked me.

I lifted my face, questioning why on earth she had to be so beautiful. It made me even more jealous, leading me to conclude that the bastard might be doing this to provoke me.

"Yes, any bottle of wine you have," I asked her with a smile, trying to show my indifference when, in reality, I was deeply shaken.

She nodded and left with her cart, leaving me alone with my husband. He still had his eyes on me, as if wondering what my problem was.

"Is something wrong, dear?" I asked sarcastically.

"I should be asking you, what's wrong?" Valentino shot back.

"And why would there be?"

"You didn't even seem bothered." He raised an eyebrow.

"Oh, that. I expect nothing less from you. You can't even surprise me." I shrugged, *thinking I should take a course to become an actress because I was nailing it.*

We were interrupted when the flight attendant brought my wine with the glass, placing it on the table in front of me.

"So, I can have sex with her in front of you and you won't even care?" Valentino asked again.

"Just let me know so I can jump off this jet," I replied sarcastically.

"So you clearly do care," he continued his investigation.

"I just don't want to see the future father of my children having sex with another woman. If you want to cheat, do it out of my sight," I declared, not taking my eyes off his.

"So you do care," he emphasized again as if trying to rub it in my face that he was right.

"I don't give a damn what I think or don't think. Just do as I said," I spoke authoritatively, causing him to tilt his head to the side.

"Since when do you give orders?" He crossed his legs as if enjoying our brief argument.

"Is it so hard for you to do something for someone else for once in your life?" I asked, wanting to end the topic.

"So what you're saying is that I can cheat on you and you won't care? I can screw other women and then come home and screw you, and you won't care?" Valentino kept bombarding me with his ridiculous questions.

"The only purpose of this marriage is to produce an heir. We'll have sex just once and pray that this child is conceived. If not, we'll try again during my next cycle. And when we do, you need to be clean for at least five days..."

"Clean?" Valentino was really enjoying provoking me.

"Yes, without having slept with other women. Also, we don't need to share the same bed; there's no need when hatred is mutual," I said promptly.

"None of this was in the contract..."

"Well, I just added it. That's what I decided, and nothing will make me change my mind." I shrugged, picking up the wine glass the flight attendant had left for me.

"You know I'm a sexually active man, right?"

"And since when is that my problem?" I turned my face, raising an eyebrow at him.

I ran my tongue around my lip, removing the excess wine, feeling the sweet freshness go down my throat.

The man in front of me focused his eyes on my lip, shifting uncomfortably in his seat as the flight attendant returned with a glass of whiskey for him.

"Let me guess, you want sex in the dark?" he asked, making me bring the glass to my lips before responding.

"And preferably quickly. I'll count the seconds until I'm away from you," I replied, setting the glass back on the table.

"Know that nothing with me is quick..."

"That's fine. It shouldn't be too hard for a man to do the job and get away quickly." Valentino continued to watch me, analyzing all my reactions.

"Are you a virgin? I could have sworn you weren't, damn, you're a virgin!" he asked and then stated, and from my reaction, he got his answer. "So it must be so easy to have sex because you're still a virgin..."

"It's all your fault, you damned bastard!" I cut him off with my irritated voice.

"Watch your words, fiancée. Know that I'm not your little buddy, and no, it won't just be sex. It won't be sex in the dark, and it won't be just one time because I want to fuck your untouched body in every way possible. Maybe you should have lost your virginity because my dick is the only one you'll ever see in your life!" he snarled, speaking without even blinking.

"Bastard!!!" I growled, wanting to grab that glass and throw it at his perfect face.

CHAPTER TWELVE

Yulia

"Damn it," I muttered for the umpteenth time, trying to remove some pins that seemed to have buried themselves in my head.

What the hell had Amélia done to my head?

"Need help?" Valentino offered.

"Help me by staying as far away from me as possible." At that moment, all I wanted was distance from that arrogant man.

The only thing separating us was the hallway. I heard him closing his laptop, but didn't even look, until I felt his hand grab one of my wrists, pulling me towards him.

"Hey!" I squeaked as his pull was so strong that I fell into his lap, grabbing onto his black button-down shirt to avoid falling to the floor.

"Stop complaining; the amount of 'damn it' you're saying is really starting to annoy me," his voice was firm.

"I get annoyed just by your presence." I tried to get off his lap, but Valentino kept me seated there, holding my waist firmly.

"Be quiet; I'm going to get these damn pins out," he growled.

I crossed my arms, sitting sideways on his lap, feeling him release his hold on my waist as he began working on my hair.

"I'm only being quiet because these pins are bothering me," I pouted as if unwilling to concede.

"You're quite spoiled too, aren't you?" he whispered while working on my hair.

"Coming from a playboy who doesn't know how to hear the word 'no,'" I grumbled.

"And I have every right to say that," he declared in a way that made me turn my face, making it impossible for Valentino to continue working on my hair.

"You don't have any right! None at all," I said firmly.

He just rolled his eyes, making me turn my face again, thus giving him the opportunity to remove the pins from my hair once more.

It was strange to be in his lap, in such intimacy; after all, I was sitting on a man's legs, a man who was my husband. I was so immersed in my thoughts that I didn't even realize Valentino had removed all the pins from my hair and was running his fingers through my long strands.

Quickly, I became alert, wanting to jump off his lap and stand up, but I was caught off guard when his arm pulled me back, pulling me close to him again, my back facing his gaze.

"Wait, do you have a tattoo?" he gasped as he spoke, feeling his finger touch the blue butterfly I had tattooed at the base of my spine, near my buttocks.

"It's not like you don't have several," I retorted, trying to escape.

Valentino turned me around, his legs parting as he positioned me over them, his face close to my stomach, where he came across the piercing pendant in my belly button, his eyes widening momentarily. Holding me with only one hand, he lifted my shirt just enough to see my piercing.

"What do you have?" His eyes rose to meet mine.

"Nothing?" I responded as a question, since his inquiry seemed ridiculous.

"Why the hell did you do that?" he declared as if against it.

"Why the hell did you do yours?" I raised an eyebrow.

We were playing a game of cat and mouse, neither answering the other's question.

The jet hit a bump, probably a brief turbulence, causing me to lose my balance and fall back onto his lap, grabbing onto his shoulder in fear, my face close to his, his eyes fixed on mine.

"I don't want you marking your delicate body with this," he whispered, his lips close to mine.

"Just because you don't want me to gives me all the more reason to do it," I whispered, feeling the warmth of his mentholated breath collide with mine.

"Is it so hard to agree with me?" Valentino's hand traveled up my waist, touching my skin, sending a tingling sensation through my body, similar to the one I felt during our wedding when he first held my hand.

"Yes, extremely hard," I whispered, closing my eyes, hoping his lips would touch mine, waiting, waiting, and nothing happened.

I opened my eyes, and he was still in the same position, watching me.

"Asshole." I tried to push him away, but he pulled me forcefully to his lips.

"You look so vulnerable, so delicate that I'm afraid of breaking you sometimes," he murmured against my lip.

Now he wanted the kiss, but the tension of the moment had passed, and I no longer wanted it.

"No!" I grumbled, locking my lips.

"What's your problem?" He pulled his face back, surprised.

"You made me look like a fool, staring at me when you should have kissed me. You missed your chance; I'm not an idiot!"

Clumsily holding onto his shoulder, I stood up, quickly trying to pull down my skirt, which was all in vain, as he saw my white lace panties.

"Butterfly, I saw your panties; it wasn't that fast," he mocked, making my cheeks turn even redder.

"Don't use endearing nicknames with me," I huffed, heading to my chair where I sat with my arms crossed. "And don't ever look at my panties again!"

Of course, I liked the way his eyes practically devoured my intimacy covered by the panties, how he had lifted me onto his lap, his lips brushing mine, the heat that coursed through every part of my body.

It made me think that maybe I could have sex with him without freaking out, without screaming, without cold sweats as if the walls were closing in on me.

Just thinking about it made my body tense, my muscles start to stiffen, and what if I failed? What if I couldn't do it? Was there something wrong with me? Why couldn't I go further? Maybe I should have seen a specialist before getting married, but now it was too late; I was already married, Valentino was already my husband, and he wanted a child, a child I wasn't sure I'd be able to have.

I focused my eyes on the jet's window. At least, for the moment, Valentino had become silent, which made me realize that in the last few minutes, we had had conversations, he talked to me, there was interaction; we didn't run out of things to say.

Was what we needed for one of us to let down our guard? If it had to be him, because I wasn't going to do it. If we continued this constant fighting, how long could we endure it?

CHAPTER THIRTEEN

Yulia

"We've arrived." I jolted at Valentino's heavy hand touching my body.

"Okay, okay!!!" I quickly woke up, getting out of my seat, dazed.

Valentino gestured for me to go ahead of him. I merely nodded, pulling down my skirt, even though it was already lowered. After having exposed my panties once, I was afraid of showing them again.

I could hear his faint laughter behind me. I held onto the jet's handrail, looking around. We were at a different airport. A black car was waiting for us, our bags were being loaded by Valentino's men. I thought there were only three, but now there were twice as many dark-suited men.

"Where are we?" I turned my face, asking him as I descended the steps.

"Just walk, *piccola*," he grumbled impatiently.

Of course, he didn't say anything else.

I walked across the tarmac, luckily opting to wear flats, heading towards the open door while still looking around for any signs, but seeing nothing. We were at an airport, but I didn't know which city. I sat in the back seat, with Valentino beside me.

"How long did I sleep?" I asked since my phone was dead. My charger was in one of my bags, and I didn't want to admit it and ask for his, even though I saw him charging his.

"Between your wake-ups and going back to sleep, you slept for thirteen hours," he replied while looking at his watch.

"You're lying..." I muttered, as if I didn't believe him.

"Why would I lie? You sleeping is almost the definition of calmness, too bad it changes when you're awake." He looked at me with the arrogance he always wore.

"Go to hell," I retorted, turning my face to the window.

Out of the corner of my eye, I noticed he was fiddling with his phone. Our bags were placed in the car's trunk. As we started driving, I saw a car in front of us and another behind us, clearly indicating that we were being escorted by Valentino's men.

"Where is your phone?"

"Dead," I answered.

"And why the hell didn't you put that damn thing on charge?" he said, as always, in his authoritative tone.

"Because I left the charger in one of my bags."

"You have a mouth to retort with quick answers but can't ask to borrow my damn charger? Now I have to deal with your idiot brother who thinks I've already killed you in our first hours of marriage." I think that was the longest sentence he's ever said to me, and it was to insult me.

"I didn't want to contaminate my phone with your toxic charger." I shrugged, saying the biggest nonsense that came to my mind, just to avoid giving in.

Valentino muttered something I didn't understand, reaching into the middle of the car where he fiddled with a holder and took out a charging cable.

"Charge that damn thing. Even though the drive here is short, it'll charge a bit and calm your little brother's nerves who's pissing me the hell off." I smiled as I took the charging cable and plugged it into my phone. "Why the smile?"

"Nothing." I shook my head.

"Yulia?" My name on his lips sounded quite sexy.

As soon as I connected the phone, I looked up and noticed his eyes on me.

"Hell of your ass? You know that phrase doesn't make sense." He must have been so irritated that he didn't notice the nonsensical phrase he had used. Valentino stopped to think, then broke into a half-smile, a spontaneous, *beautiful, very beautiful* smile.

"I hate admitting you're right." He lowered his eyes, the smile fading as quickly as it had appeared.

I left my phone charging beside the seat and looked out the window. It was late afternoon, and it seemed like it was starting to get dark wherever we were. I focused on the signs, noticing that most were in Spanish, which meant we were in South America?

Damn it, I hated all this suspense.

I noticed the car slowed down as we stopped at what seemed to be a dock with many anchored boats. I swallowed hard at the magnitude of it.

He parked, and my door was immediately opened. I grabbed my phone and walked around the car, feeling the breeze hit my body, looking to the side and seeing Valentino waiting for me. I felt his hand cover mine as he held my fingers, guiding me along the long concrete dock, past numerous boats, until we stopped in front of a sleek, black, beautiful boat.

On the side, it was written, *San Juan – Puerto Rico*, and that's how I found out where we were.

"Get on, Yulia," he ordered in his serious tone.

"Where are we going? I'm not getting on this boat with a man I barely know, and what if you decide to kill me at sea?" I turned my body to face him, feeling the wind play with my hair, making it flutter gently.

"I'm not going to kill my wife." He frowned in a funny way.

"Then give me proof, or drag me inside by force." I crossed my arms.

"Why do you always have to complicate everything?" he grumbled, irritated.

"Because you've given me plenty of reasons not to believe a word you say," I retorted.

"Then let it be by force." When he said that, I wanted to run, but I didn't even get a chance, as his arms were already grabbing me, lifting me onto his shoulder, my face pressed against his back.

"Damn Italian," I grunted, punching his back with my fists.

"Your punch feels like a flea bite, the most it does is tickle," he said mockingly.

"DAMN, IDIOT, EGOCENTRIC, BOSSY!!!" I started shouting, doing what I said I would.

Valentino didn't stop carrying me onto the boat. I felt his body tense as he easily passed the side of the huge boat, entering it, going down a flight of stairs, and opening a door which I noticed was a bedroom, quickly throwing me onto the bed.

"Shut your damn mouth." I flinched, retreating behind the bed.

His finger pointed at me, making me tremble. Even the veins on his forehead were bulging. I swore he was going to raise his hand and hit me, his breath ragged, making his chest rise and fall.

"I'm your damn husband and so far I've been patient with you, but another one of your little games will be punished. I don't have patience for spoiled girls. Either do what I say or face the consequences, and know that the consequences can be quite painful, and that's not a bluff." There was the out-of-control husband I knew would show up eventually.

"I'd rather face the consequences than deal with a lunatic like you," I spat out.

Valentino moved his hand. I closed my eyes, bracing for the slap that was coming, but it didn't come. I opened my eyes again when I heard the door close, and he left me alone there.

CHAPTER FOURTEEN

Valentino

I slammed the door shut, leaving that part of the boat and instructing them to leave the luggage in the kitchen since I wanted to keep that insolent woman locked in the room.

Damn it! It took all my self-control not to punch her in the face; it wouldn't have been a slap, not a simple slap—nothing with me was simple. I could still feel the sting from my nails digging into the palms of my hands.

I remembered my father's words: "Don't do anything you might regret, don't measure your strength against hers, don't do what I did with your mother."

If it hadn't been for that damned voice in my head, I would have done it. I know I would have; deep down, I was just another out-of-control Vacchiano.

I stopped outside the boat, taking a deep breath, closing my eyes, and feeling the night air hit my body.

"Don?" one of my men called me. I masked my expression, turning my face. "Everything is ready, can we leave?"

"Yes," I nodded, knowing it would be five days with that insolent girl on an island.

Damn, I was starting to regret doing this, but I just wanted to get her away from my family, knowing there wouldn't be any privacy to do what I wanted with her.

But I didn't expect all this insolence. I didn't expect my wife to have a sharper tongue than I'd ever seen. It was as if there was a barrier, a wall separating us.

This had to be life's punishment. After laughing at my brother for having a no-filter wife, I ended up getting my dose of daily stress.

The boat started moving through the waters, and I stood there watching for long minutes, knowing it would be the longest three hours until we reached Mosquito Island.

I needed to bring the luggage to Yulia. I knew her phone had charged, but I had to give her the boat's Wi-Fi password since there was no signal out here. I refused to send one of my men to do it.

I turned my back, unbuttoning my shirt as I headed toward the kitchen where her two pink bags were. I grabbed them and went downstairs, stopping in front of her door, removing the lock, and opening it to find everything dark. I fumbled for the light switch and turned it on.

My eyes immediately focused on the girl curled up on the bed, her head resting on her knees, which she hugged with her arms. A sniffle was audible—was she crying?

What the hell, why was she crying? And why did it affect me?

"Your bags," I said into the boat's silence, seeing her lift her face, her eyes red, desperation evident in her gaze.

"You locked the door, you left me alone, you left me scared. I'm afraid of the dark. Damn it, damn it, damn it..." Yulia let out a loud sniffle, wiping her nose with her hand.

"Who's afraid of the dark at 22?" I raised an eyebrow, thinking it was just another one of her tantrums.

"I AM! I'M AFRAID!" she shouted in a way that really seemed like fear; she wasn't throwing a tantrum.

"Then why didn't you turn on the damn light? Enough with the drama," I grunted.

"Because when the boat started, everything went dark, and I couldn't get out of bed, couldn't move. Damn it, I'm afraid, simple as that. My body freezes up. Apparently, you're not the only crazy one here." She looked dazed.

"Your problems are solved, the light is on," I said insensitively.

But at that moment, the last thing I wanted was to take her pain on myself. I wasn't obligated to do that. No, I wasn't.

I left her bags there, turning my body, hearing her call my name:

"Valentino." My name on her velvety lips sounded almost like a song.

"Yes?" I turned, looking at her again.

"Leave the door open, I promise I won't get upset, but don't lock it," she asked, making that lost puppy face, blinking her eyes as if trying to persuade me not to close the door.

"What do I get in return for not locking the door?" I raised an eyebrow, putting my hands in my pockets.

Yulia stretched her legs, sitting on the edge of the bed, wiping the tears that had stopped falling from her eyes.

"I have nothing to offer you in return," she murmured, sounding like a puppy about to be trained.

"Oh, butterfly, you do. Many things." I tilted my head, examining every inch of her body, stopping at that white skirt.

"I'm not going to sell myself for sexual favors, just so we're clear." She crossed her arms, all her sweetness disappearing as she realized I wanted more from her.

"Your sweet smile and soft speech don't affect me. It seems all your attempts to persuade me have been in vain." I gave a wicked smile, and the girl's eyes widened.

Tommaso told me not to hit her, but he didn't say anything about punishment.

Holding the doorknob, about to close it, I heard her say:

"Know that this egotistical attitude of yours will only make me hate you even more."

"Love me or hate me, I don't care about either feeling. After all, as you yourself said, I only care about myself," I said in the most cutting tone, closing the door and hearing her banging on it from the inside.

"YOU IDIOT, ARROGANT, EVERYTHING THAT'S WRONG, I HATE YOU, YOU STUPID ITALIAN." I shouldn't have, but I smiled at her insults.

"You'll need much more than a soft-spoken tone and a delicate smile to make me fall for your tricks," I said before turning my back and heading upstairs, stopping in the kitchen while still hearing her banging on the door.

I knew she could call her brother and complain about what I was doing to her, but what would Ferney do? I wasn't hitting her; it was just a punishment in the room, and that girl wasn't foolish enough to call the authorities, after all, her brother was also a man living in illegality.

Yulia would likely be hungry soon since she hadn't eaten on the jet in the past few hours. I stopped in front of the fridge, opening it to find two ready meals for us.

Perhaps I'd leave my wife locked in that room for another hour, and then I'd go to open it, allowing her to eat.

CHAPTER FIFTEEN

Yulia

I texted my brother, pretending everything was fine. After all, he didn't need to know what I was going through. Ferney had enough problems of his own without me adding more. I also messaged Billie briefly, but she was traveling to California; her mother needed to uphold the perfect family image.

If only there were a bathroom here for a shower, but there wasn't even that. I sat on the bed, looking at my charging phone, folding my legs, and retrieving my sketchbook from the suitcase.

Along with the pencil, I opened to my latest sketch. Even though I couldn't work in the field I wanted due to my new responsibilities as the Italian mafia's first lady, which made me roll my eyes.

I heard the door lock click, then it opened to reveal Valentino.

"Come eat," was all he said before leaving the door open and walking out.

At that moment, I felt my stomach rumble, maybe I really was hungry.

I could play hard to get and not go eat, but I was indeed very hungry. I got up from the bed, slipping on the sandals I had taken from one of my suitcases.

I walked down the corridor; the yacht was moving, which made me think we were heading far away. We had been on it for over an hour. Since my phone had battery, and with the real-time map update, I knew where we were.

I climbed the stairs, looking around, finding Valentino in front of the sink, arms crossed, fiddling with his phone. He was shirtless, giving me a view of his chest. Why did he have to be so defined?

For God's sake! This man looked almost sculpted, his abs defined, as Billie would say, you could almost wash clothes on that washboard. With his arms crossed and the other resting on the crossed arm while fiddling with his phone, he looked even bigger.

I quickly turned my eyes to the table, seeing my plate of food. I sat down in silence, picked up the utensils quietly, and Valentino left, leaving me alone.

Once again, we were playing strangers, probably never having any meaningful conversations or desire to talk.

I ate in silence, devouring the plate of food. Finally, I washed the utensils, tidying up my mess.

The door to the outside was open; the Italian hadn't said anything about me not being able to leave, so I went out.

The yacht was ridiculously beautiful. I walked through the door, crossing the narrow corridor to the back, where I saw my husband sitting on the mat. There was a dim light, and I could see the tip of a lit cigarette. I hadn't seen him smoking yet, but I could already smell the nicotine from him.

Everything around me was dark, only the sea visible, no trace of light, which made me swallow hard. I turned my gaze back to Valentino, who at that moment had his eyes fixed on me.

"I let you out?" he whispered, his voice getting lost in the cold wind that made my body shiver.

"You didn't say I couldn't leave." I shrugged.

"Do you want to sit here?" He looked to his side, and sitting next to him might open a chance for us to talk.

Without agreeing or refusing, I moved toward him, sitting beside him on the mat, feeling his arm brush against mine. I remained still, not knowing what to say, until I felt his hand move, resting on my shoulder and pulling me closer to him.

Even doing this, he remained silent.

His scent enveloped me, the cigarette smoke dissipating into the wind. I shivered again with the cold wind coming from the moving yacht, pulling my legs to my side and curling up more.

"Are you cold?" he asked, seeming to enjoy himself.

"And you, aren't you? Or are you going to tell me that having a defined abdomen keeps you warm from the cold?"

My question made him laugh softly.

"Not really, but part of my training for serving my mafia was in Switzerland during the harsh winter, often testing our endurance, so my body is somewhat adapted to it." I raised my face, meeting his gaze.

"Why training?" I asked, curious.

"We need to be ready for everything that comes with the burden of joining a mafia. We need to be strong, resilient, and never flinch. And since I wanted to be my father's successor, I had to be perfect, good at everything, absolutely the best at everything," he said with such conviction that even I was impressed.

"But you know no one is perfect," I said, giving the most clichéd response ever.

"I am, I need to be." From his words, I realized Valentino was very hard on himself.

I turned my face, noticing his hand on my shoulder, where his wrist was resting, his free hand relaxed. But what caught my attention was seeing that as he moved his hand, the yacht's light reflected the visible bruises and cuts on it, the same cut that had bled onto my hand.

I raised my hand, holding his, wanting to see it more clearly, wondering how he managed to get so many cuts like that.

Valentino noticed what I was doing, pulling his hand away abruptly. I turned my face toward his stern green eyes.

"What's that on your hand?" I asked, worried.

"None of your business," he growled, sounding irritated that I was intruding on his precious life.

"Of course, nothing that concerns me." I shifted, kneeling as I looked at him. "Is it always going to be like this? Cold and distant? One minute you want me by your side, the next you're tense as if it's forbidden to invade your precious privacy!"

"I just thought if you sat here, we could finish with me fucking your pussy." I opened my mouth slightly at his crude words. "But you've always been such a stuck-up."

"Stuck-up, me? Do you really think you're going to get anything from me like this? Being egocentric and wanting me only for sex? Once we have our first time, know that it will only happen again if I don't get pregnant." I jumped off the mat.

"Maybe I should use a condom, then." His wicked smile lit up in the dim light.

"I loathe the damned day they married me off to a jerk like you." I stamped my foot on the ground.

"That's not what your eyes say when they're on me."

"That's obvious, and clearly, you must know you're handsome, but your character overshadows all your physical beauty. And you can wipe that stupid smile off your lips because it's not something you don't already know." I gestured with my hand.

"Get lost, Yulia. Just take that sassy mouth of yours away from me before I shut it with my hand." There was the controlling husband I always knew I'd marry.

"Yes, majesty, that's a favor I'm doing for myself, staying away from you." I made a dramatic bow, practically running away when I saw him move, wanting to come after me to at least punish me.

CHAPTER SIXTEEN

Yulia

I ran down the stairs, my breath ragged as I entered the room, closing the door and holding it with my body weight.

I could hear his footsteps coming from outside; I held my breath in vain, as he obviously knew I was there. I looked around for something I could use to defend myself but found nothing.

The door moved as if someone was trying to enter—it was him.

"You know, little butterfly, I love playing hide and seek with rats—or should it be hide and seek with butterflies?" he said from the other side of the door, in a mocking tone.

"Stop calling me butterfly!" I declared loudly.

"Do you want to test your butterfly strength against mine?" The bastard knew it was me holding the door, that it was my body weight there.

With just a shove that seemed almost casual, he opened the door, making me dash toward the first thing I found—the porcelain lamp by the bed.

"Don't touch me." I pointed it at him, my yank pulling the plug from the socket.

"What are you going to do with that lamp? Throw it at me? My position as Don can't be threatened by that..."

"Is your position really that insignificant? Because you don't know me at all!" I growled, still threatening him with the lamp.

"Go ahead then, wife, throw it..." he continued walking. "Go on, butterfly, throw it..."

Valentino was provoking me; he thought I'd hesitate. With a quick move, I smashed the lamp against the furniture beside the bed, shattering it into sharp shards and pointed it at Valentino.

He smiled in a masochistic way, as if he didn't care about the pain I might cause him.

"Go on, wifey, isn't that what you want? Hurt me." My husband stood in front of the broken lamp in my hand.

He took a step slowly, letting one of the sharp points graze his chest. I looked at the scene, terrified.

Blood began to stain the sharp point, a satisfied smile appeared on his lips.

My body, already tense, became even more numb from the situation. I pulled the lamp away, letting it fall, and quickly moved my slippers over the porcelain shards scattered on the floor.

"Ouch!" I screamed as his hand yanked me forcefully, throwing me aggressively onto the bed.

My eyes fixed on the man in front of me, blood running down his chest, his masochistic smile on his lips, as if nothing frightened him, as if the pain I had inflicted on him didn't even faze him.

"Did you like what you did?" he growled amidst his question, wiping the blood off his chest. "Did you enjoy drawing blood from your husband?"

"N-n... no," I stammered for the first time.

Valentino moved closer to me, his bloodied fingers rubbing against my arm. A squeal escaped my mouth; the scene left me horrified.

"Stop! Stop!" I begged, one of my hands pinned by his, while the other was smeared with his blood, my legs immobilized by his feet.

"Aren't you the warrior princess? Where's your pride in drawing blood from your husband?"

"I'm not proud of it, I hurt you, but it wasn't on purpose; you put yourself in my way. I didn't want to do this..." I closed my eyes in fear. "No, I didn't want to, I don't do these kinds of things..."

"I saw the desire in your eyes, the anger you have towards me, deep down you wanted it." I opened my eyes again, meeting those vast green ones, which were now half-closed.

The blood on his chest had stopped flowing; the wound was there, small, but it must have been stinging.

"How can you not be feeling anything?" I murmured, terrified.

"Who said I'm not, but it's just a scratch, made by the delicate wings of a butterfly." His lip curled to the side, revealing a small, mocking smile.

"You're insane... INSANE..." I screamed, feeling something snap sharply against my face.

I closed my eyes, a cry of pain coursing through my body. Valentino, at that moment, released me and quickly got off me. I sat on the bed, terrified, pushing my body back against the wall, my frightened eyes meeting his stunned ones.

I felt the tears burning my face, streaming down from the pain of his open-handed slap.

"Damn it!" Valentino grunted as if to himself. "Sorry... sorry..."

I didn't say anything; I could even feel that he stammered the apology. I raised my hand, touching the sting of the slap, a sob escaping my mouth.

No one had ever hit me before, and it caught me off guard—the pain, the sting, the fact that my own husband had slapped me.

"Go to hell! You big idiot!" I growled in my rage. "I should have shoved that damn lamp into your chest. You're right, I don't regret it; I liked it. Maybe next time I'll push it all the way through."

In that moment, I didn't even recognize myself; that wasn't me. I didn't do those kinds of things. Valentino had awakened a sadistic side in me, a side that wanted to destroy him.

My husband, who seconds ago had a guilty expression, changed, his face hardening, his lip curling, making it clear that this was just the beginning of our endless war, a war until the end of our lives, as we were bound and sealed by this damned marriage.

"I take back what I said, I'm not sorry. Next time, I'll hit you harder," he roared through gritted teeth.

"Go ahead, because that's what cowardly men do—hit women," I retorted, focusing my eyes on his hands.

He was clenching his hand so tightly that the knuckles turned white, the blood clearly visible through the side, confirming what I had already suspected. Valentino was self-harming; he didn't even seem to realize it was bleeding.

"Valentino, your hand..." I whispered, terrified as he lowered his eyes as if realizing I had seen and quickly turned his back, leaving.

I was left alone, hugging my knees, thinking about how we had gone from a tender embrace on the yacht to a bloody fight.

I hadn't even noticed that I was holding my breath until I released it with difficulty. At that moment, alone, I let the tears fall from my eyes, letting them wash my face.

Allowing myself a solitary vulnerability.

CHAPTER SIXTEEN

Yulia

I lay on the bed after locking myself in the bathroom to take a shower, washing away all the blood Valentino had left on me.

The scene was still vivid in my mind as I lay on the bed, staring at the ceiling, remembering the blood on his chest, his hand, his masochistic smile, and how he reacted to everything.

It was madness on my part; should I talk to his mother about this? After all, no one had told me that he was self-harming, and what if he did worse things?

I noticed the yacht starting to slow down. My bags were all packed, and I knew we must be almost there since we had been on this yacht for about three hours.

I waited until someone came to get me as I had been waiting for him. He came. Valentino appeared, opening the door, wearing his button-up shirt with only the top buttons undone.

"We've arrived, come on," he said briefly, turning away and leaving me alone.

I got up from the bed, adjusting my loose dress. I couldn't find my bras, so I chose to go without them, as the straps were thin on each of my shoulders. I climbed the steps, passing through the kitchen and heading outside, holding only my phone. As soon as I stepped outside, my mouth fell open a million times. Wow! It was beautiful; in the distance was an island, and a car was waiting for us.

I approached the exit. Valentino went out first, extending his hand to help me down. I didn't want to take his hand, but with a huff of air, I accepted it, feeling those damn electric sparks every time he touched me.

As soon as I placed my feet on the ground, I wanted to pull my hand away, but as expected, he prevented me. It was nighttime, and all I could see were lights in the distance.

A car was waiting for us with the door open.

"Sir, we'll take you to where the car can go, to the resort entrance. From there, you'll take the mini jeep to your house on the highest and most private part of the island," Valentino nodded to the man.

I sat in the back seat, my husband next to me. He didn't say anything. I took out my phone, trying to find a signal to figure out where we were, but obviously, there was none.

"Can I finally know where we are?"

"Mosquito Island, part of the British Isles," he answered without opening up for further conversation.

Since he wasn't talking, neither was I. The atmosphere was tense. If someone threw a match, it would probably catch fire from our tension.

Our bags were stored, and we proceeded in silence until we reached the resort entrance, where three mini jeeps were waiting for us. Some staff were already there, offering congratulations to the newlyweds. Little did they know, we had almost killed each other and hadn't even had our honeymoon.

I looked around. There were some chalets, the sea was nearby, everything was well lit, with gravel forming the street and white pebbles at the chalet entrances.

Noticing my admiration and the fact that I wasn't moving, Valentino grabbed my arm. The jeep only had space for two people and their luggage, so our bags were placed in the other two jeeps. Valentino's security followed us while a resort guide led the way.

My husband drove our jeep. I didn't say anything. If we had any semblance of intimacy, I might have made a silly joke, but I didn't.

We climbed several hills, passing various types of chalets and houses, until we stopped at the largest one, with an elegant beachfront entrance. My God, I was so fascinated that I could have sworn I was drooling.

I got out of the jeep and saw my husband heading toward his men, giving them orders. I walked toward the open door of the house and pushed it open.

The lights were all on. The back of the house was entirely glass, with the doors open, revealing a beautiful starry sky. I approached, seeing the infinity pool, with a lawn beside it, and even a private bar for the residents of the house.

In the middle of the living room was a huge white sofa. The living room was open to the kitchen. I walked around, observing everything.

With all this, I could even judge that Valentino was romantic, if only he hadn't slapped me a few hours ago.

I heard his footsteps and turned, feeling my body shiver from the night breeze—or was it his intense gaze?

"The bedrooms are on the second floor..."

"How do you know? Have you been here before?" I asked impulsively, feeling a pang of jealousy.

Valentino furrowed his brow, confused.

"No? Why do you ask?"

"Then how do you know they're on the second floor?" I raised my eyebrow.

"The resort guide briefly told me about the rooms." Valentino seemed to notice my brief outburst, as he opened a small smile. "By the way, I think I'll hide your bras. Your breasts look beautiful without them, and when we're here alone, I want to have a full view of your body."

I instinctively lowered my face, not realizing that my nipples were erect. Damn it! Was this the effect of his stupid look? How could I be so vulnerable to that?

"Dream on, you Italian *idiot*."

"Silence!" He raised his hand to cut me off. "Every time you call me any name that offends me, you'll be punished, and know that I brought many torture instruments in one of my bags."

"You're bluffing," I murmured, even though I knew he wasn't.

"Wanna bet?" At that moment, I lifted my face and saw Valentino's men coming through the door with our bags.

Two of mine and two of his. A man always has fewer clothes than a woman, so obviously, Valentino wasn't bluffing.

"So, wife?" I turned my face away from him in fear.

"I won't be your submissive, or whatever you want me to be. I won't play *Anastasia Steele*." I shook my head in horror.

"Who's that?"

"The protagonist of the book *Fifty Shades of Grey*," I answered, leaving him even more confused.

"Whatever, I don't know what you're talking about. Just know this isn't a honeymoon. I'm not romantic, I don't want your love, nor your concern for me. All I want is you, physically you, your body, your pussy, and to put a baby right there in your belly." He pointed a finger at my stomach.

I took a step back, frightened by this man.

Seeing that staircase as an escape route, once again running from my crazy husband.

CHAPTER EIGHTEEN

Yulia

I spotted the last door in the hallway open, walked up to it, and closed it as soon as I entered. Looking around, I recognized it as the couple's room, with many red rose petals scattered on the bed, which felt ironic given the out-of-control man who was my husband.

I pushed away from the door after standing alone in silence for a few long seconds, not hearing any sound from the outside.

Walking with trepidation, afraid he might come back to chase me, I noticed that the only wall in the room seemed to have the bed against it. On the other two walls, it looked like there might have been curtains, and on the fourth wall, there was the entrance door to the room, the suite door, and a third door leading to the closet where our bags were. I saw only one of Valentino's bags—where was the other one?

I tried not to focus on it, pressing the button in the corner of the wall to open the curtains, revealing two walls entirely made of glass. I could see nothing but darkness and the starry sky in the distance; I deduced that it must be all ocean.

I approached the glass, my eyes lowering to see my husband below, sitting at a glass table for four with a laptop open and a phone to his ear. I focused on the laptop screen, wanting to see what he was looking at, but all I saw were numbers, probably just a spreadsheet.

Until he opened a new tab, which seemed to be a security camera feed from somewhere.

I didn't know much about these mafiosos' assets, but it looked like a nightclub. Valentino was skipping through the cameras, still with the phone to his ear, until he stopped at a scene with a couple—no, not a couple, there were three women. I couldn't count the number of men because he quickly closed the laptop, abruptly standing up from the chair, looking like he was even arguing with the person on the other end of the line.

It might have been a honeymoon, but not a vacation, as it was clearly a nightclub they had control over.

I quickly stepped back when Valentino hung up the phone, throwing it on the table. Without realizing it, I was breathing heavily, stepping away from the glass wall. I thought he might come to the room afterward, but he didn't appear—perhaps he had left.

Would he have the nerve to sleep with someone else on our first night as a married couple?

Well, if he wanted to do that, so be it, because I didn't want to see him in front of me.

I entered the closet, bending down next to my two bags, opening them and searching for my baby-dolls. I picked a white satin one. Since I had recently showered on the boat, I quickly changed my dress, fearing he might come in.

Grabbing my toiletry bag with all my personal hygiene products, I went to the suite. The sink there was double. I stood in front of one, tying my long hair into a bun to have better access to wash my face. I applied my cleaning creams to my face.

I was almost done when I heard the sound of the door. Through the mirror's reflection, I saw Valentino walking into the room. He passed by the door, unbuttoning his shirt.

He went into the closet, then came out with his hand luggage. I saw through the mirror's reflection that he sat on the bed, opening the bag and pulling out his phone charger. He seemed distracted, but

I knew he was aware of my presence; I was making noise with the water.

Valentino plugged in his phone to charge, then took the fabric from the bed, pulling it down and removing the red rose petals. Clearly annoyed by it, he shook everything to the floor, throwing the blanket haphazardly on the bed, which now no longer had romantic petals.

What a big insensitive idiot.

I packed my things back into my toiletry bag, holding it in my hand. I turned around as he took off his shirt, passing by me without saying a word, practically pushing me when he closed the door.

What a jerk. One moment he was playing the sadomasochistic husband, wanting to lay down his stupid rules, and the next he was fighting or, like now, pretending I wasn't even there.

I rolled my eyes, going into the closet and letting my long hair down. Since I was kicked out of the bathroom, I brushed my hair in front of the closet mirror. Maybe this ignorant version of Valentino was better; it kept us from talking.

When I finished with my hair, I grabbed my skin creams and went to the bed. There was nothing better than sleeping smelling good.

I walked past the petals. I was sure that if Valentino were at least a bit more approachable, less ignorant, and maybe a little romantic, I might have tried to give myself to him. But none of that was viable; nothing about it was easy, and it made me hate him.

Not to mention what he did over the past two years. Even though it was in the past, he participated in an orgy to affect me and made sure I knew about it.

I picked up one of those petals and left it on the nightstand by the bed.

I sat on the soft mattress, folding my leg over the bed, putting a bit of cream on my hand and smoothing it over my skin, enjoying the nutty aroma that touched my sense of smell. It was wonderful.

One of my favorite creams. I was finishing the second leg when I saw the bathroom door open, but I didn't even make the effort to lift my eyes. Only when he entered the closet and came out again did I look up, seeing him walk around in nothing but white boxer shorts—white fucking underwear... WHITE!

Who wears white underwear unless they're trying to provoke?

"Aren't you going to put on pants? Shorts? Anything?" I asked, trying to keep my eyes on the cream, a task that was becoming difficult.

Valentino didn't answer my question, as if I had spoken to the wind, as if he were alone there.

I turned my face, noticing that he had laid down on his stomach and was turning his face away from mine, remaining silent.

Great, we were practicing the silent side of my husband.

I finished applying my cream on my arms, neck, and stomach. I got off the bed, left the lamp on the bedside table lit, went to the light switch by the door and turned it off, keeping only my bedside lamp on. I closed the bedroom curtains, not bothering to look at Valentino.

I went back to my side of the bed, realizing he had indeed fallen asleep. His slow breathing betrayed that. I could kill him now, and he wouldn't even have a chance to retaliate—a silly theory, as I would never have the courage to do that.

I lay down on my side of the bed, not before placing the pillow between us to divide us.

Would it always be like this? Either silence, or aggressiveness, or ignorance, with no conversation, no intimacy...

CHAPTER NINETEEN

Valentino

I squeezed my eyelids, feeling something brushing against my back. I slowly opened my eyes, looking at the closed door. My body shivered from the cold air conditioning inside. I was without a blanket, turned my face, still lying on my stomach just as I had fallen onto the bed. I was so exhausted, over 24 hours without sleep, I don't even know how I managed to sleep. I only remembered throwing myself onto the bed and, to avoid any possible argument with my wife, I chose not to talk.

I'm good at the art of ignoring.

My eyes focused on the girl lying with her eyes closed, her black hair spread out on the pillow. In the middle of the bed was another pillow, and despite it being there, her arms over it touched my back. Yulia was also without a blanket and seemed to be feeling cold.

Carefully, I sat up on the bed, grabbing my phone next to her. Being there was like going back in time, with the time zone being almost five hours ahead of Sicily.

I had to check the local time app to realize it was five in the morning. Damn, I had hardly slept, and outside, the day was apparently beginning to break through the light curtains.

I got up, running my hand over my thighs, encountering the damn morning erection.

I was heading to the suite when I heard the girl moving on the bed. I turned, noticing she was searching for something. Her sleep must have been light, as Yulia opened her eyes, looking around as if wondering where she was.

Until her eyes met mine, half-closing them, then quickly closing them again when she realized I was in my underwear. Her cheeks flushed red, and a smile formed on my lips.

"Put on some pants. Nobody's obligated to look at you in your underwear," she mumbled, still sounding sleepy.

"Well, then turn your face away." The fact that I spoke made my wife open her eyes again, trying to focus them only on my face.

"Am I invisible today?" Her voice was low and hoarse.

"Never was. I just sometimes wish I could hit a mute button on you." I shrugged, heading to the suite, where I locked the door.

I stayed there for a long time. After brushing my teeth and washing my face, I left the suite. By that time, my morning erection had gone away, but it returned when I saw my wife sitting on the bed, performing the simple task of tying her hair into a bun on top of her head.

Her arms raised, the satin pajamas clinging to her nipples, which were slightly erect, her stomach slightly exposed due to the raised hand. I tried my best to ignore the tempting sight of my wife, but it was nearly impossible.

Yulia's eyes turned towards me when she finished her bun. She even tried to ignore me as she got off the bed. My eyes trailed down her small body, the short shorts making me wonder what she looked like naked. Damn, how I wanted to see her naked.

"Lost something?" she asked, making me lift my eyes to meet hers.

"Just analyzing what's mine." I shrugged.

"I'm not yours." She crossed her arms.

"That's what you think, because in the agreement I made with your brother, you're mine, like property—my property." I gave a brief mocking smile.

Yulia stamped her foot, doing what she did best—throwing a tantrum. She walked past me into the bathroom.

I entered the closet, putting on one of my black nylon shorts. I didn't take a shirt; that was enough. I needed to call Matteo and see how things were going in Sicily.

Last night was chaos on earth. At our Vegas nightclub, some new associates thought they could abuse two of our dancers. We didn't deal with any kind of girl sales or escorts. Our club had sexual female dancing, and that was it. In terms of sensuality, the main focus was on illegal gambling, with people who thought they'd get rich but ended up getting deeper in debt.

Fortunately, it was all resolved. I asked the manager there to take a hard line, and if that didn't work, to expel them, stripping away any privileges they once had with the Cosa Nostra.

This always happened, but when the client was persistent, a more aggressive action was necessary.

I went down the stairs, noticing a hearty breakfast on the table, just as I had ordered to be prepared every morning. At the door was one of my soldiers. I asked him to come to me, and we both headed to the back.

I asked for the night report, and everything was calm. He was responsible for all the nighttime security. We stayed there for a long time until I decided to go in. Since Matteo hadn't sent me any messages, I decided I would call him later.

We both went back home. The glass doors were all open. My eyes lifted when I saw my wife coming down the stairs in a tiny bikini top.

"If I catch your eyes on my wife, I'll rip them out," I growled at my soldier.

"Yes, Don." At that moment, the man walked behind me to his post at the door.

"Stay outside," I ordered, as the sight of Yulia in that bikini top, exposed for everyone to see, was making me furious.

On the bottom, she had put on a skirt that seemed made of some kind of fabric, full of holes. What the hell did this woman think she was doing?

"Where do you think you're going dressed like that?" I grunted.

"We're in a beautiful place like this, with a pool and the sea. Do you think I should dress like what? A burka? No, husband, I have too beautiful a body to keep hidden." Her smile was smug while all I felt was anger at her audacity.

"A body that's mine!" I snarled as she lowered her face, raising her hand, pulling the fabric of her bikini even tighter.

It shaped her round breasts even more, marking them perfectly.

"Well, you don't like to keep your hands off other women? Maybe my view is pleasing to other eyes. From what I saw, there's a restaurant downstairs. I'm going to have breakfast with civilization, not here with a caveman like you." She turned away.

Giving me a perfect view of her round, well-endowed ass, too much for her small size. Damn, Colombian woman.

I just crossed my arms, waiting for her to try to leave, smiling at my little victory when she tried to open the door and found it locked, beside it, a keypad. Her face turned towards me.

"Where exactly do you think you're going, wife? I believe the only civilization you'll find is this." I pulled out a chair and sat down.

Yulia stamped her foot in her tantrum, making that pout of hers, which, even though it was out of anger, was deliciously tempting.

Damn it, all I wanted was that little Colombian riding my dick, and she knew I couldn't resist feminine curves. She was probably teasing me.

CHAPTER TWENTY

Yulia

I turned my body, observing the triumphant expression of my idiot husband. I couldn't believe it—despite all my effort to look beautiful to provoke him and make my dramatic exit, it was slipping through my fingers.

Damn!

And the worst part was that I was hungry; the smell of the food on the table was making me even hungrier.

Valentino picked up a slice of cake, put it on his plate, took a bite, chewing without taking his eyes off mine.

"You don't know how delicious this is..." he taunted.

I rolled my eyes, leaving my handbag on the sofa and heading to the table, where I sat facing him. I didn't say anything; maybe the silent version of Valentino was better, as the provoking version made me lose my composure quickly.

I filled my glass with orange juice, took a slice of cake, and tried not to look up, even though it was hard to ignore the perfect view of my husband with that sea in the background.

He had brought me to this paradise and still thought I couldn't explore it, and on top of that, he made me think about what it would be like to enjoy a real honeymoon, but as he himself said, this wasn't a honeymoon.

"What's making you stay silent?" he asked.

I didn't want to answer; I wanted to do what he did to me last night—pretend I was alone in my world.

"I know your tongue is itching to say something," his provocation was endless.

I was determined to be strong, raised my eyes only to grab a small dish with chopped fruit, putting some pieces on my plate, then putting it back. I took small sips of my juice, leaving it on the table, my eyes briefly meeting Valentino's; he still kept his gaze curiously on me.

"Fine," he whispered, getting up and passing by me. At that moment, I thought I had won that round.

"AH!" I let out a scream when my chair was pulled back, his hand gripping my shoulder to keep me seated.

"No one ignores the Don," he roared, and I thought he had taken it in a good way.

"Let me go," I pleaded, raising my hand, trying to remove his hand from my shoulder, which was now sliding down my skin.

"You didn't want to provoke me? Didn't you want to come down in these tiny clothes just to show off your delicious body to all the men? Is that what you wanted, Yulia?" His reprimanding tone made me tremble with fear. "Come on, damn it, answer me!"

He growled, making me scream when he roughly yanked at my bikini, the force tearing it apart. I raised my hand to cover my bare breasts, and Valentino released my shoulder, holding my bikini. Despite my fear, I got up from the chair, looking at him.

"I don't want you wearing these tiny things anymore; I don't want another man thinking about my damn wife. You're mine, understand? Mine, only mine!" he said harshly, tearing the bikini into millions of pieces, his forehead veins bulging.

Valentino threw the pieces to the ground and came towards me. It was as if my feet were glued to the floor, unable to run, I stood still.

His large hands gripped both sides of my face, with aggression, his lips touched mine. Either I pushed him away or held my breasts.

"Kiss me, damn it!" The mobster growled with his lips pressed against mine.

"No!" I stayed resistant, as I wouldn't give in to him during a jealousy crisis.

My husband tried, even biting my lip, but all I did was keep it clenched and my body vulnerable to his, no matter how much I wanted, desired that incredibly handsome man, I wouldn't give in—not that way. I could endure the shivers running through my body; we wouldn't surrender to the man who ruined my last two years in college. *Not easily.*

He pulled away with his eyes half-closed in my direction, then glanced down at my hand holding my breasts.

"What's your problem? Why won't you kiss me, damn it?" He ran his hand through his hair while the other hand clenched.

"I said there would be nothing from me with aggression. Want me? You'll have to force me because I won't give in!" My voice came out breathless, my body on fire, absolutely hot.

"Things could be different. I can make your first time not be bad..."

"The problem isn't that. The problem is that you're egocentric, only thinking about yourself. You came to my college and ruined it. Made all the men stay away from me, even my friends. And I haven't mentioned the damn orgy that my fiancé insisted on participating in, branding me as *The* campus's cuckold. Do you have any idea, Valentino??? For two years, TWO DAMN YEARS!? Do you think I have a flea's memory? I remember everything, everything!!!" I lost it at that moment, shouting, throwing all my anger at him.

He fell silent, both of us staring at each other, as if there was an electric current between us, my chest rising and falling uncontrollably.

"You're being resentful," he declared amid the silence that surrounded us.

"I can be resentful, but I can't simply erase the fact that the man who claimed to be my fiancé went to my college, slept with various women, just to hurt me. If that's being resentful, then yes, I'm very resentful. I hate you, Valentino Vacchiano, I hate you with all my strength. I abhor the day my brother crossed your path, I hate the day you went to my college, and I dare to throw it in your face. YOU ARE NOT PERFECT, ALL I SEE IN YOU IS JUST A MAN WHO THINKS HE'S GOOD, BUT HE'S NOT!!!" I screamed so loudly that I could swear the whole island heard.

My husband didn't react; it was as if I had found his weak spot. Valentino remained still, his eyes lost on me but his mind distant, so distant that I even moved, and he didn't notice.

I seized that moment to leave, running for the stairs, climbing the steps breathlessly.

When I reached the top, I looked back at him, still standing in the same place, but what worried me most was the fact that his hands were dripping with blood.

"I don't want your concern." Those were the words Valentino had said to me when we were on the boat.

But I couldn't help but worry. Valentino quickly moved, grabbing a knife from the table. He thought he was alone, assumed I was in our room, and pressed it to his wrist. My heart squeezed so tightly, a feeling I had never experienced before—desperation, pained by the suffering he felt or thought he needed to feel.

I raced down the stairs, filled with concern, needing to get that knife out of his hand.

CHAPTER TWENTY-ONE

Yulia

I positioned myself in front of him, seeing Valentino's dazed expression.

"Let go of that," I pleaded, afraid of what he might do if I approached.

His jaw was clenched, as if he wasn't even hearing what I said, holding the serrated knife to his wrist. He was going to cut himself; it wouldn't be just a small cut, that knife had serrations!

Acting impulsively, I grabbed his arm where he held the knife.

"Please, Valentino, let go of that..."

"No," he said with a choked voice, as if his teeth were clenched.

"You're going to hurt yourself, for God's sake, your hand is already bleeding." I squeezed his hand hard, trying desperately to make him stop, but nothing could deter him.

His muscles were so tense, and quickly my mind flashed back to the confrontation my sister-in-law had with my brother. When he was out of control, she kissed him to bring him back to reality.

God was my witness to my torment, as I tried to make him release that knife.

"Valentino, please, look at me, don't do this." My eyes widened when he pressed on, even with my pleas, my strength was nothing compared to his. "Damn it..."

I murmured, releasing my only hand that covered my breasts, holding his face with both hands, standing on tiptoe, my stomach in front of his arm with the knife, my hand over his wrist.

Without thinking, I pressed my lips to his, trying to do as Amelia did, knowing it might not have the same effect.

"Kiss me, my husband," I murmured with my lips against his.

It seemed my words had some effect; I heard the knife clatter to the ground, his arm moving quickly, wrapping around my waist, lifting me effortlessly, my legs circling his waist, my arms sliding over his neck, feeling his hair between my fingers.

Valentino's tongue touched mine, sliding with lust, I didn't stop him, as my husband's hands traveled up my back, his touch was firm, hard, aggressive, taking me somewhere.

His kiss was strong, intense, using his tongue as if he wanted to transfer his pain to me, laying me down on the large sofa. When he pulled away, he tried to cover my breasts, as they were exposed to him.

"No!" he growled, holding my wrists above my head.

I lowered my face, and when I looked down my body, my eyes widened seeing his blood smeared across my waist.

He didn't say anything, just stared at it.

"Valentino," I whispered his name.

My husband closed his eyes, then opened them again, as if the blood didn't affect him, he lowered his face, catching me off guard when he bit my breasts, with force, sucking aggressively, using his teeth on the tips of my nipples.

"Ah," a little squeal escaped my mouth, but he didn't stop, continuing to leave hickeys all over my breasts.

Releasing my wrists, he let my hand free. I placed it on his neck, feeling his body still tense, his fingers that were holding my wrist moved down to the middle of my legs, reaching my intimacy, and through my bikini, I could feel myself wet for him.

Even though his actions were aggressive, even causing a bit of pain, it made me want more of his hand.

I was giving in to that frenzy of emotions, starting to think I might actually go through with it for the first time in my life, but as soon as he touched my pussy, everything became clouded.

My body that was surrendered became tense, sweat appeared, and trembling coursed through me.

"Stop, Valentino, stop," I pleaded, wanting to pull away from him, but he didn't stop, crossing my limits of calmness. "STOP, STOP, STOP..."

I began to scream, desperately, unable to see anything in front of me, closing my eyes tightly, hearing cries of children in my mind.

My scream didn't cease, my eyes filled with tears even with them closed, and they started to fall down my face.

Valentino released me, I recoiled, opening my eyes to everything around me without being able to focus on anything, everything was blurred, I hugged my knees, feeling that pain that always overtook me, tearing me apart, sniffing in my sobs.

"I... I'm sorry..." I could hear his apology beside me.

I blinked several times, the torment slowly leaving me, managing to focus my eyes on my husband.

"Looks like you're not the only crazy one here." A forced smile appeared on my lips.

"Did I do something?" My husband wanted to know.

"It's me, okay? I'm the problem. How do I tell you that to have your heir you'll need to annul our marriage because I'm a failure?" I said, placing my hand over my breasts as I stood up from the sofa.

Looking at him, who still had that questioning expression.

"Don't get it? Want me to spell it out? I can't have sex, I have a defect. I tried, I thought it might work with you, but it didn't, it doesn't, I can't. Annul the marriage, you'll need to talk to my brother." I smiled amidst my desperation.

Maybe I had never really envisioned having a child since it wasn't meant for me, I couldn't, there was a block within me.

"So you're not going to question the fact that I covered you in blood?" he asked, still dazed.

"Well, what's your madness compared to mine? See, no one is perfect..."

I blinked several times, wanting to leave, feeling useless. How did I think it could be different? That it could go forward.

"You're perfect, Yulia." I heard his voice, but I didn't listen, because at that moment all I wanted was to be alone in the room, maybe a bath to clear my head.

Even though all that came to my mind were his strong hands, his aggressive grip. No one had ever taken me that way before; the few men I had been intimate with had only offered gentle touches, nothing compared to that, to the hickeys, the bite on my nipple.

Damn, I shouldn't have liked it, because he was going to leave me. Valentino wanted an heir, one I could never give him.

Maybe I should have talked about this before the marriage, it would have spared everyone that embarrassment, and I wouldn't have to worry about that man. Thinking Valentino was a perfectionist seemed easier, but now knowing he had weaknesses and vulnerabilities affected me in ways it shouldn't.

CHAPTER TWENTY-TWO

Valentino

We needed to leave the house so it could be cleaned, with blood on the floor and the sofa. I took Yulia to the beach, and throughout the trip, she remained silent, which made me even more curious.

Even though I had torn that damn bikini, she had another one, flaunting her beautiful body on that beach.

I rented a tent, where I was sitting inside but with a view of everyone around us, keeping an eye out for anyone approaching my girl.

If Yulia thought she was going to annul the marriage, she was very mistaken. It was impossible for someone to simply be unable to have sex; something had to be wrong.

I closed my laptop when a resort waitress brought my whiskey, leaving a drink for Yulia as well.

She quickly turned away, leaving me with the sight of my lovely wife. Her body was completely illuminated by the sea droplets, her wet black hair, the vision of perfection.

I wanted to pull that damn tiny bikini and rip it off. The bottom part marked her pussy, making me wonder what it would be like to touch her. I was almost there, almost touched her, but then everything happened suddenly.

The atmosphere between us was tense. Yulia grabbed her glass and sat on the edge of her lounge chair. I kept wondering how I lost my control so easily around her; I had never done that before. It was as if she made me step out of my comfort zone.

I was startled when my phone rang. I picked it up from the table, seeing Ferney's name on the screen for a video call.

"It's your brother," I declared, drawing her attention.

"So what? Answer it, he probably wants to talk to you." The girl shrugged.

"No, he wants to talk to you."

"You didn't do that, did you? You told him? Are you crazy? I didn't tell anyone in your family about your problem." Yulia quickly started to lose control.

"Well, he was quite concerned when I briefly mentioned what happened. My problem isn't something that affects us both. Your problem does affect us both because I want my heir," I roared, grabbing the phone and answering the call. "Talk to him, stubborn girl."

With no other option, Yulia took the phone. I had no idea what he was going to say to her. All I knew was that Ferney was worried when I told him that his sister had lost control when we tried to be intimate for the first time and kept repeating that she had defects and couldn't give me an heir.

Ferney asked to speak to his sister, as if he had something serious to say.

"Sister, how are you?" I could see Amelia in the background of the call. Yulia stayed by my side, which allowed me to hear their conversation.

"I'm fine," she whispered, quickly putting the phone aside, putting on her cover-up to hide the hickeys I gave her on her breast, which looked so beautiful.

Yulia picked up the phone again, looking at her brother.

"Since when has this been happening?" he asked directly.

"Do we really need to talk about this?" she wanted to avoid the topic.

"Yes, dear," Amelia said in her sweet voice.

"Well, I've never been able to go further; it's always just kisses. When things start to get more intimate, I freeze. My therapist tried to get to the root of it, but nothing, simply nothing appears, nothing I can remember, and no, I'm not a lesbian," she said, assuming they had considered that possibility.

"Oh, dear, we know you're not." Amelia smiled warmly.

It was funny because if she really liked women, I would make her like men by force.

"Come on, Ferney, there's no easy way to say this. You hid it from her, now is the time for Yulia to know..."

"Know what?" Yulia interrupted Amelia.

"Sister, I initially apologize. I thought by doing this I'd be sparing you from a past you didn't need to know about. You were so small, an innocent child." Ferney cleared his throat, and even I started to feel concerned.

"Brother, you're making me worried," Yulia declared, placing the tip of her finger on her mouth.

"Do you remember that our mother was an addict?" he asked, and she nodded. *"Every time I came home from work, she was high somewhere. Until one day I came home, and one of her boyfriends was at our house, she was passed out somewhere. I started looking for that miserable boyfriend and found him in your room. You were just a baby, only two years old. I didn't see him touching you, but I don't know if there was another time before I caught him. I asked Aunt to take you to the hospital, and nothing was found. You were never touched, but somehow it must have stayed in your subconscious. If I hadn't arrived in time, only God knows. But I killed that bastard; I made him feel what it's like to touch my sister. I'm sorry, Yulia..."*

The girl fell silent, and at that moment, so did I. I didn't know anything about their past, which made me believe that I didn't know anything about my wife either.

I grew up in a large family with many cousins. There was never a shortage of love amid the chaos that we were, and it seemed that with Yulia, it wasn't quite the same.

"So there was always a reason?" she whispered, seeming confused.

"Apparently, yes..."

"Is there anything else I need to know?" She seemed bitter.

"No, I don't think so," Ferney said in a guilty tone.

Yulia threw the phone at me and simply started running. I grabbed the device.

"Take care of my sister, whatever she needs right now, I beg you," my brother-in-law asked.

"I will," I said, ending the call and leaving the phone there.

I got up from my lounge chair, seeing that Yulia was heading towards the end of the island, where it was divided by many rocks. I didn't know how to deal with her demons, as I couldn't even handle my own, but at that moment, I needed to keep my calm. After all, she had just discovered that she was almost abused at two years old and that her mother, who was supposed to protect her, was high somewhere.

After that, Ferney had all my respect; he honored his sister and killed the bastard.

I had to pick up the pace because my little wife was running faster than I expected.

CHAPTER TWENTY-THREE

Yulia

It caught me off guard. It was like taking a punch to the stomach and not knowing where it came from. Running was all that came to mind, trying to escape, wanting to wash away the bitter taste that pervaded my whole body.

I wanted that ball that had formed inside me to come out, something that had been there all the time, my subconscious trying to alert me that there was always a small tip of the iceberg that made me this way.

What a fool I was; everything could have been resolved earlier if only I had opened up to my brother, but how could I have imagined?

By God, how was I supposed to foresee that something like this could have happened to me?

Even with my eyes fogged, with thick tears escaping, I could see that I was approaching the large rocks that marked the end of that part of the beach.

The sand getting between my toes, what was going to happen to me now?

How could I deal with something that had always been there? All I wanted at that moment was to escape, to leave this reality. Ferney had no right to hide this from me, but deep down, I understand that my brother had his reasons, given his past, wanting the best for me, thinking that this fact would never torment me.

But it did torment me; it had been there all my life, and I didn't know the reason. I thought I had some pointless flaw.

Am I a flaw?

I reached the front of that enormous rock, realizing there was nowhere left to run...

"Ah!" I let out a small scream when I felt strong hands sliding around my waist, pulling my body backward, pressing my back against that hard chest.

"*Bambina mia*" his voice was breathless, he had been chasing me and I hadn't even noticed?

"Let me go, Valentino..." I grabbed his strong hand that was splayed across my belly.

"No..."

"I want you away from me." A sob escaped my mouth.

"I may be insensitive, but I know when someone needs help," he whispered firmly, without even letting go of me.

"I don't want you, I didn't ask for your help, I want you away." The tears kept falling, fear tormenting me, my vulnerability completely at his mercy.

Valentino didn't let me go, holding me tighter against his bare chest, against his warm skin. My body started to go limp, pain and exhaustion taking over. And as if he felt I was about to give in to exhaustion easily, he lifted me into his arms.

"Let me take care of you, *bambina mia*..." his voice trailed off as I dragged my fingers across his chest.

My husband started walking, taking us back to our tent. I said nothing; at that moment, even talking was becoming a difficult task, my mind wouldn't stop.

The tears had stopped, until the thought of me being only two years old, a little girl, crossed my mind...

Valentino entered our tent easily, laying me down on it. Inside, no one could see us from the sides except for the front entrance, which was open.

The Italian sat next to me, I lifted my hand to cover my eyes, feeling foolish for exposing myself so vulnerably to that damned man who knew nothing.

"Do you want to say something, butterfly?" His tone was calm, as if he was trying to soothe the situation.

"Just leave me, leave me..." I cleared my throat, still with my face covered.

My body briefly tensed when I felt his hand touch my belly. It soon turned into a shiver that spread all over me, an act he felt, as his hand gently caressed my skin.

"I'm not going to leave you, or did you forget what the pastor made us promise?" he murmured, reminding me of our wedding vows.

"All I remember is handing myself over to a man who didn't even promise his fidelity," I muttered.

"Even so, my loyalty is to you, regarding your torment, your health; you will always come first in my life, Yulia Vacchiano." That made me remove my hands from my eyes, and I realized that no more tears were coming from them.

"Except for your pleasure, because it was clearly evident that you might betray me whenever it suits you," I retorted, my anger surfacing again when the subject was brought up.

"I'm a sexually active man..."

"I'm sorry, Valentino, but this doesn't sink in for me. What if I were a sexually active woman? They wouldn't let me run around like a crazy woman with my husband. Just because I'm active doesn't make you immune to anything; these rules are indeed sexist." I pressed my hands against the lounge chair, wanting to get up, but was stopped by his hand that had moved from my belly to the middle of my chest, his fingers touching the top of my breasts.

"Rules that benefit the Don, because I'm the damn boss, I carry the weight of having a clan on my shoulders. I need to be perfect, and if there's something that satisfies me, it's good sex, with one, two, three, regardless of how many women there are. It's crossed my mind to go out and seek sex because I'm tense. I'm showing you what I'm not, what I've never done with anyone before. This coexistence is destabilizing me, so if you can't be the damn woman who gives me pleasure, I'll find another one"—he roared at me, making me even more furious.

"Go ahead, if that's what you want, go, Valentino, get one, two, three, even four if you want. I don't care what you do with your dick. I hope you catch a disease and die, or if possible, it would be a huge pleasure if you got sick and lost your dick. That would be suffering in paradise"—I spat the words out in my anger.

"You're saying you don't mind being betrayed?" His tone sent shivers down my spine in my fear.

"I'm saying I want you to go to hell, to wherever is far from me." I tried to futilely evade his hand, raising mine and hitting his arm. "Let me go, or I'll scream..."

"Scream, and you'll find out what it's like to take a second slap."

"Go ahead, you coward, hit me, maybe I'll become like you, take pleasure in feeling pain. What does that make me? A masochist? CRAZY!" I shouted the last word.

A scream escaped my mouth when his hand flew to my neck, gripping it tightly.

"Don't provoke me, don't defy me. You think you know me, but you don't know anything about me. And I'm not a masochist; I'm a sadist. I love fucking to the limit, I hurt my partner for pleasure. I've wanted to see you suffer, I've imagined you tied up in various ways, and know that one more defiance from you will have you completely bound, not even touching the ground with your feet, and your mouth..." He touched my lips with his other hand, his aggressive fingers sliding over them. "Will be silenced by tape that, when removed, will make you feel even the pores coming off..."

My husband abruptly released me, standing up. My eyes went directly to the bulge in his shorts.

"I wanted to help you, but in return, you chose to get the worst of me, and now you will have it" he snarled, turning his back and leaving me there alone.

I didn't doubt a single word he said, as in front of the erect member, he was aroused by the thought of torturing me.

CHAPTER TWENTY-FOUR

Yulia

Valentino left me alone on the beach, but that didn't make me afraid. I got up from the lounge chair, grabbed my beach cover-up, and put it on, covering my breasts and those horrible hickeys he had left on me, which reminded me of his mouth on my skin, his tongue sliding over me, the way he pressed against me.

Now that I knew the reason for my block, would I be able to move forward?

It was leaving me very confused. Our constant fights made me feel excited for the next ones; should I think of myself as crazy? Probably.

But all I expected from Valentino was this: fights, *and more fights*, with no connection, just fights.

Maybe there was physical connection, but we had no conversations, always ending with one of us saying something the other didn't like. His aggression didn't move me at all; that's how those mobsters resolved their disagreements.

I continued walking on the sand, holding my bag in my arm, stopping in front of the sea, taking a picture of the crystal blue water and posting it on my Instagram stories.

I replied to Ferney's message, calming him and Amelia, making it clear that I was okay, that my husband took care of me. Technically, I didn't lie; what came next was a consequence.

Since we were on the lower part of the island, even though my husband had sent one of his men to keep an eye on me, I pretended not to know anything, heading towards a song playing in an *electro house*.

My sandals clicking on the loose stones until I found a little bar with the music I had heard; it was late afternoon, people were dancing with drinks in hand, many seemed to be drunk, like a *social gathering*, with cushions in the corners revealing couples kissing.

Noticing the bar, I went to it, pulling up a stool and sitting on it.

"Would you like something, cutie?" the bartender asked in a dragged-out Spanish, my native language.

"Please, a strawberry gin," I said, looking at the young man working behind the bar.

Even with the huge ring on my finger, it didn't stop him from hitting on me. He continued to prepare my drink, and I looked around, noticing someone familiar in the back, in a group of women, apparently doing nothing, just chatting, with that cocky smile, which was never directed at me. He always gave me that mocking look.

As if he knew he was being watched, Valentino turned his face, and I quickly turned mine. If he thought he could hide in a circle of women, I was capable of doing something much worse.

I gave the bartender my most convincing smile.

"Thank you," I said as I took the drink.

"It's on the house, cutie." He winked at me, making me wish my damn husband had seen that wink.

Let him go around giving his cocky smiles to all the girls. I knew how to play that game of mischief.

I held the glass in my hand, bringing the umbrella-shaped straw to my mouth, getting up from the stool, thinking about where to go, noticing that the circle where my husband was also had men. Why not pretend I didn't know him and go over there as well?

Without looking in Valentino's direction, I approached him, heading in the opposite direction, passing close by, hoping one of the men would see me and pull me over. Then I felt an arm on mine. I knew that grip wasn't from my husband because there were no damn electric shocks. I turned my face and met a pair of brown eyes.

"Lost, cutie?" the man said in English.

"Just taking advantage of the fact that my husband left and decided to check out the place." I smiled, pretending to be innocent, leaving the statement with a double meaning. I knew Valentino heard what I said because the music was ambient, not loud.

"Join us, but I still think you're wearing too much clothing." His eyes dropped, coveting my body.

"Do you think so?" I joined their circle. If Valentino thought I was going to play the suffering wife, crying over him, he was very mistaken.

I diverted my eyes from the man, wanting to glance at Valentino, noticing that at that moment, he had placed his hand on the shoulder of a girl in a tiny bikini.

"Well, I can hold your bag so you can take off your cover-up..." he said, already reaching for my cover-up.

"Trust me, what stays a secret is much more satisfying." My voice was sweet, the most sensual I could manage, making the man think he had won the night. Little did he know, I was just playing with my idiot husband. "By the way, you called me Yulia, what's your name?"

"Mick." He lowered his face, trying to kiss me, and I turned mine because I wasn't crazy enough to let him kiss me on the mouth.

But Mick continued towards my face, trying to kiss my mouth, when I heard a growl beside me. There, I had unleashed the monster that was my husband.

I felt the electric fingers gripping my wrist, knowing who it was.

"Didn't you see the damn ring on her finger? Did you think her husband was a damn old man who doesn't know how to lift his fucking dick?" I was startled when Valentino yanked me into the commotion.

Out of the corner of my eye, I saw the men in black approaching, not even removing their dark suits despite the heat.

"She seemed pretty loose," that Mick said amidst his drunkenness, which made my husband growl like a caveman.

"Since when does her seeming loose mean you can hit on a married woman?" My husband took a step towards him, Valentino's men were practically on top of the group.

The shit was hitting the fan; my husband could order that poor man's death at any moment, and he wasn't even sober.

"Valentino, if you do something, I'll never look at your face again," I whispered in Italian, knowing that few people there spoke that language.

"Shut the fuck up, Yulia. Why didn't you go back to our damn house? Did you need to come here and flaunt yourself?" His angry eyes met mine.

"Oh, and the damn arm of yours on that woman was all good? I didn't do anything, didn't touch any man, which I can't say about you!" I tried to pull my arm away, but he wouldn't let me.

Acting quickly, he grabbed me by his shoulder, causing my head to hit his back due to his rapid movement.

My bag fell to the ground.

"Get her bag and take it home," he ordered one of his soldiers.

Valentino walked through the crowd, heading towards our mini-jeeps, and I started hitting his back, that arrogant bastard.

"Why can you and I can't? I'm disgusted by your hands being on another woman's body," I continued, feeling his hand slap my ass at his mercy.

"So you care if I'm with someone else?"

"OF COURSE I CARE, YOU ASSHOLE!" I screamed, hearing his loud laughter.

We stopped next to our mini-jeep, where he promptly sat me down, his face moving close to mine.

"The next time I see a man touching my wife, I'll tear off every finger that's been on your body," he growled, his breath mingling with mine.

"The next time I see you with your arms around another woman, I'll rip your dick off!" I murmured, even though my entire body was trembling with fear, overwhelmed by exceeding all my limits. "You're my husband; if I have to be yours, it's your duty to be mine..."

"That wasn't what was in our vows." He tilted his head to the side.

"But that's what I'm demanding..."

"In exchange, will you give me your virginity?"

"I'm not merchandise to be sold like that." I crossed my arms, turning my face away from his.

"Alright then, we'll stay at the same impasse. You want me to be yours, I will be, but in return, you need to surrender completely to me," he said, fastening me into the seatbelt, he literally tied me up, what a fucking bastard. "Take her home; I'll come later..."

"No! You're not doing that! I won't look at your face again if you do that." I turned my body, realizing he made a move for his man to take me away.

Without diverting his eyes from me, as if he wanted me to beg him to come, saying I would give myself to him, but by God, I had never begged for anything, and at that moment, I was almost doing it.

My eyes burning with tears, but I wouldn't let them fall, gathering all my pride, I turned forward, biting my lips hard, but I didn't ask him to come along. Let Valentino go to hell!

CHAPTER TWENTY-FIVE

Valentino

I asked to have Yulia taken home, and of course, my wife thought my intention was to betray her. But damn it, when I had my arms around those two girls, all I could think about was that they weren't my wife. They didn't have her nutty scent from the cream she used, nor her challenging gaze, and not even her sharp mouth that wasn't afraid to challenge me.

Yulia Vacchiano was the only girl outside my family who had the courage to confront me, and damn it, that excited me. It made me want to be near her, to touch her, but not in a tender way, rather with aggression, possessiveness, because she was mine, and only God knew how much I was controlling myself not to punish her, not to bind her with one of my cuffs, chain her up, and silence that delicious mouth with mine.

"Don?" I turned my face when one of my men called me. "Mrs. Vacchiano is already at the house, and we are keeping an eye on her."

"Alright. Have they arranged a private room for me?" I asked, as I needed a calm place; Santino and Matteo had been requesting a meeting for over an hour.

My man nodded, leading me through gravel paths towards a chalet that should have been vacant. The door was opened for me, and I saw my laptop on the table, along with my cigar box and a glass of whiskey.

"Close the door, and don't let anyone come near this chalet. I want complete privacy," my soldier confirmed, doing just that.

I turned on the orange light, pulled out a wooden chair, and sat down while opening my laptop and preparing a video call with my men, continuing to light my cigar.

After a few minutes, the two appeared in the same room, in my office, with Santino sitting in my chair and Matteo beside him.

"Any problems?" I asked immediately, bringing the cigar to my lips.

"Yes, we have issues in Las Vegas, a new nightclub, products being sold that are attracting the attention of local police," Santino said.

"Drugs? Any chance it's Serbia?" I asked casually.

"We don't know yet. Could they be doing this to draw attention to us?" Santino questioned.

"Darko Cosic is acting sneakily; I wouldn't be surprised if he wants our downfall to enter our territory," Matteo reported. He was always a good observer, analyzing everything before acting.

"Based on this, we need someone in Las Vegas, someone who can investigate everything calmly and find out more about this new nightclub," I declared, placing my hand on my chin, scratching my beard.

"Who do you have in mind?" my brother asked, giving me that same questioning look I used to give.

Looking at him was always like looking into a mirror. We were physically identical; if it weren't for our tattoos differentiating us, we would be exactly alike.

"Matteo, I know this isn't your usual role, but right now I trust only your judgment to be there. I want you to go to Las Vegas," I asked my *consigliere*.

"Yes, Don, I'll pack my bag and arrange for the jet to be ready," he confirmed my order promptly.

"Keep an eye on everything. Report any suspicious activities you find. We need all the details; we can't risk one of our nightclubs, active for over thirty years, being caught by the police or even having our spot stolen," I ordered, and Matteo nodded in agreement.

It was the first time I was stepping away from my mafia, and it was obvious that it could happen. However, even from afar, I could work for my clan.

"For now, we're set with this. Matteo needs to go there, talk to the nightclub manager, gather all the information our men have, and then we'll take the appropriate actions," the two nodded in agreement with my command.

"And now, since we're on a video call, how's the honeymoon going? Do I have a nephew on the way?" Santino asked in his mocking tone, knowing he wouldn't miss the chance to needle me.

"Look, I never thought I'd say this, but what an impossible woman. I must have mocked your marriage a lot to end up with a half-meter that barks like a Chihuahua," I grumbled, bringing the cigar to my lips as I heard my brother's loud laughter.

"Don't tell me that the Colombian girl you bragged about, saying you wouldn't last 24 hours without taking her virginity, is still pure?" I raised an eyebrow, hoping he'd understand my gesture as the answer to his question.

And of course, my brother understood, shaking his head while continuing to laugh, even Matteo was laughing along with the bastard.

"You both can go to hell. I'm not going to fuck a girl full of trauma. I just touched her body, and my wife started screaming as if I was killing her." I remembered the time I had her delicious breasts in my hands; even though she was small, she had perfect breasts for her size, big enough to fit in my hands.

"So you care about her, brother?" Santino asked, stopping his laughter and paying attention to what I had to say.

"I can't help but care. Yulia is my wife; I promised to protect her, even though I've already pushed all my limits around her. I just ordered that they take that little thing to our house because the Colombian girl manages to irritate me with her always accusatory remarks, even though I give her reason to judge everything wrong about me. We always end up in some fight, and damn it, I like fighting with my wife, and that's not healthy at all." I opened up to them, without mentioning the delicate fact about her childhood.

"Well, I have only one thing to tell you." Santino gave me his mocking look. "You got screwed. You laughed at me, said that my wife deserved a good spanking, and now you've got one too. Did you think the Colombian would spread her legs just because you're the Don of the Italian mafia? Brother to brother, if you don't lower your guard, you won't get your heir so easily."

At that moment, Santino was giving advice, even if it was in his twisted way, but I didn't want to admit it. That would mean lowering my guard, admitting defeat, and making her realize she won when I was always the one who won.

After a long discussion, with my brother talking about family matters and showing a photo of little Bella, my niece, we ended the call, and I stayed there, savoring the essence of my cigar, thinking about my delicious wife, her tongue sliding over mine.

How I desired her, I wanted that Colombian girl, but I wanted her my way.

CHAPTER TWENTY-SIX

Yulia

It was late at night, close to midnight, and my husband still hadn't shown up. I went to the end of the pool, diving into the water that enveloped my body.

I was bored. What was the point of being in such a paradise if I couldn't do anything?

Bored and angry, the thought that my bastard of a husband might be cheating on me kept running through my mind. Not might be—he was definitely cheating.

I resurfaced, gripping the edge of the pool, opening my eyes slowly as the excess water cleared from my sight. I was briefly startled when I saw a pair of white sneakers in front of me, looking up to recognize one of his tattooed legs—my husband.

I looked up, the pool light illuminating him. Valentino was still wearing the same board shorts and a V-neck shirt. The strong scent of cigars emanated from him. He crouched down to my level.

"Shouldn't you be asleep?" he asked, his green eyes fixed on me.

"Do I look like I'm sleeping?" I countered.

"Why are you in the pool?"

"Why not be in the pool?" I raised an eyebrow, noting that he exhaled a long breath. Clearly, I was irritating him.

I might be developing a new addiction—irritating Valentino Vacchiano.

"Answer my damn question," he growled.

"Did you answer mine?" As I noticed his hand move, I dodged to the center of the pool, swimming where my feet couldn't touch the bottom.

When I returned to the center, I heard a splash. Opening my eyes quickly, I panicked as I saw him leap into the water, his clothes—shorts, shirt, and sneakers—left at the edge.

I began to move, kicking my feet, trying to reach the edge, my breathing becoming rapid as I noticed him swimming toward me.

A momentary relief washed over me when I realized he was getting closer, which was as fleeting as I imagined. I felt his hand grab my ankle, pulling me toward him.

"You bastard!" I shouted.

"Where's that smart mouth of yours?" he grunted, pressing his chest against mine.

I started to struggle, his hands now gripping my stomach, his chest pressed against my back. One of his hands moved to the middle of my breasts, resting on my neck and applying just enough pressure to make me gasp.

"Still brave?" I felt his breath against my neck as he spoke close to my ear.

"Let me go, you damn Italian." I kept writhing, desperately trying to escape his strong arms.

"The Italian who's your husband, the only man who can touch every part of your body," he murmured with possessive tone.

"I'm not your property..."

"That's where you're wrong. You're mine—my property, mine to use until I'm bored," he pressed his member against my buttocks.

"I'm not going to give in to a man who's probably been with other women." Anger consumed me—the thought of him with someone else, the frustration of having a husband who cared more about others than me.

"What makes you think I was with someone else?" His hand that had been on my stomach made a move toward my pussy.

Moving my hands, I grabbed his fingers. We were underwater, and I wasn't going to let him touch my intimate parts.

"The fact that you had your hands on the shoulders of two of them?" I closed my eyes, trying to erase the image of him smiling at one of them.

"But it could've been you there. Just give me your virginity," he murmured, rubbing his cock even more against my ass.

It was the first time I felt a member so close to me, even though his underwear prevented it from being directly on my skin.

"You'll have me only once, just to conceive our child," I whispered with a brief gasp.

"The word 'our' fits your lips. Give me your virginity, little butterfly," he requested, his voice thick with desire.

I tilted my head against his chest, knowing I was about to give in to that rough tone, to the extremely sexy man rubbing against me. I wanted it—I wanted my husband's lips.

My hands, which had been holding his, began to release them. I wanted to feel his touch on my pussy, to know what it was like to be touched down there by a man—something that had never happened before in all my experiences.

Freeze... the word made me tense, but it wasn't that which brought me back to reality. It was the thought of giving myself to the man who had ruined the last two years of my life, who came home without explaining where he'd been. How could I trust him when he had said outright he would betray me?

That he preferred to talk to anyone but me. The anguish filled my chest, the desire replaced by the feeling of vulnerability, as if I were something superfluous to him.

Valentino saw me only as the woman who would bear his child, and that hurt—it hurt so much to know that I was just a sexual image to him when I knew I was so much more.

"No!" I growled through gritted teeth. "Don't touch me! I won't give myself to you, not when I'm not sure where you've been, not when you might have been with other women. You ruined me, destroyed my last years in college. You're unreliable. I don't trust any of the words that come out of your mouth..."

I continued to struggle, shouting, my desperation catching him off guard. He really thought I would give in to him, that he could persuade me with his hot, sensual body.

His hand, which had been around my neck, moved to cover my mouth.

"Shut up, you bitch," he roared, his tone making me tremble, but not stop.

My husband started walking within the pool, dragging me out of it. He didn't let go until we were on the floor of the house. As soon as we touched the ground, I practically ran away from him, turning to face him from a safe distance, my chest heaving up and down rapidly.

"I'm not a bitch. I hate you, HATE! Why do you want me? I don't want to be just another sexual object in your hands. I have feelings, opinions, a life—a life you've never cared to understand. You only want me for sex, to procreate your heir. But know this: if you want your heir, you'll have to take him by force, because I won't willingly submit," I declared in my anger, pouring out my anguish on him.

Valentino clenched his hands, his eyes narrowed at me.

"Go to your room, NOW!" For the first time, I saw him shout at me, increasing my fear, causing me to run.

I stumbled on the stairs, grumbling in pain as I felt my knee hit the edge of a step, but I didn't stop. I continued to walk as fast as I could, even while limping.

CHAPTER TWENTY-SEVEN

Yulia

I emerged from the shower, drying myself with a towel and then wrapping it around my head, seeing a small bruise where I had bumped my knee on the stairs.

I wrapped myself in a robe and opened the suite door, finding my husband standing in front of the open bedroom door, looking out at the sea. He had his phone to his ear, talking to someone.

"Damn it, Santino, I spent an hour on a video call with you and Matteo and not a word about this guy?" Valentino growled at his brother. "It's fucking honeymoon, my clan always comes first. You should have told me, damn it, we're talking about a Serbian mafia member here."

He fell silent, and I stood there listening. Could it be that he wasn't lying? He had just mentioned spending the last hour on a video call with his brother.

"Don't kill him without extracting any information. I want this bastard alive. Don't send any remains to Darko, we don't know what the bastard is up to. Stay alert in our territory. I want updates every hour. If they don't come, I'll head to Sicily immediately," he growled at his brother, ending the call and roughly running a hand through his hair.

He turned towards me, our eyes meeting.

"Is there a problem?" I asked nervously, unsure if I should be there, if I should step in front of him.

"I spent almost two hours on a video call with my brother and Matteo before coming home. Not a single word was mentioned about them being with a Serbian mafia member. The excuse was that they didn't want to worry me. Damn it, how can I not worry when I just found out about it from a soldier!" Valentino started pacing. "I knew they would try to make me think everything was fine, which is why I left one of the soldiers on watch to pass on all the information."

He vented everything without even looking at me.

"Are we going back to Sicily?" I bit the corner of my lip, thinking that maybe going back would be better, having his mother around.

"No. I intended to return, but Santino said he has everything under control and will send me reports every hour." Valentino turned, his eyes fixed on my body.

"Oh..." I cleared my throat, as deep down I wanted to go back. I headed to the closet. "Valentino?"

"Yes?" My husband raised an eyebrow.

"You haven't been with other women, have you?" He seemed to analyze my reaction, as if searching for any sign that I would believe him.

"No, I haven't been, but that doesn't matter." He walked quickly, passing by me and entering the bathroom, the sound of the lock clicking behind him.

I entered the closet, wearing one of the white silk nightgowns that fell slightly below my buttocks. Feeling too lazy to dry my hair, I just combed it and went to the bed where my lotion was. I started applying it to my legs, hearing the sound of the shower being turned off.

The glass doors were still open, allowing the delicious sea breeze to refresh the room. We were at the tip of the island, so no one could see us there.

The bathroom door opened, and I ignored it, focusing on massaging my sore knee until I noticed Valentino's shadow beside me.

"Did you hurt your knee?" I quickly looked up and then down. He was right beside me in white underwear.

"It was just a stumble. It will leave a slight bruise," I declared, feeling my cheeks warm. This would be our second night sleeping together, and nothing was going to happen, even though at that moment, my entire body was tense.

"Let me see." I didn't have time to say "no"; he was already sitting beside me, touching my knee, his fingers examining as if searching for any dislocation. "It seems fine..."

"As I said." I shrugged, noticing he turned, his eyes meeting mine.

"You always have to confront me, don't you?" he said without removing his hand from my knee.

"You irritate me just by existing," I grumbled, pouting.

"Do you think I wanted an arranged marriage? Do you think I chose a union I didn't want? To seal the union with your brother, he had to give me something in return, and you were given to the Don. I wanted to be the Don; I love power, I love being at the center of everything. And if to be the Don I had to marry a spoiled little girl, I wouldn't think twice. That's why you're mine, but not because I wanted it, but because of a duty to my clan, a clan I lead, and for that, I need to be an example to everyone." Valentino moved his hand up, squeezing my thigh.

"If you didn't want me, why did you go to my college to ruin me?" I brought up the same issue, needing his version.

My husband was silent for long seconds before finally speaking:

"That wasn't my intention, but since I saw you on Instagram, I realized that anyone who laid eyes on you would desire you. I tried for a long time not to go to your college, but eventually, I couldn't stand it anymore. Even though I'm blocked on your social media, I have another account I use, and when I saw that asshole next to you, I lost control. I went to see you, I was enraged, jealous, furious, and did things I'm not proud of. Not the part where I ruined you for everyone, but I don't regret that. Since the day your brother handed you over to the Italian mafia, you became mine. I'm a fucking selfish person, and everything about you belongs to me. But as for the orgy—" *well... I.* — He cleared his throat, opening up to me. "Well, I regret that."

"So you're saying you did that to hurt me?" I pulled my legs together, covering them with my nightgown.

"Yes, Yulia, I did. But when I ruined you, I did it for my own benefit. I wanted you from the beginning, and I couldn't bear the thought of knowing another man touched you first. It had to be me; I will be your first man." There was my possessive husband, the one I had known from the start I was marrying.

"Do you realize I was branded as 'the cuckold'? Having to hear in the college corridors for almost an entire month how my fiancé was a maniac in bed? I hate you, I hate you for all of this." Valentino remained still, silent, analyzing me as he searched for the right words to use.

"Sorry?" He raised an eyebrow in a way that made him look guilty.

"An apology won't make all the humiliation you caused me go away..."

"I need sex, Yulia. I'm fucking sore. I'm trying to understand you, but I need to fuck you." His sudden words made my eyes widen.

"So you're making it clear that you only wanted to understand me to have sex? You never cared about my feelings?" That was the last straw.

"What feelings? Damn it, I've never had to deal with that, not even with my sister's hysterical episodes. What fucking feelings are you talking about? I'm pragmatic!"

"Then go to hell. I just wanted you to show a shred of interest in me. Is it too much to ask that my husband ask questions about the person next to him? I bet you don't even know what course I took."

"Fashion, I know you're 22, your birthday is February 2, your favorite color is yellow, the cream you always use is chestnut, that's while you're with me, your best friend's name is Billie Harris, she took the same course as you, you love to hum along to English songs, you have a habit of biting your lip, your eyes are so black I don't even see your pupils, you move like hell when you're sleeping, you don't sleep with the lights off, you're afraid of the dark. Want anything else?"

I opened my mouth in surprise; he knew more about me than I knew about him.

"How do you know all this?"

"I also know the names of your parents, your aunt... I know everything, Yulia. I'm good at remembering names and I'm a great observer. I know more about you than you think..."

"But I'm not a good observer, and I don't know anything about my husband." I pouted in my sulk.

"Can we make a deal?" he asked, sitting closer to me.

"Depends?"

"Let me take your virginity, and I'll tell you everything you want to know." His green eyes scanned my face.

"I said I wouldn't sell myself..."

"We're making a trade; technically, it's not a sale." His fingers touched my thigh.

At some point, I would need to give myself to him, so it might as well be for some benefit of my own.

"Just promise me you'll be gentle and that you'll let me be calm. I'm still scared I won't be able to..." I pleaded.

"I can make that exception for your first time..."

CHAPTER TWENTY-EIGHT

Yulia

"I don't believe you." We were still at an impasse.

"Well..." My husband was reconsidering his decision.

"Unless you give me it in writing." I bit the tip of my lip.

"In writing?"

"Yes, write it on a sheet with your signature," I requested, my anxiety evident.

"Okay." Valentino shrugged as if it were an easy task.

I leaned over the piece of furniture next to the bed where I knew my sketchbook was, grabbing it along with my pencil case. I placed the sketchbook between us while opening my pencil case and taking out a pencil. I turned my gaze to Valentino, who had my sketchbook in hand, looking at my drawings, which ranged from sketches and landscape drawings to people.

"Wait, did you draw me?" He turned to me, the sketchbook showing the drawing I had made of him sitting on the boat from one of the times we ended up fighting.

"Yes." I shrugged slightly.

"Wow, you're really good at this." Valentino was genuinely surprised, observing the pencil and shading work I had done. My husband looked like a model when I saw him in that position, which is why I wanted to draw him.

"Was that a compliment?" I asked, as his eyes lifted to meet mine.

"Yes."

"Thank you, then." I widened my eyes when he pulled the sheet away, keeping the drawing intact. "Hey, what are you doing?"

"If I'm in this drawing, it means it belongs to me." He shrugged, stretching out and putting it in the drawer by his side of the bed.

"You know if you'd asked, I would have given it to you without tearing it up like this." I rolled my eyes, taking the sketchbook back and finding a blank sheet to hand to him along with a pen. "Write."

"What exactly do you want me to write?" he asked mockingly, as if it were too childish.

"I, Valentino Vacchiano, solemnly swear..."

"Are you serious?" My husband frowned.

"Come on, Italian, just write it, or I'll keep fighting with you," I said firmly, noticing he shook his head in contradiction but started writing, prompting me to continue. "To be understanding on my wife's first time, attentive, caring, patient, not aggressive, and after the sexual act, to answer all the questions Yulia has about me... and to be faithful as well."

I cleared my throat, adding a little extra, and he surprisingly wrote it down without hesitation, not caring about the content.

"Anything else?" he asked, extending the sketchbook to me. I shook my head. "Now it's your turn."

"My turn?" I was puzzled as I took the sketchbook.

"Yes, or do you think I was out of my mind when I wrote the part about being faithful to you? You'll write what I tell you." I sighed deeply, starting to write. "I, Yulia Vacchiano, promise to be less quarrelsome, less sharp-tongued, to be more understanding without flying off the handle..."

"Is this serious?" I interrupted, stopping my writing.

"Come on, stubborn, just write it. Also, add 'less stubborn.'" I rolled my eyes, writing what he requested. "To be more open, not to hide anything from my husband, and to stop flashing delicate and innocent smiles at other men, as they belong only to my husband, whom I am faithful to."

I bit my lip, finishing the writing, trying not to burst out laughing. It was so typical of Valentino, as if he wanted me to wear a collar declaring myself his.

I signed below, handing it back to him to sign as well. Valentino signed, handing the sketchbook back to me. I left it on the page of our agreement, placing it beside the bed, ready in case he wanted to find an excuse for not fulfilling his part.

I put the pen back in the pencil case, leaving it in my drawer.

"And now what do we do?" I felt my body tense as I looked at Valentino, who was gazing at me with desire.

"We can start with you taking off that nightgown." I swallowed hard, afraid of being so vulnerable to him.

"And what about the understanding part?" I murmured fearfully.

"Well, I can take it off if you prefer. Luckily, we know you're afraid of the dark, so you won't be asking for sex in the dark," he said mockingly.

"But we could make the room darker, what do you think?" I started coming up with excuses.

Valentino got up from the bed. I studied his legs, one completely tattooed, the other without tattoos. His back was covered with a skull. When he turned to turn off some lights, I noticed the name Verena written on the side of his waist, his mother's name.

I found it quite sweet, a sign of respect for his mother.

Only the lights from the two bedside lamps remained on, with the nightlight from the moon coming in through the windows. He didn't close the windows, allowing the night breeze to continue entering our room.

"What was your first tattoo?" I asked nervously, knowing I always talked too much when I was like this.

"My mother's name, to tame the beast and show that I got another one on my thigh, and started the skull on my back." He showed me on his thigh a woman's face. I hadn't noticed the woman tattooed there because it was above the line of his shorts.

From a distance, I couldn't see it well, so I got up from the bed and went toward him.

"Is it a woman?" I declared, not looking closely.

"Yes." I lowered my face, about to ask who the woman was, already thinking it must be someone he had loved and couldn't have.

Until I widened my eyes and noticed my own features there. It was my black hair, my lips, my eyes—it was me. He had tattooed me on his thigh?

"What is this?" I whispered, taking a step back, stunned.

"When Amélia showed me your photo on your Instagram page, I didn't have any tattoos. Having you tattooed on me, seeing it every day on my thigh, would remind me of my commitment to my mafia." He shrugged as if having my face there was just a commitment.

"A commitment to your mafia? Was I always just that to you? A commitment?" I realized I was starting to lose patience.

"And isn't it?"

"You slept with all those women for years with my face tattooed on your thigh?" I began to feel dirty, just because of a damn tattoo.

"Do I need to remind you of our agreement?"

"Damn agreement, right now all I can think about is the women who sat their asses on my face." I noticed a small smirk on his face—"I... I need some time alone. This is too much for me, and I'm about to explode, idiot. You had no right to tattoo my face right there! Asshole..."

I turned my face away, feeling anger in every part of my body. It was supposed to be something I was proud of, but it was nothing more than a commitment. He did it to remember that he had a fiancée, but didn't think of me when he slept with countless women.

I ran out of the room, down the stairs, feeling the tears streaming down my face, anger, pain...

Why did Ferney have to hand me over to a bastard like this?

CHAPTER TWENTY-NINE

Yulia

I sat on the lounge chair, wiping the damn tears from my eyes when I heard footsteps approaching me.

Why did it have to be this way? Why did everything irritate me? It was as if Valentino's entire past was getting on my nerves, a past we couldn't change.

"Butterfly," he whispered, sitting down next to me.

He didn't argue, just stayed patient, sitting on the lounge chair.

"I don't want to look at your face," I grumbled, pouting my lips.

"Well, I'm making you look." Valentino easily lifted me into his arms, placing me on his lap, my legs wrapped around his waist.

I didn't hold onto him, keeping my hands clasped in the middle between us, staring out at the distant sea until I felt his finger on my chin, turning my gaze to his.

"Bambina, are you realizing that you're angry about my past?"

"A past I hate," I huffed, pouting, noticing his half-smile; the bastard was enjoying my distress.

"Well, you can sit on your own face then." He shrugged.

"After millions have sat there?"

"Millions is a pretty high number; I don't think it was that many." I raised my hand and gave his shoulder a playful punch, noticing his amused, big, and beautiful smile at that moment.

"You think? You think? Bastard!" My eyes widened, making Valentino move quickly, laying me down on the lounge chair, his body covering mine.

"Bastards don't promise to be faithful..." His sentence trailed off as he moved my hair aside, lowering his face, starting to trail kisses on my skin.

"I only believe it when I see it," I gasped, feeling every inch of my skin tingle from his wet kisses.

"If there's one thing I am, it's loyal," he murmured, dragging his tongue through the middle of my nightgown's neckline.

"That wasn't what it seemed when you told my brother not to trust your promises." I closed my eyes as he pushed the neckline aside, feeling the breeze touch my nipples, causing them to harden.

"A promise is different from loyalty." He blew on my nipple, and I slightly parted my lips, letting out a sigh.

"Valentino," I moaned, feeling his tongue trace around my nipple. He didn't bite it like he did last time. Sucking gently, he took my breast in his mouth while caressing the other with his hand.

"Moan for me, my butterfly," he whispered, moving to the other breast, which he began to suck with lust.

While sucking on my nipple, he slid the strap of my nightgown down my arms, pulling it down, releasing my nipple from his mouth, passing the fabric around my waist, until I was left in only my panties, which were now completely wet because of him.

"May I, wife?" he asked, holding the sides of my panties, his eyes completely intense on me.

"And if someone sees us?" I looked around.

"No one enters without my permission," he declared, just sliding it off when I allowed.

"Yes, you can," I whispered, knowing I needed to do this, and, God, I wanted to.

Avoiding looking directly at me, he removed my panties, his gaze fixed on my vagina, which I wanted to cover in the face of his thorough inspection.

"You are so incredibly delicious." His eyes traveled over my body, stopping on my face.

"What if I freeze up?" I murmured, thinking of the worst.

"I will insist and not give up; I am your husband and want the best for you," he whispered, rising from the lounge chair, adjusting the lever, laying it back, then lowering his underwear.

It was impossible not to look away. Damn, his member touched the top of my belly—large, hard, veined, strong, and robust.

My husband was naked in front of me, coming between my legs, spreading them. I bent both of them, feeling the breeze touch my wet vagina, his fingers touching my intimacy, rubbing his thumb over the folds.

I closed my eyes. This was the first time a man had touched me there, and he knew exactly where to touch to give me pleasure, my body starting to tense, the darkness dominating my mind.

"Stop, Valentino!" I grunted as everything seemed to close in again; it was happening once more.

"I'm not stopping. I'm your husband, open your eyes now, Yulia, keep them on me, on your man." I opened my eyes despite the blur and focused on him, everything soon becoming clear in my vision. "It's me, just yours..."

His sentence trailed off as a sigh escaped his mouth.

My husband withdrew his fingers from my vagina, bringing them to his mouth and sucking them, as if savoring my taste.

"I'm only not sucking you off right now because I know you'd close your eyes and wouldn't focus on me." He moved between my legs. "Are you ready to be mine forever?"

He asked with his member touching my vagina.

"I'm already yours, Titi." A sigh escaped my lips.

"For God's sake, don't call me that," he grumbled. "It takes away all my credibility as a ruthless Don..."

"Well, that's exactly what I'm calling you now," I teased, loving the smile displayed on his lips.

"If I push any boundaries, tell me to ease up," he whispered, holding his penis which was now pressing firmly against my vagina.

I said nothing, closing my eyes against the pain that was coursing through me. Closing my eyes made my body tense, everything coming to the surface...

"Damn it, Yulia, open your fucking eyes, you stubborn girl, don't close them, damn it," he muttered through clenched teeth.

"You said you wouldn't be insensitive," I whined through the pain, opening my eyes.

"It's quite complicated to fuck your incredibly tight and delicious pussy gently," he murmured as a moan escaped my mouth, feeling his penis touch the depths of my vagina.

"Is that it?"

"From my cock?"

"Yes." A smile spread across his lips.

"No, there's more, but your pussy is already mine..."

"Is there going to be more?" I widened my eyes.

"In time, yes. Not now. Your little pussy still needs to adjust to my size, don't be scared." My husband withdrew his member, then started to penetrate me again.

Our eyes stayed locked, as if we were one, placing all my trust in him.

"I'm going to increase the pace," he whispered, and I nodded.

I raised my hand, sliding it under his arm, touching his back, pulling his body closer to mine, merging our bodies together.

In my hands, I felt his movements, his penis entering my vagina, the initial pain turning into pleasure. My face was turned to the side, his eyes locked with mine, not straying, being patient, claiming me as his own.

If this was sex, maybe I wanted more of it. Valentino was making it possible, perhaps because he knew the center of my blockage. My husband wouldn't let me close my eyes, making me know it was him there, my husband.

His movements became more urgent, loud moans escaping my mouth, my nails digging into his back, knowing I was about to explode into an orgasm, a sensation I was familiar with from when I touched myself.

But now it was different, better; it was my man...

"Titi," I whined, using the nickname I knew he hated, surrendering to the moment, feeling my walls tighten around his member, spasms running through my body, shivers overwhelming me at that instant.

"Damn it!" He roared, thrusting hard inside me, feeling his liquid hit the bottom of my vagina, his muscles tensing, holding me tightly, as if he was releasing every last drop inside me.

At that moment when everything ended, I allowed myself to close my eyes and relax. He had taken my virginity; I managed it; I wasn't problematic. Deep down, I wanted to shout for giving my husband his heir, happy to know I would be able to have my long-desired child.

I opened my eyes when he pulled out of me, noticing that he had placed his white underwear under my intimacy, lifting it to reveal a small red trace, proving my virginity.

"Why did you do that?" I whispered, sitting on the lounge chair, covering my breasts.

"I needed to make sure you were a virgin," he said naturally.

"But I told you I was." I widened my eyes.

"Well..." He shrugged as if to say he didn't trust me.

"You don't trust me, typical of you." I reached for my nightgown, pulling it in front of my breasts as I stood up, covering my intimacy. "Ouch!"

A cry escaped my mouth when I felt his hand pull me by the waist, lifting me into his lap.

"No, I don't trust you, just as you don't trust me. Only time will make us capable of trust..."

"But we're talking about my virginity, a much more peculiar matter." I squeezed his chest tightly as he carried me up the stairs.

"Well, we made a deal. I promised to be patient on our first time. It's late now. I'll clean you up and put you to sleep so I can say I kept my part." I rolled my eyes as we entered our bedroom.

CHAPTER THIRTY

Valentino

I squeezed my eyelids shut, quickly opening my eyes without remembering how I had fallen asleep so fast. I turned my face, searching for my wife, only to find the bed empty beside me.

I immediately jumped out of bed, pulling up my boxer briefs, seeing the bright day and the windows still open.

Yulia had slept with me; I, who usually had a light sleep, hadn't even seen her leave my side. I went out of the room, quickly descending the stairs, finding my little wife by the pool with her phone to her ear. I sighed with relief. Damn, I immediately thought something might have happened to her, that she could have been kidnapped.

I dragged my steps closer to her in silence, smelling the delicious aroma of breakfast that was served on the table.

"Billie, I really don't know, friend," Yulia said on the phone as if enjoying the conversation.

Gently, I placed my hand on her waist.

"Oh!" My wife jumped, turning her face when she saw me there. "I'll check with him and call you back... okay... okay... friend, you're crazy."

She said a few more words, ended the call, and turned to face me, her beautiful face lifted towards me, blinking her black lashes.

"Your friend is in Las Vegas?" she suddenly asked.

"Friend?" I feigned ignorance.

"The one who was with you; I don't remember his name." Yulia subtly furrowed her brow as if trying to recall the name.

"Matteo?" she confirmed. "Yes, he is. I sent him there to take care of some things. Why?"

"Well, Billie spent the night with him, but she has a terrible habit of getting drunk and not remembering people. I think he was also drunk. My friend said she left early and kept looking at him as if she remembered him from somewhere until she recalled our wedding. Now she wants to know if he will remember her." My wife made me think that story was just like Matteo.

"Well, I can ask." I shrugged.

"Probe, Valentino. If he doesn't remember, she doesn't want him to be reminded of her." I found that request strange.

"Doesn't want him to?"

"Yes, Billie said she must have made a fool of herself. She shrugged.

"Look, Matteo does have a terrible habit of getting drunk when he wants to forget something, but if there's one thing he doesn't forget, it's sex, even when he's drunk," I declared, curious to know what my friend had been doing to end up in bed with Yulia's friend.

"And what did he want to forget?" My wife seemed curious.

"A year ago, Matteo ended a relationship. She wanted to get married, but he didn't. So Marina pressured him, and Matteo told her to choose—either him or the marriage. She chose marriage, so they broke up. My friend thought he didn't need marriage, that he felt nothing for her, until he saw her with someone else, with a wedding planned. Since then, he's been jumping from bed to bed, keeping up with me. When we're together, he doesn't get drunk like a lunatic, well, not this time…"

"And he won't in the future; that's in the past now," Yulia cut in, making me laugh.

I slid my hand down her leg, lifting it onto my lap, her legs fitting around my waist.

"So, that's all I know," I declared, feeling her hand brush over my shoulder.

"Billie woke me up early with her craziness. I think I'm still sleepy," my wife grumbled as I stopped by the table.

"I'm hungry." I lowered my hand, lifting up her nightgown and pressing it against her butt.

"I'm still mad about you putting your underwear underneath me," she complained with that delicious pout on her lip.

"Lucky for you, we have a contract that requires you to control your tongue," I teased, bringing my lips close to hers, biting her lower lip and pulling it back with a bit of force.

"Jerk," she cursed, giving me a little punch.

"And there's more. We're not going to sleep; we're going to another island nearby by boat," I declared, remembering one of the plans I made.

"Another island?" She raised an intrigued eyebrow.

"I heard there's a club there." A suggestive smile formed on my lips.

"Club?"

"Yes, a swingers' club..."

"I don't want to swap partners," Yulia cut me off quickly.

"So you know what it is?" I forced my eyes wide.

"Of course I know."

"Anyway, we're not going to swap; we're just going to check it out. The owner is an acquaintance of mine and said he has private rooms in a world I want to introduce you to." My hand continued to slide over her butt.

"World you want to introduce me to?" Yulia seemed to know what I was talking about.

"Yes, little butterfly, and yes, that's what's on your mind. Are you excited?" Her curious eyes became bright.

"At most curious, maybe a little wet." She bit the tip of her lip, not wanting to admit it.

"I need to feel it with my fingers." I slid my hand between her buttocks, moving towards her pussy, so small and delicate. My finger brushed luxuriously over her folds, finding her wet, damn.

Yulia parted her lips, letting out a rough moan. She always gave in, even when she didn't want to admit it; my Latina always softened in my arms.

"Will you come with me without hesitation? Want to satisfy your curiosity?"

"I thought you were a masochist." She forced her eyes on mine, even though her body was limp.

"I am, but I don't find sexual pleasure in it. I use it to punish myself. Pain makes me feel vindicated for my failures. I'm sadistic; I get sexual pleasure when I see a woman crying out in pleasure, even if she's numbed, hurt, giving herself up to masochism, to pleasure. Pain can accompany sexual pleasure, and I want you to experience it."

"Will you hurt me?"

"Possibly," I spoke the truth.

"Will there be blood?"

"Definitely," I wasn't hiding anything.

"Will I enjoy it?" she asked, still fearful but curious.

"You will enjoy it if you surrender to the process," I replied, hoping she would accept.

"And if I don't like it? What if I get scared?"

"We won't cross your limits, but know that I want you to at least try it."

"And if I like it?" Yulia bit the corner of her lip.

"You will be fucked brutally for the rest of your life and will come numerous times like a crazy woman," I teased, almost coming in my underwear just from the sight of my wife's innocence exposed to me.

"Okay, let's test it..."

CHAPTER THIRTY-ONE

Yulia

I'm still apprehensive. How could I agree to this?
I know it was out of curiosity, to understand his world, what he liked, but deep down, my curiosity was tinged with fear.

I sat at the back of the boat, feeling the breeze on my skin, closing my eyes and tilting my head back, my hair moving with the wind. Valentino was on a call. Surprisingly, he was sticking to his part of the deal, answering everything I asked.

I felt something touch my leg, pulling it mid-reflection. When I opened my eyes, I saw Valentino there, kneeling and spreading my legs, positioning himself between them.

"Any problem?" I asked, watching his hand slide under my dress.

"Everything is in perfect order. As for your friend, tell her Matteo remembers every one of her embarrassments." Valentino turned, pulling me onto his lap.

He was wearing a black button-up shirt and matching dress pants, impeccably dressed like a mobster. I settled on his lap, holding onto his shoulder.

"I hope they don't see each other anytime soon," I declared, knowing how much my friend talked when she was drunk. This wasn't the first time she got drunk and ended up in bed with someone, despite my constant warnings that she could end up being abused one day.

"If I may ask, isn't this dangerous? Why does she do it?" Valentino asked, sliding his hand up my legs to my panties.

"She's the daughter of famous actors who always neglected her, and she kind of does this to get attention. When I'm around, I control her, but Billie went to Las Vegas on a trip with her parents, trying to present a perfect family image, and when she's with them, this always happens. It's as if she wants to disconnect from reality, or end up on some sensationalist site as the wayward daughter of Cassandra Harris." I rolled my eyes mentioning her mother's name.

"I'm not trying to discourage you, but Matteo said he's staying at the same hotel as her, even if they went to a motel or wherever. He told me he won't drink anymore; it was a slip-up after I pestered him about not working and drowning his sorrows." Valentino made a move to remove my panties. "Take them off..."

"We can't do that here; your men are up front." I widened my eyes.

"I told them not to come back here." His smirk was clearly visible on his lips.

I shook my head. Valentino was giving me little things without me even begging for them, and for God's sake, I wanted my husband's warm hands on my body.

Slowly, I removed my panties, watching him take them from my hand and bring them to his nose.

"You're crazy." I grimaced.

"Are you excited, wife?" he asked, looking at my wet panties.

"Tell me who can stay dry with that smirk of yours." I rolled my eyes.

"Smirk?" My husband raised an eyebrow, finding it amusing.

"Look, you're turning into a cocky bastard." I pointed a finger.

"And now?" Valentino flashed a different, wide smile, showing his perfect teeth.

"Oh, I don't know..." I bit the tip of my lip.

"I just invented the 'sit on my cock' smile." It was impossible not to laugh at my husband's depravity.

Seeing the genuine smile dominate his lips, I lowered my hand to the button of his pants, noticing the double clasp, which this type of pants has to keep the stitching more secure. Since he had a toned stomach and didn't wear tight pants, it was easy to open them.

"You have a knack for this," he said, sounding jealous.

"Forgot I'm a designer? I've removed plenty of mannequins' pants; it's not like you, who tested your skills on human bodies." I huffed, lowering the zipper.

I raised my eyes, seeing that he wanted me to continue.

"Everyone gains practice in their own way." I gave him a playful punch on his shoulder.

"I can increase the strength of my fist," I pouted.

"What a relief, I was thinking you might have a problem with strength." My husband's light-hearted and teasing side was showing. "Now lower my pants, since you've practiced on mannequins, put it into practice with me..."

"You can do that yourself." I felt my cheeks heat up. "The mannequins didn't have erect members..."

"Now, Yulia, that's an order..."

"You know I love being a naughty girl..."

"And I love spanking disobedient girls." He squinted his eyes at me.

I held his pants, pulling them down, making his member spring out, hard, eager, veins prominent, the tip glistening with pre-cum.

"Hold it with your little hand," he asked, and I did, gripping it at the base, sliding my hand, feeling the texture and how incredibly hard he was.

"So hard, so hot," I murmured, looking up at him as he studied my curiosity.

"And it's begging for your pussy. Sit down, little butterfly," he whispered, lifting my dress without removing it.

I rested my body on my knee, guiding his cock into my entrance, sliding down onto him gently.

"Keep your eyes on me," he requested, and I nodded.

I lowered myself as far as I could, gripping his shoulder tightly.

"Move that part." He held my waist, guiding me on how to move, as if I were grinding.

"Like this?" Valentino removed his hand, and I continued on my own, grinding and seeing the smug smile on his lips.

"Fuck, perfect." His hand held my neck, flattening it with my hair, pulling it back, bringing his lips close to my neck. "Don't close your eyes, bambina..."

He had noticed that closing my eyes triggered my crises, so he asked me to keep them open. Surprisingly, it always happened when I closed them, maybe because I knew the source of the problem was him, my husband...

Valentino alternated between kissing and sucking on my neck, his other hand touching my pussy, making me moan loudly, as I was intoxicated by the pleasure of being on top of him.

With my head tilted back, I released my grip on his shoulder, moving my neck away from his mouth, while I held the back of his leg, raising my face and noticing that his eyes were fixed on my pussy swallowing his cock.

"Don't stop, ragazza, don't stop..." he ordered, locking his gaze with mine, making me drunk with pleasure and lust, his fingers sliding over my pussy.

I should have been taking it easy; it was only my second time, but it felt like years of being deprived of sex were coming to the surface.

Contracting around his penis, I surrendered, noticing Valentino closed his eyes tightly, as if he didn't want to give in that way, gripping my thigh hard, my husband came inside me.

"Fuck." He opened his eyes dazed, as if he were intoxicated. "What do you have, huh?"

He pulled me by the neck, pressing my lips to his as our bodies went through spasms, entwining, just letting our breathing calm down.

CHAPTER THIRTY-TWO

Yulia

The car stopped in front of a house; it looked like a normal vacation home, but that was only from the outside.

My husband held my hand as we walked along the sidewalk, his men waiting for us in the car. I still felt tense, my hands cold with sweat. It wasn't necessary to knock on the door; it opened on its own as we approached.

A beautiful tall woman opened it, flashing a look of desire at my husband, who did not reciprocate.

"Sir, here it is." She picked up a basket, something I only deciphered when she brought it closer to us.

A collar?

No, Valentino must be going insane— a collar?

I turned to my husband; he took the collar in his hands. Its material was leather, shaped like a human collar, with hooks around it.

"You're going to keep quiet and stick to our agreement," he whispered between his teeth, as if anticipating my state of alarm, wishing him to hell.

"I'm not wearing a collar," I muttered.

"Now, Yulia," he growled, as he always did.

He pulled my hair back, placing it around my neck and fastening it. My eyes met his.

"Turn around," he ordered.

"Why?" This was going too far.

"Now, Yulia!"

Rolling my eyes, I did as he said, feeling him grasp my hair.

"Do you want me to do it, sir?" the woman asked beside him.

"No one touches my wife but me," he snapped impatiently at the woman beside us.

Not even a woman was allowed to touch me; when I said he was crazy, it was this level of madness I meant.

From the corner of my eye, I noticed he was doing something with my hair, until I realized it was a braid. A braid? What was with this madness now? Was he going to take me to the "red pain room"? I felt like Anastasia Steele, but without a CEO.

Valentino ended up tying the end of the braid with an elastic band the woman handed him. Then she took a chain and gave it to the mobster.

"Valentino Vacchiano, no! You didn't mention chains, collars, and braids in my hair." I turned quickly as he swiftly hooked it onto one of the collar's hooks, securing the chain there.

"Calm down, bambina, these are just house rules." He winked at me, lifting his hand to touch my cheek. "You look like a beautiful submissive like this..."

"On the verge of shouting and kicking like a rebellious girl," I muttered as he started pulling me by the collar.

My husband was a step ahead of me. We passed through an entry hall with few people, stopped at a new door, which opened as soon as they recognized the mobster. Here, unlike the entrance, it was darker with red lights in some spots.

I swallowed hard when I saw four people on a sofa with two women bound to each other, and then two men penetrating them from behind. Turning my face, I saw sofas with a pole dance bar in the middle, a woman dancing while another was penetrated by two men.

It didn't look like a swinger club at all.

A sensual music played in the background. I felt a hand touching mine, guiding it behind me. I was numb from everything I was seeing when I felt that person leading my hand to touch something.

"Ah!" I let out a startled squeal, turning my face to see a woman making me touch her pussy through her panties, and I quickly pulled my hand away.

Valentino stopped, looking back to see what had happened.

"My lord loved your wife and would like to know if you'd like to join us?" I noticed she also had a collar like mine around her neck, but unlike mine, it was loose.

"No!" My husband growled, without even looking where the woman pointed, not even lowering his eyes to her body.

He pulled me by the collar again, this time with a stronger tug, catching me off guard and making me stumble.

"Hey!" I grumbled.

"Damn, why does everyone want to touch you?" he declared, slowing his pace so that I walked beside him.

"It's not really about me; I think it's more about you." I shrugged, seeing him lower his eyes toward me.

"Do you really think that? I'm just another man when you have Latina beauty, a body with curves in all the right places, delicious breasts, legs that drive me crazy, not to mention your ass, so enticing, everything about you screams lust, and the best part is that it belongs entirely to the Don of the Cosa Nostra." He stopped walking, holding my neck above the collar, lowering his face.

Sticking out his tongue, he licked my lip. I jumped, pressing my body against his in shock when his hand landed on my butt, lifting my dress and exposing my rear to everyone there.

"Let these vultures see what only I can have," he growled, his mouth close to mine.

"Valentino," I whispered his name.

"Speak, bambina..."

"I don't want to do this with people watching us." I moved my hand to his waist, gradually feeling him release my butt.

"We won't do it, I'd never let anyone else see your beautiful pussy, my little butterfly," he whispered, giving my lower lip a wet kiss, then pulling it with his teeth. "Walk by my side before I end up using my weapon..."

Wanting to avoid that, I walked beside him.

A new door opened, and we entered a dark room. But unlike the first space, it was lit with yellow lights. My eyes widened when I saw various torture devices, and no one else was in that space.

"Sir, do you need anything?" the woman asked in her sweet voice, as if wanting to participate.

My husband looked around. I noticed a table with some drinks. Without looking at Valentino, I heard him say:

"I want to be undisturbed. Everything I want is here; just give me the key to the door. I paid for the entire room and don't want to be interrupted." The woman nodded and handed the key to my husband.

As soon as we were alone, sensual music started playing.

"How do you know there are no cameras here? What if we're being filmed?" I turned my face away.

"There aren't any. I know the owner, and he knows who I am. He wouldn't be crazy enough to do something like that." He narrowed his eyes at me, bringing me to a corner where he practically tied me to a wooden beam with the chain.

"Great, this is exactly what I wanted to feel like a dog." I crossed my arms, pouting, watching Valentino turn toward me.

"Do you trust me, Yulia?" he asked, and I shivered at his tone. "I need you to trust me. I might push you to your limit; you might think it's not me, but deep down, I can always stop. We just need to choose a safe word."

My husband looked at me, waiting for me to say something.

"Yes, I trust you. You're going to hurt me, aren't you?" I swallowed hard.

"Probably," the same word he had used last time.

"How does the safe word work?"

"I need you to choose a word that will make me stop..."

"Yellow." It was the first thing that came to mind when I looked around.

"Okay, the safe word is yellow," he said, and I nodded quickly.

"And now?" I was so anxious that I could feel my chest rising and falling rapidly.

CHAPTER THIRTY-THREE

Yulia

"Give me your hands," he commanded. With apprehension, I extended them, and Valentino guided me to a table covered with an array of utensils.

Okay, maybe I was being a bit dramatic, but there were so many objects, including things that resembled nipple clamps, chains, vibrators of various sizes, and anal plugs of different shapes.

"You're not putting that on me," I declared, horrified by the plugs.

"Quiet," he growled, grabbing a pair of handcuffs, opening the leather buckle, and placing them on my wrist. He tightened them firmly, then did the same with my other wrist.

My eyes followed his every move, questioning what the hell had possessed me to get into this situation.

"Valentino..." I murmured as he held a ball connected to two chains in his fingers.

"Wrong." Placing the ball on the table, he grabbed the first whip he saw and brought it down on my butt. The whip was black with many leather strands, and even though I was still in a dress, the crack of it on the fabric made me let out a squeak.

"Wrong?" I asked incredulously. "What the hell did I do wrong?"

"Again?" He smiled with that typical mocking Italian grin, slapping the whip on the ground beside my feet. "I'll give you a break since it's your first time, but every time you're bound and in a room equipped like this, address me as 'my Don.'

"My Don?" I squinted. "I thought being your wife meant I could call you whatever I wanted..."

"Not here."

"Ouch!" a squeal escaped my lips as my husband cracked the whip on my butt, letting one of the strands touch my leg, causing a stinging sensation.

The Italian placed the whip on the table and, with just one step towards me, began to slide my dress down my leg, leaving me naked, as I wasn't even wearing panties after our quick sex on the boat.

I stepped out of my heels, standing barefoot. Valentino picked up the ball again.

"With this ball in your mouth, you won't be able to talk. So snap your fingers and I'll stop, okay? You know how to snap your fingers, don't you?"

I raised my hand to show that I knew how to do what he asked.

Smiling like a child who had just received a sweet, I opened my mouth, felt it touch my tongue, and he closed it behind my head, holding the chain, pulling me as if I were his little dog.

All of this was making me anxious and wet. Even though I knew he could do whatever he wanted, I also knew that if I asked, my husband would stop.

"Do you see that instrument?" He pointed to what looked like a rectangular box on the floor, with six iron bars along the longer sides, and at one end, two bars with a piece of wood that reminded me of the medieval era when they used to put a person's head there, their arms at the sides, and then behead them.

The iron bars had many small holes, as if to pass bars through them.

Despite my fear, I shook my head, as there was no way to see it clearly.

"I have an exactly identical one in my apartment, and I'll take you to see it." I swallowed hard, not knowing if I'd be able to endure it even once, let alone more. "Sit here at the end."

I did as instructed, gripping my thighs tightly, pushing myself back slightly, spreading my legs and placing them behind the iron, feeling a brief pain in my groin from the force with which he made me open my legs in that way.

He released the chain that held my hands, moving them behind me and securing them, one on each side of the bar behind the one where my legs were trapped.

"You see, little butterfly, this way I have you completely vulnerable to me." He smiled wickedly, stepping away and returning with clamps in his hand, both connected by a small golden chain.

Kneeling in front of me, my husband placed one on each nipple, a mild pain spreading through my body, not too painful.

"It doesn't hurt, does it?" I shook my head in denial.

I hadn't realized, but those clamps were adjustable, and he began to tighten them, one hand on each nipple. My head tipped back as the pain intensified, and I searched for my fingers, even though my hands were restrained, I had some freedom with my fingers.

"Just snap your fingers when you reach your limit, when you can't take it anymore," he growled, as if he knew what was going through my mind.

Valentino stopped adjusting the clamps, and that pain drove me mad, high-pitched moans escaping from my muffled mouth.

Catching me off guard, his fingers touched my pussy, his face coming close to my sensitive skin. Valentino didn't even care that he had already come inside me before; at that moment, he buried his face in my pussy.

My mobster dragged his tongue along my folds, my body on fire from the pain in my nipples and the pleasure he was giving my intimacy, the slaps of his tongue against my pussy echoing with the background music.

With wet, sucking motions, he brought me to high peaks, his hand reaching up and gripping my breast tightly. As the clamp tightened on my nipple, the pain increased, and I wanted to scream, to thrash about, but the pleasure he was giving me in my pussy prevented me from snapping my fingers.

I felt two of his fingers penetrating me forcefully; he wasn't gentle but intense. Soon, I felt a new finger, as if inside me, three fingers moving aggressively within my walls.

I wanted to move, but that position prevented me. Sweat began to accumulate on my skin.

The corner of my groin burned, the tight nipple made me want to scream, but the mobster between my legs made me want to suffer in paradise.

"Go on, my butterfly, come in my mouth, give me your honey..." he growled as if he were controlling my pleasure. "Now, come..."

And like a command, I collapsed, surrendering, coming hard, feeling tears well up in my eyes from the madness, without even closing them, keeping them locked on my husband the entire time.

In that moment, something I thought could never happen occurred—I was submissive to a man.

He better not think this would get out of here, because if there was something I wouldn't give up, it was my freedom of speech.

CHAPTER THIRTY-FOUR

Valentino

My wife's head was tilted to the side, clearly showing she had an orgasm that she felt even at the tips of her toes.

"That was just a taste, what I'm going to do now will be entirely for my pleasure." I smiled wickedly.

Yulia tried to speak, but the device in her mouth prevented her from doing so.

Moving, I positioned myself between her legs, running my hand down her neck, lowering her head, I removed the tape holding her mouth, freeing her to speak. Stepping back, I watched my wife shift her jaw, uncomfortable from the device that had been there.

But those intense black eyes didn't focus on me; she was still apprehensive about what I was going to do. Damn it, all I wanted at that moment was to punish her—for not being obedient, for always wanting to disobey me, to punish her even for the damn male eyes that kept lusting after my wife, the woman who was uniquely and exclusively mine.

Before removing her from her current position, I adjusted the opposite end of the guillotine, opening the latches, raising the part of the guillotine where my wife would place her head.

"What are you planning to do?" At that moment she spoke; she must have felt she needed to ask because her curiosity wouldn't let her stay silent.

I didn't answer her question; it was obvious what I was going to do. Opening one latch of the handcuffs, I released it from the iron bar, did the same with the other, freeing both of her hands. I easily grabbed her waist, lifting her and removing her legs from behind the bar that had kept her standing.

"Ouch," she whispered, reaching between her legs where it must have been sore from the stretching.

Before placing her on the guillotine, I lowered my face, taking her lips with mine in a fierce, urgent kiss, our teeth even clashing during the act. I slid one of my hands down her buttocks, squeezing them tightly.

"Do you trust me, butterfly?" I asked again. I might be sadistic, but I knew this was her first time here.

"Yes, husband..."

"Wrong." At her mistake, I delivered a hard slap to her buttocks with my open hand, the sting echoing on her sensitive skin.

"Asshole," she murmured, but didn't call me "my Don," I felt she was starting to do it to provoke me.

"Come on," I called, making her kneel on the box. "Put your hands here, your head on the larger part."

I ordered, and my wife looked at me for long seconds.

"Do you want to stop?" I asked, even though I didn't want to stop.

"No, I agreed to enter your world, so I'll go all the way." Yulia tried to sound calm, but there was nothing calm in her tone.

"That's my girl," I declared proudly.

My Latina placed her head down, and I secured her wrists in the guillotine. In that position, Yulia couldn't move freely. I walked over to the table where the equipment was, grabbing two ankle restraints. I returned to my wife and secured them to the two iron bars on the sides, completely immobilizing her and making her get on all fours.

My fingers itched as I caressed her little, smooth, and entirely mine buttocks.

I didn't close her mouth because I wanted to hear her moaning, crying, begging for more.

Returning to the table, I spotted a plug with a fluffy tail. I picked it up, feeling the cold metal. I knew everything I had to use with my wife was new, as that was what I had requested.

Yulia couldn't see what I was doing. When I moved behind her, I slid my hand down her still-swollen, delicate, and small pussy, my fingers getting enveloped by her folds. I passed the plug over her moisture, lubricating it.

"Valentino, what are you doing?" Again, she spoke incorrectly.

"Wrong, I'm starting to think my reprimands are too few." I moved, leaving the plug on the box, stopping in front of a wall with many whips, choosing one with only the tip having several leather strands, knowing that it would hurt depending on how hard I struck.

I positioned myself behind her buttocks, delivering the first lash without warning. Yulia gasped, recoiled, and moaned in pain, but she didn't say anything.

"What am I, wife?" I asked, giving another lash to the same spot, wanting her to feel the burning sting.

"Damn it..."

"Not going to speak? I'll only stop when you do." Without changing position, I continued to whip my wife's buttocks, delivering one, two, three...

"My Don, you are my Don!" With her voice choppy, she screamed, and I stopped.

I could feel my cock begging for attention, it was so hard that I was afraid of coming too quickly.

I left the whip on the ground, picked up the plug, and resumed what I was doing before. Even after the whippings, my wife was wet—damn, Yulia liked this...

I pressed the plug against her anus, feeling her clench as I pushed it in.

"My Don," my wife whimpered as I inserted it completely, seeing the tail exposed.

"You haven't forgotten the safe word, have you?" I asked, walking around the box to find her flushed face.

"No." In front of her, I stripped, becoming completely naked, holding the base of my cock.

"Open your mouth, my submissive wife..."

"Valentino..."

"Wrong." I grabbed her braid, pulling it hard to the side as I pressed my cock into her mouth. "Open your mouth now!"

I growled as I spoke, my wife complied, her face red. Roughly, I shoved my cock into her mouth. Yulia didn't know how to give a blowjob—it was evident when I felt her teeth scrape my skin. But I didn't stop; the pain turned into pleasure, fucking her mouth while watching tears well up in her eyes, making her gag repeatedly. Damn, no one had ever made me cum like this, and I felt like I was at the peak, coming in and out even though she wasn't doing much, the braid wrapped around my hand, pressing hard to the back of her throat.

"I'm going to cum, and as a good submissive wife, you'll swallow it all. If you let even one drop escape, I'll slap your ass hard until I see it bleed," I roared through clenched teeth, feeling the spasms course through my body as I came hard. "Fuck!"

My eyes never left her mouth, watching her try to take it all, but she couldn't. Yulia tried, it was clear. I pulled my cock from her mouth, kneeling and watching my cum leak from the corner.

"Didn't swallow it all, wifey?" I smiled in the most twisted way I could.

"I-I couldn't," Yulia stammered.

"What a shame, for you it's obvious, but for me, it will be paradise, your little ass completely at my mercy..."

CHAPTER THIRTY-FIVE

Yulia

I closed my eyes, quickly feeling the impact of the whip on my buttocks. I kept them open at all times, so nothing prevented me from having my outbursts. I knew he was waiting for me to call him "my Don," but saying that would mean giving myself to him completely in submission, and by God, I loved being a naughty girl.

The clamp on my nipple burned so much it felt almost numb. I still felt the pain on my scalp from the tugging on my head, not to mention the taste of him in my mouth, his cum going down my throat. I tried to swallow it all, but I couldn't.

"Come on, Yulia, say it!" My husband roared, delivering another lash.

"Hit me, Valentino, go on, hit me... I know that's what you want." I whined as another lash struck my buttocks.

This time he didn't strike just one side but alternated between both, the plug in my anus making me clench with each lash. Tears streamed down my face; it was such a wild pain, burning and stinging on my skin. But I also felt the plug tightening in my orifice. Was I actually enjoying having a plug inside me?

"Yulia Vacchiano, what am I?" He roared, and at that moment, I was at the peak of my pain.

"I am a girl, very... very... naughty," I murmured, trying to smile but barely managing.

A final lash was delivered, and then he stopped. Everything fell silent, with music playing softly in the background. Suddenly, I felt my husband's tongue on my buttocks; he was licking me as if I were an ice cream.

Approaching me, I noticed his legs in front of me as he knelt, matching my height.

"Taste this." His lips met mine, his tongue sliding against mine, and all I could taste was the metallic flavor of blood from his mouth.

"Are you bleeding?" I asked, genuinely concerned it might be him.

"No, *mia bambina*, that's from your buttocks. I hit you so much that it caused small, superficial wounds. Tell me, what am I?" His finger traced down my cheek, wiping away my tears.

"My Don, with you looking into my eyes, it's not hard to say that." I winked mischievously.

"You haven't forgotten the safe word, have you?" He asked, genuinely concerned for me but wanting to push me to the edge of my pleasure, and his.

"No, my Don," I murmured, biting the tip of my lip.

"So provocative, just need to be more submissive..."

"There are things in this life that cannot be how you want them," I whispered, still under the anesthetic effect of the moment.

My body was hot, a mix of burning and pleasure. Perhaps once all this was over, I would truly feel the pain as it was meant to be. But at that moment, it was as if I wanted to provoke all of Valentino's senses, making him realize that I wasn't like any other woman he had ever had, because I was Yulia, his wife and first lady.

Taking me there might have been Valentino's worst mistake, because if he wanted to tame me, he didn't know that I could also tame him.

"But I am not a man to make exceptions, and you will not be my first exception." He lifted his fingers along my back, stopping behind me.

I felt the tip of his cock brushing against my entrance, entering gently, without removing the anal plug, penetrating me until he reached the depths of my pussy.

My head hung down, my arms numb from the position. I futilely tried to move my legs, which were fixed in that contraption. Valentino's hand gripped my waist tightly as he began to fuck me forcefully, like a savage, roaring loudly. I felt his cock hitting every corner of my pussy. I didn't close my eyes at any moment.

"My Don..." I whimpered amid my moans.

"Speak, my butterfly..." He declared with a choppy voice.

"Just don't stop." I clenched my toes.

My husband's fingers slid down my waist, touching my pussy from underneath, stimulating my clitoris. It made me collapse, reaching a point of pleasure I had never imagined.

His fingers strummed my folds; I wanted to move, push my buttocks against his cock, but I couldn't due to my limited mobility.

Valentino didn't stop, fucking me hard, roaring loudly with each thrust.

All I could do at that moment was moan loudly, bite my lips, every part of my body numb, surrendered to my sadomasochistic husband.

"I can't take it anymore..." I moaned, surrendering, feeling the spasms even in the tip of my little toe, clenching my hands and biting my lip. "Mine, only mine, Don..."

I felt the tears streaming down my face as I came, giving myself completely to that wild, hallucinatory process.

"*Fuck, my wife, mine, only mine...*" With one final brutal thrust, he came, and I felt his warm jets inside me, holding firmly in place.

And here I was, having said it would be just once to have his heir, finding myself in a guillotine, experiencing a powerful orgasm as my sadistic husband fucked me for the third time...

I could feel his breath crashing against my skin, his hands caressing my back.

"*Yellow*, I need water," I murmured, closing my eyes, wanting to get out of it.

"My beautiful wife, you were simply fantastic." I felt his fingers undoing the clip on my ankle, then removing the anal plug from my ass. "My cock will still be fucking this little ass, that was just a sample..."

"Oh God, what have I gotten myself into," I whispered, laughing.

Valentino let out a faint laugh, moving around to open the guillotine and helping me out of it. His skilled fingers undid the clamp on my nipple. I lowered my head, noticing my nipples were completely red and incredibly sore.

"They're sore," I murmured.

"Just as I wanted them to be, so you'll remember which man can touch you—only me." He easily lifted me into his arms, and I rested my head on his shoulder.

"My husband, so sick with control... I don't need to call you my Don anymore, do I?"

"Game over," he whispered, his hands sliding down my back. "You can call me whatever you want."

"I'm hungry."

"Let's go to a restaurant on this island."

At that moment, the atmosphere between us was calm, and it didn't even seem like just seconds ago we had been fucking uncontrollably.

CHAPTER THIRTY-SIX

Yulia

My husband pulled out a chair for me to sit in; we were at a seaside restaurant.

"Ah..." I whimpered as I sat down, feeling the soreness in my butt.

"Is something wrong, wife?" he asked, with a hint of mockery.

"Asshole," I whispered, crossing my legs.

Valentino sat beside me, his hand resting on my thigh. A waiter approached, and my husband ordered from the evening's menu. As we left the house, I was confronted by the night; I hadn't even noticed it.

We had spent nearly an entire afternoon in that room, and time had passed without me realizing it.

"Is there anything you don't eat, *bambina*?" the Italian asked after the waiter finished listing the menu.

"No."

He then placed an order for both of us, still in control even here, making even my order. Lastly, he requested a wine, and once the waiter left, we were alone again.

The sea breeze brushed against my arm, causing a brief shiver on my skin.

"Are you cold?" he asked, turning to me.

"No, it was just the breeze," I said with a shrug.

My husband had the top buttons of his shirt open, revealing the beginning of his defined chest—an imposing man, always well-groomed.

"Since you owe me so many questions, I'll start my interrogation." I gave him a sly smile.

"Go ahead, curious lady." His extroverted side thrilled me.

"Your favorite brother? They say that anyone with more than one brother always has that one we'd ask to help hide a body, for example." He smiled at my question.

"To hide a body, I know that both Pietra and Santino would do that for me, but to reveal my secrets, without a doubt, it's Santino. We share the same womb; he's my other half. I love both of them, but San is the one who knows the most about my life." He shrugged, raising his eyes as the waiter approached with our wine.

The waiter set two glasses on the table, opened the bottle swiftly, and gave my husband the first taste. He took a small sip and then approved.

The waiter filled our glasses, left the bottle on the table, and departed.

"I guess that question was pretty obvious; of course, it would be your brother," I grumbled. "Does he still ride a motorcycle?"

"Why?" I picked up my glass as he asked another question about mine. I took a small sip of the wine, savoring its delightful essence.

"When you came to my college, I saw you were on a motorcycle, so I got curious." I shrugged my shoulder.

"I have a motorcycle. The one you saw at your college wasn't mine, but I've had one since I was sixteen. Actually, now I have three."

"So you like them?"

"Yes, I love motorcycles. Santino and Enrico and I always ride together. Well, it was Enrico who taught me how to ride a motorcycle, after almost killing ourselves together." He seemed to drift into distant thoughts.

"Have you ever had an accident?" I asked, curious.

"Yes, numerous times, but always minor falls. The most serious was when I fell off a motorcycle with Enrico. That bastard protected me from getting hurt, but it was many years ago. Why all this curiosity?" My husband removed his hand from my thigh, sliding it around my waist and pulling me closer, our chairs touching, our bodies pressed together.

"Just wanted to know. I know how to ride a motorcycle, you know?" I smiled, raising my eyes to his. My husband narrowed his eyes at me.

"I don't like that at all; how do you know?"

"Well, during these holidays, Billie bought a motorcycle and said she wanted to impress one of her father's security guards, but it didn't even make an impact. And since I have a license and had never ridden one of those, I wanted to satisfy my curiosity," I declared, excited, remembering the motorcycle my friend bought just out of vanity but lacked the courage to ride because it was too big.

"Tell me you had a motorized bicycle," he grumbled, somewhat apprehensive.

"I'm sorry to inform you, it was a 300. I don't remember the model right now..."

"And you rode it? Without ever having been on one before, were you alone?" Valentino released me, holding my face.

"Does Billie count?"

"Damn it, of course not, do you have any idea how dangerous that is?"

"I'm fine, and besides, I was very good at it; otherwise, I wouldn't have gotten my driver's license." I lifted my hand, trying to move his off mine.

"You're crazy. I will never let you ride a motorcycle again, unless you're on the back with me, but never driving!" His possessive way of speaking made my eyes widen.

"Don't you trust my ability?" I confronted him.

"Look at your size, you probably can't even touch the ground..."

"Sure, as if a motorcycle could do what you just did to me. Do you realize how absurd that is?" I noticed that both of us were starting to lose patience, something that happened very easily.

"I said no, you will not ride a motorcycle again, not while you're my wife..."

"While? While what? What do you mean by that?" I dug my nail into his hand in my anger.

"It was just a figure of speech. Besides, you'll only leave my side if you're dead. Otherwise, you'll be mine until my last breath," he growled in his way of speaking.

"Then let one of us die before we grow old together, because if we reach old age together, I'll go insane." Valentino released my hand.

Our argument was interrupted by the arrival of our dishes. I moved my chair away from his, our relaxed moment was broken by a silly little fight in response to my husband's authoritative tone.

I kept wondering, would it always be like this? Relaxed moments replaced by petty arguments? We both ate in silence, and I didn't ask any more questions as the mood had already shifted.

As I chewed, I got lost in the vastness of the sea in the distance, feeling a slight knot in my stomach just at the thought of being pregnant—pregnant by a possessive man who always wanted everything his way, treating me like a fragile crystal that could break at any moment.

Despite feeling unwell, I finished eating everything because I was very hungry.

"Are you done eating?" my husband asked as I took the last sip of my wine.

"Yes."

"Then let's go." He stood up in silence and then pulled out my chair. I rose, feeling his hand on my wrist.

"I can walk on my own," I grumbled.

"Did I ask you anything?" Without looking at me, he continued walking, pulling me as if he were dragging a dog against its will.

It seemed like we were back to square one, with a husband who was extremely arrogant and thought he owned the universe.

CHAPTER THIRTY-SEVEN

Valentino

Yulia arrived at our vacation home, stomping her feet. Every time I wanted to touch her, the little minx would swat my hand away or quickly dodge, doing everything she could to stay away from me.

I put my hand in my pants pocket, letting her go up first, and took out my phone. I called Santino several times, and that bastard only answered after I had called a few times.

"Damn it," I immediately complained.

"It's so wonderful to keep you waiting. So, how's the honeymoon going? Do I have my nephew on the way?" His mocking genius usually irritated me.

"What's the situation? And our guest?" I rubbed my forehead, wanting him to provide useful news.

I sat on the couch, looking out at the distant sea, the light reflecting off the water.

"We're in the same situation. You said not to touch him, so we're keeping him there, feeding him scraps when it's convenient for us. Everything is normal, as normal as it can be, considering we have a Serbian prisoner in our hideout..."

"That doesn't make me happy at all. We know Serbs don't talk; I highly doubt this one will. What worries me is what Darko is planning in Italy. What the hell is that bastard up to?" I sighed deeply, once again considering cutting my vacation short. After all, I only had two days left in paradise.

"I can't shake the feeling that sooner or later that unfortunate soul will attack. We hope it's soon because the longer the Serbian mafia's godfather takes, the stronger he will become," my brother declared thoughtfully.

"If only we knew where that bastard was, operating in the shadows, being sneaky without leaving any evidence. Only a few men are caught and they never say a word." Like me, Santino sighed deeply.

The Cosa Nostra, along with the Los Sombríos Cartel and the In Ergänzung mafia, were investigating those Serbs, but nothing was being found. They had been found on their territory, men just like ours, always the same thing: they stayed silent and said nothing, or spoke in their native language, too quickly for anyone to understand.

"Valen?" My brother called me out of my reverie.

"What is it?"

"And your wife? Aren't you going to say anything?"

"Have I ever told you what a busybody you are? What do you want to know about my wife?" I huffed in irritation.

"I want to know if the job is done. Can we expect the next heir?" As a good busybody, he was playing his role.

"Just because you're nosy, I won't give you that information." I ended the call, standing up from the couch. But before I could throw the phone, I read Matteo's message that had just arrived.

"You should keep an eye on your wife's friends. That friend of hers is a complete nutcase..."

My *consigliere* wasn't the type to get attached easily, but at that moment I was almost sure Matteo was concerned about Billie, who, from what I knew, was a bit unhinged, as if she were missing a few screws.

I didn't reply to his message at that moment; we were talking when I was on the boat. Matteo had sent the Las Vegas report, but there was nothing that worried me. We only needed to find out who was trying to enter our territory with that cheap drug, trying to draw attention to us.

If this wasn't a Serbian operation, I don't know who it could be.

I took out my pack of cigarettes, brought one to my lips, and lit it with my lighter. Standing by the pool, I got lost in the view in the distance, remembering my little wife's body, the blood that stained her skin after I whipped her so much, the taste after licking her.

Damn it, I licked my wife's bloodied ass and got turned on by it. I fucked her hard and saw pleasure tears streaming from her eyes.

Yulia surrendered, wanting to feel everything, and even though she felt pain, she reached her peak of pleasure. If that wasn't submission, I didn't know what was. Even though she would never admit it, knowing how well I knew that little creature, she would confront me even knowing she wasn't right.

I turned my face when I heard footsteps coming from the stairs. Yulia was now with her black hair wet, wearing a robe, clearly having just come out of the shower, heading toward the kitchen.

Without even finishing my cigarette, I left it in the ashtray and went toward her.

"What do you want?" I asked, noticing her small hands opening the cabinets.

"A painkiller. My body aches." She turned to look at me, raising one of her dark eyebrows.

"I have one in my carry-on bag." I shrugged.

"Could you give me one?"

"Are you talking to me now?" I put my hand in my pants pocket.

"It depends on my level of anger, because right now all I want to do is punch your perfect face for leaving me with a cut-up ass, not to mention the bruises on my breasts from last time, and just to top it off, I got new hickeys on my neck." She turned her neck, showing the red marks I had left.

Maybe I had gone a bit overboard with possessiveness, marking Yulia as mine, wanting everyone to see it explicitly.

"Do you realize that? Anyone who looks at me this way might think I was run over by a car or attacked by a vampire... For God's sake, you licked my blood." Her mind wandered off, which made me let out a loud laugh.

"Bambina, come back to reality. I almost thought you were going to say I'm a vampire. I'll take care of your problem. I have ointment and painkillers..."

"Great, give them to me and stay away. Every time you touch me, you manage to leave me with bruises. I don't want that. Maybe now I'll put into practice what I said I would do: we'll only have sex again if I'm not pregnant." She crossed her arms, pouting.

"Are you saying you didn't like the sex we had today?"

"What's the point of liking it if we always end up in a fight? If every moment you want to be right, I'm made of glass to the world, not to your aggressive hands, right?" My Colombian was irritated.

"So you're saying you enjoyed being dominated by me?" She was silent for a long few seconds before finally speaking:

"Yes, I enjoyed it, but I hate the aftermath, the pain I'm feeling, and the fact that you only care about the sexual act. How could you not predict that I would end up like this, all sore? Like I've been run over by a truck." My little wife crossed her arms, holding back her tears of anger.

"I knew it, which is why I have the ointment and painkillers. It'll pass and soon you'll be ready for the next time..."

"Give me the painkillers, and don't talk about the next time for now." Yulia walked past me, or tried to, but I easily grabbed her arm, pulling her to my chest and lifting her effortlessly.

"I said I would take care of *mia bambina*, and I will..."

"I want to strangle you, damn Italian." It was impossible not to smile at her pouty face, her rosy cheeks, full lips, not to mention the intense black orbs of her eyes that fascinated me.

CHAPTER THIRTY-EIGHT

Yulia

My eyelids felt heavy, exhaustion taking over, and I only remembered falling asleep after a lot of protest, losing the battle with my husband as he applied cream to my ass after giving me the painkiller.

I opened my eyes slowly, finding the room lit, the bed empty beside me. I sat up on the mattress, feeling the pain shouting from my ass. Damn Italian, how could I ever think that would be enjoyable?

I was shattered, destroyed, as if I had been in an accident.

I got out of bed, still in my nightgown, dragging my feet toward the bathroom, where I did what I needed to do, stopping lastly in front of the mirror. I lifted my nightgown, seeing the scratches the whip had left. They were superficial scratches, something I knew would heal soon.

With some bruises on my ass, as well as on my chest, and hickeys on my neck, I knew they wouldn't go away quickly. I even knew I needed to hide them with makeup. I left the bathroom and headed for the door. The house was always empty, so I didn't mind walking out of the bedroom in my nightgown.

Distracted, I reached the first step, turning my body when I noticed my husband with his men in the living room. They all kept their heads down when they saw me.

"You can leave now, with your eyes down," he growled at his men.

"Yes, Don," one of them responded while the others followed him out.

I stayed there, quiet, watching my mafioso get up from the sofa. He was wearing one of his suits, without the jacket, with the first buttons undone.

"You know we're going to be living in a house where people come and go all the time, don't you?" he murmured in his controlling way.

"And is this already the house?" I raised an eyebrow in my best smug manner.

"You seem to have woken up much better." Our eyes met as he stopped in front of me.

"I woke up ready to claw my face off your thigh." I smiled, still hating that tattoo.

"I love it when you're wild, but I love it even more when you're submissive." His fingers touched my neck, gently squeezing as if questioning whether he should tighten his grip.

"I bet you want to choke me right now, don't you? Want to punish me? Then punish me, *my Don*," I provoked him in the best way I knew, speaking in a low, drawn-out voice.

Valentino let out a growl in response to my provocation.

"You're too sore; I'm not going to fuck your pussy after having fucked you hard three times..."

"Is that what I am to you? Just a sexual object? Then punish me. Isn't that all I am to you? A semen deposit?" I took a step toward him, losing my fear, confronting him, feeling the pressure on my neck grow stronger.

"You know it's not like that." Valentino also took a step toward me, our bodies pressing together.

"Then why did you bring me to this place if not for that? You brought me here with a purpose, and you achieved it. You had my virginity, you had my submission, and now what more do you want? My pussy again? Then fuck me, Italian, isn't that how you treat me with these vulgar words? My intimacy is just that for my husband—a deposit for semen." I felt tears burning my face, anger taking over.

Valentino released his hand from my neck, brushing his finger down my cheek, wiping away the tears that were falling.

"*Mia bambina*, you are my first lady of the Cosa Nostra. How can you be just a semen deposit if you'll be by my side for the rest of my life?" he whispered tenderly, making it clear he wanted to calm me down.

"Then why does it have to be like this? Always commanding, always ordering, never revealing almost anything, of course, unless I ask. And why do I need these hickeys? *Why? Why? Why?*" I punched his chest, catching him off guard and taking a step back, then grabbing my wrists to stop my tormented actions.

"Enough, Yulia, I'm not good at this. I've never had to explain my life to anyone. So if you're not clear with me, I won't know what you want, what you want from me?" My husband seemed impatient, nervous.

"I want everything. I want you, fully, body and soul, not just the sexual part. I want affection, I want ointments on my ass, to wake up next to you, have coffee together while we discuss the day's plans. I want to be your confidante, just as you will be mine. I want your devotion to me." I slumped my shoulders.

"You're asking too much for just four days of marriage," he declared, but he didn't deny it.

"So what do you have in mind?" I asked, feeling tired even after a full night's sleep.

"We can start with the coffee, and I'll tell you about our plans for the day..." He intertwined his fingers with mine, leading me to the coffee table, pulling out a chair where I sat, letting out a groan of pain.

I prepared my coffee in silence. At that moment, the tears had stopped, and Valentino had only made plain coffee, his eyes meeting mine.

"Eat well, because we're going back to Sicily." It was impossible to hide my shock.

"Weren't we supposed to be here for five days?" I asked, astonished.

"Yes, but given the circumstances, I prefer to return. I can't stay away; my mind is there, my clan needs me with them, even though my family wants me to stay here."

"Okay." I shrugged. Even though we were always fighting, this was our bubble, and it was about to burst. We were going to return to reality, to live in a huge house with his family, who would now be mine as well.

"Is everything okay, *bambina*?" he asked, noticing my daze.

"Yes, just a bit apprehensive..."

"Apprehensive about what?" He cut in, wanting to know what was going on with me.

"What if your family doesn't like me? What if I'm not good as the first lady? What if..."

"Schii." My husband raised his hand to touch my lips. "You're perfect, born to be my wife."

"I don't believe that." I rolled my eyes.

"Just stay calm. I should be the one scared. After all, you'll gain allies who will do everything to keep you away from me." He gave a sly smile that made me melt inside.

"And aren't you afraid?"

"I know how to handle the women in my house." He winked, referring to the women in his household.

"Well, I'm sorry to say the same doesn't apply to you." I shrugged.

"I'll still learn to handle you, butterfly, and when you realize it, you'll be my submissive."

"That's something we'll see, Italian." I smiled slyly; it hardly seemed like minutes ago I was exploding at him.

CHAPTER THIRTY-NINE

Valentino

Yulia spent most of the trip lying in her seat, sleeping. It was incredible how easily she could fall asleep. My family didn't want us to leave yet, even though we had two more days on Mosquito Island. However, I couldn't stand being away any longer; it was as if they were hiding something from me. I needed to be at the center, to know everything, even the smallest details.

Matteo was in Las Vegas, gathering everything we needed, but nothing was leading us anywhere. My *consigliere* even managed to find a *mule* who bought the drugs they were selling there, and it was nothing like the Serb's product. Was there a new organization we were overlooking? Or was it a Serb strategy to mislead us?

We were already sharing Las Vegas with Los Sombríos; we couldn't handle more competition, especially of this type, which attracted attention, leaving many users out of control, even ending up in the hospital, causing two deaths.

"No..." I turned my face. Next to me, with only the aisle separating us, was my wife. She murmured as she slept.

I waited for her to say something else, but nothing came. Her small, full lips twitched, her eyelids tightened.

"No..." she murmured again, as if in the midst of a nightmare. "I don't want..."

It was the first time I'd seen her dream so vividly; perhaps it was an intense dream that made her whisper as if she were living it.

"No, Valentino..." Her mentioning my name in her trance unsettled me. I wondered why she said she didn't want something; what the hell was I doing in her dream? Was she beginning to hate me just for hurting her in her dreams? "Don't leave me... don't leave me... I'm afraid of the dark..."

She continued to repeat it until her eyes suddenly opened, scared, focusing on me, the first person she saw, blinking several times. I lowered my notebook onto the table in front of my seat and stood up.

Yulia didn't say anything, only watched my movements. Carefully, I held her slim waist, lifting her with ease. My wife was so dazed she didn't even know what was happening. I sat down in her seat. Yulia swung her legs around my waist, holding onto my shoulder.

"Kiss me, please..." she requested, still with a hoarse voice.

I slid my hand along her neck, drawing her lips close, wanting to touch hers gently, but what came from my wife was an aggressive act and a fierce kiss, as if she needed it to breathe, a moment of relief.

I gripped the back of her neck, opening my mouth, letting her tongue devour mine. It was Yulia claiming that kiss, my little wife, hot and delicious. Her pussy rubbed against my leg, her loose dress causing her panties to rub more against my pants.

For the first time, I was letting a woman take control, and this woman seemed out of her mind. I moved my other hand down her back, touching her ass, lifting her dress, feeling her skin against mine.

"Hold me, Valentino, be aggressive, let me feel you," she begged amid the urgent kiss.

"*Bambina*, please don't ask me for that," I whispered, knowing that if she asked one more time, I would fuck her hard right there.

My men were a little further away, but the sounds of my first lady's moans could be heard.

"I need it, I need it... take me... make me yours," her urgent voice made me slide my hand between her buttocks just to feel her pussy, and damn, Yulia was incredibly wet.

Removing my hand from her ass, I grabbed the curtain that could separate us from the rest of the jet, providing visual privacy.

I knew she was out of her mind, but if this was what Yulia wanted, this is what I would give her. Holding both sides of her face, making those intense black eyes meet mine.

"Are you sure?" I asked breathlessly against her lips.

"I've never been so sure of anything. Fuck me already, please, take this bad dream out of my mind, do it the way only you know how," she pleaded, returning to devour my lips as if she wanted to drown in them.

Quickly, I unzipped my pants, releasing my extremely hard cock, demanding that she take it.

Yulia didn't even bother to remove her panties, pushing them to the side, and sat down on my cock. Fuck, my girl, she rubbed her hot, tight pussy against me, making me stifle a groan.

"Keep your eyes on me, okay?" I commanded, splaying my hand through her hair, pulling it back, seeing her swollen, red lips.

"Yes, my Don." She bit her lip in a sensual way that took me to paradise. What the hell kind of woman was she?

How did she manage to captivate me with just a small smile?

With my free hand, I gripped her round ass, thrusting deep into her pussy. Yulia rolled her hips on my cock; she knew exactly how to do it, her prowess driving me insane.

I saw a tiny bead of sweat forming at the corner of her forehead, her wild black hair cascading over her shoulder, her seductive eyes locked on mine, my Latina wife driving me to fucking delirium.

I knew I was about to come any moment, and my sex nymph was about to come too, her eyes rolling back, biting her full lips, hoarse moans escaping her mouth.

"My Don..." she contracted, her walls tightening around my cock.

"Fuck," I roared as I came hard inside her. "*I'm yours... yours...*"

I spoke instinctively, not realizing it, just pulling her lips to mine, kissing her aggressively until I tasted blood on my lip, but I didn't stop kissing her and claiming her.

Without breaking our lips, the kiss became slower. Yulia didn't even mind the taste of blood I took from her, as if she were getting used to my aggressive way, or even enjoying it.

Gently sliding her lips over mine, my wife pulled away, resting her face on my shoulder, a sigh escaping her mouth.

"Do you want to talk about it?" I whispered, removing my hand from her ass, running it through her hair, caressing her.

"It was a horrible dream," she murmured, giving only the basics.

"*Bambina,* what did I do in your dream? You spoke while you were asleep..."

"Did I?" She lifted her head, looking at me scared.

"Yes." I touched her rosy cheeks.

"You left me, you left me, just like my brother left me at that boarding school to study, away from family. I know Ferney loves me, but he never wanted me close to him." Her eyes filled with tears.

"Butterfly, what part didn't you understand is mine? I will never let you be away from me." I pulled her face close to mine, giving soft kisses, calming her until her body relaxed completely.

CHAPTER FORTY

Yulia

I had to apply makeup to my neck before getting off the jet; after all, I didn't want anyone seeing my neck like that.

We landed at the Sicily airport, and my husband's cars were already waiting for us. We quickly headed towards the open door. I sat in the back seat with Valentino beside me. Four cars were escorting the Don to the mafia headquarters.

I was anxious. This was the moment when our life together was really going to start, with his family and the daily challenges.

I could still feel the slight burning in my intimate area, not something bad, but something delicious that made me recall our spontaneous sex. An act that I demanded and he granted, and I didn't even know how I went from zero to sixty in a matter of seconds.

That dream felt so real, the fear of another person leaving me, being left alone again. Everyone said they loved me, but in reality, they didn't want me by their side.

Sometimes I just wished for a normal life, a family, people I could wake up beside, busy breakfasts with lots of conversations, like those romantic comedy movies where everything is chaotic.

"Are you quiet, any problems?" my husband asked, squeezing my thigh.

"Just anxious. We're finally going back to our reality, and what if it doesn't work out?" I swallowed hard, my eyes fixed on his tattooed hand on my leg.

"What exactly if it doesn't work out?"

"If you realize I'm annoying, after I give you your heir, if you send me away..."

"*Schii*..." His finger touched my mouth, making my eyes meet his. "Butterfly, you are mine. I won't send you away. Why this insecurity now?"

Valentino noticed my insecurity, all because of that damn dream where he left me.

"I'm scared, very scared. The first person who really wanted to be with me, day after day, was Billie, and she's my friend, my other half, we're like sisters. Now I feel alone, and after that dream, it was like tormenting thoughts came to mind. And if you realize how annoying I am, even I judge myself as irritating, who is the person who feels obligated to tolerate someone else's annoying behavior?" I spoke without stopping, realizing how nervous I was.

"*Bambina*, I'm not going to leave you. Simple as that." He winked, giving a small smile.

"And with what guarantee do you say that?" I felt his finger touch my chin.

"With this." His lip touched mine, sliding over the lip gloss I had applied, a smile forming on his lips as he kissed me slowly, our tongues touching. "I feel like I'm kissing something sticky, and strangely, it's good."

"Can I have your kiss as a guarantee?" I pressed my forehead against his.

"We could make a blood pact." He shrugged.

"A blood pact?" I was taken aback.

"You've never done it?" I shook my head. My husband took a small object from his pocket, opening it to reveal a small blade. "Give me the tip of your finger."

I did as he asked, extending my hand. With skill, he made a quick cut on my finger, making me flinch at the brief sting. Valentino did the same to his finger, cutting the tip, pressing it against mine, our blood mingling as our fingers stayed connected. He turned his hand, holding our hands with the fingers joined by blood.

"I, Valentino Vacchiano, promise on my life that I will never abandon you or leave you aside. You will always be my number one priority, Yulia Vacchiano," he declared, his eyes locked on mine.

I wasn't sure if I needed to promise anything, so I just stayed silent, waiting for him to tell me if I needed to say something, but he didn't say anything.

"Now suck my finger." He released our hands, bringing them to my mouth, his finger with blood on the tip.

Opening my mouth, I let his finger touch my lip, which I licked, tasting the metallic flavor of the blood. Valentino took my finger, bringing it to his own lips, licking it as well, wiping away the excess blood, cleaning our fingers.

"I'm starting to realize that our marriage has a lot of spice, based on blood," I declared with a smile.

"Maybe in another life, I was a vampire," he joked in a lively manner, bringing his lips close to mine, giving a soft peck while speaking. "Feeling calmer now, *mia ragazza*?"

I nodded, shaking my head. My husband straightened up, and I found myself looking at my finger. The small cut there didn't even hurt anymore, no longer bleeding. I had just made a blood pact. What a crazy thing.

His words were engraved in my mind.

I noticed the car entered a gated community, the same one I was in when we got married. This was the headquarters where his family members lived.

A whole gated community just for members of the Cosa Nostra. The car slowed down as it approached the largest house, or rather the headquarters, without parking in the garage, stopping in front of it.

Both doors were opened simultaneously. Holding the extended hand of the mafia soldier, I got out of the car, my feet touching the ground, the gentle breeze revealing the salty smell of the sea behind the house.

Going to a paradise island with my husband was crazy. Now knowing I was going to live right next to the sea made me radiant, seeing the waves every day. I didn't know much about Sicily, but the little I learned from news sites made me curious to spend a day sightseeing in the city.

Of course, if my husband allowed it—damn sexist mafia rules.

I walked past the car, hoping Valentino would at least extend his hand to me, but it didn't happen. He was soon intercepted by one of his men who began speaking, making a gesture for me to follow him towards the door of his house.

He could have waited for me, but he didn't, which left me with a slight pang of anger.

CHAPTER FORTY-ONE

Yulia

I walked through the door right behind my husband. Luckily, something must have happened to make him stop, turn his face, and notice me alone and lost. He extended his hand, took mine, and our fingers intertwined.

"I thought we'd have a big argument about this," I murmured, lifting my face.

"Sometimes I forget that I have someone to worry about. You can give me a reality check when that happens, just not in front of other people," he whispered, winking at me.

I could hear voices coming from the room we were heading to. Everything was very bright and well-lit, just like the last time I was here, with all the windows open. We made our way to the room where my husband's family was gathered, clearly waiting for us.

"My son." The blonde lady rose from the sofa and came towards us. She had well-brushed hair and blue eyes that looked like a clear sky.

"Mother." Valentino released my hand and embraced his mother. It was clear how well they got along and how much he cared for her.

"This house is not the same without you," she said as she pulled away, still holding his hand.

"That's because she keeps complaining that there's no one authoritative to yell at, even her own shadow." The spitting image of my husband came from the corner. It was strange to look at him and see that even their hands had matching tattoos.

"I'm almost sure of that." Valentino pulled his mother into a shoulder hug and kissed the top of her head. Mrs. Verena was about my size; we were both short.

"Sister-in-law." Santino placed a hand on one of my shoulders and gave a loving kiss on my cheek, as one would for a family member.

"I think it's going to take me a while to get used to this," I murmured, looking at my husband's look-alike in front of me, although his perfume was different from Valentino's.

"If I weren't so well-married, I'd take pleasure in getting back at you for what you did to my wife." Santino gave a mocking smile.

"A kick in the middle of your legs, and you'll never have a child again," Valentino declared in his usual possessive tone.

"What happened?" I asked, curious.

"Oh, she doesn't know?" Santino had that mischievous gleam in his eye.

"It's not something I go around telling everyone," my husband responded.

"And by the way, it was all your fault, husband." The blonde woman appeared, sliding her hand down her husband's arm as she came towards me. "In my defense, it was entirely intentional. Valentino was just a ploy to get back at my jerk of a fiancé."

"I'm still not understanding," I murmured, confused, receiving a kiss from Cinzia, the blonde who was a bit taller than me, even though we were both wearing heels.

"You don't need to understand... you don't need to." My husband made a face at his brother and sister-in-law.

"Just from his face, I'm going to tell." Santino did it on purpose. "Your husband kissed my wife at our engagement dinner."

"*Oh, our, wow...*" I looked at Valentino, then at Cinzia, amazed.

"Dear, it wasn't anything major. Everything happened because my beloved husband had his brother impersonate him, and I found out. When I saw him coming out of a corner with a girl, I decided to get even. I kissed the wrong twin, but that was it, there was no second intention..."

"Besides, my kiss is much better," Santino declared mockingly, making Valentino roll his eyes.

I had barely arrived and was already being bombarded with so much information about my husband. Perhaps something this family lacked was a filter.

Mrs. Verena took a step towards me, extended her arms, and gave me a hug, her sweet scent filling my senses.

"How are you, dear?" Her hand moved towards my neck, making my eyes widen as if she was searching for traces.

"I... I'm fine." I cleared my throat as her finger rubbed over one of the hickeys I had tried to hide with makeup.

"I did a lot of that when I got married. I know the men I saw grow up." She turned her face towards her son in a disapproving manner.

"What's a hickey?" Valentino shrugged.

"Did she turn into a prisoner's wife to be marked?" Mrs. Verena wasn't afraid to confront her children.

"You just said you went through the same thing, which means Dad wasn't any different," my husband had that nonchalant tone of voice.

"Did he hurt you?" Mrs. Verena asked, her blue eyes fixed on me.

Out of the corner of my eye, I noticed Valentino's father approaching, placing his hand on his wife's shoulder as if to control her protective instincts.

"No, ma'am, I'm fine," I declared calmly, not mentioning that he had whipped me enough to leave wounds or the slight burning sensation I still felt in my backside.

But I believed that no one needed to know that right now.

"Dear, remember that we were newlyweds too and that we nearly killed each other for a long time?" Mr. Tommaso rested his chin on his wife's head.

"And for that reason, I wouldn't want my son to repeat the same mistakes," Mrs. Verena said again.

"I don't remember you being like this with Santino and Cinzia," my husband muttered beside me.

"That's because I had Pietra to bother me." Santino got a nudge from his wife.

And at that moment, I realized that the older sister wasn't there.

"Well, I need a report on the recent events. Mom, stay with my wife, show her around the house, and all that boring stuff," Valentino spoke with a hint of impatience.

I raised my eyes searching for his, but I didn't find them as he exchanged a brief glance with his father, who apparently gave a nod for him to follow him out.

My husband turned, about to follow his father, but I instinctively cleared my throat, catching his attention.

"Hey." My husband's eyes met mine, a small smile appeared on my lips. He said I should alert him when he was forgetting something, and in my view, he should at least give me a kiss before going wherever he was headed.

"*Oh,* I have a wife," he teased in his way, lifting my face as he held my cheeks and gave a quick peck before turning and heading out with his father and brother.

I was left alone with my mother-in-law and sister-in-law, my eyes meeting hers as she gazed at me with admiration.

"What did you just do? I've never seen Valentino act like that," Cinzia declared, amazed.

"Well, he just said that I could give him a nudge when he forgets that he has a wife. Isn't that what husbands do? They give a kiss or something when they go away?" I said, not understanding.

"The issue is that he doesn't care about anyone but himself, and apparently, my brother-in-law cares about you." Cinzia had that mischievous smile. "I never thought I'd see this, Valentino on his knees for his wife. I'm loving this, mother-in-law."

They exchanged smiles, pulling me along to show me around the house.

CHAPTER FORTY-TWO

Valentino

"Man, what was that?" I turned my face at Santino's question.

"What do you mean 'that'?" I asked, walking across the lawn beside the pool as we headed to the hideout.

"She snapped her fingers and you went running like a trained dog to your wife." My brother had that mocking tone, while my father beside us was struggling not to crack one of his jokes.

"Shut the fuck up, it was just a kiss. Don't you two kiss your wives?" I asked, looking from one to the other as I was caught between them.

"Yes, of course I kiss my hurricane, but I love my wife, unlike you. Unless you also love her? Already in love, Valentino, after just five days of marriage?" Santino stopped walking, making me stop too, turning my body towards his.

"No, I don't love her. It's just a good relationship." I shrugged.

"Knowing my son, he wouldn't do that just for a good relationship. We all know he never cared about anyone. He's too egocentric for that," Dad said, making me look into his eyes.

Tommaso always knew everything about us. With just one look, the bastard could even unravel our souls. That's why I never held his gaze, quickly averting my own.

"It's not ugly to admit you love your wife." My father shrugged.

"It gets a little strange when it's only after five days..."

"Fuck off, Santino." I raised my fist and punched his shoulder.

"Brother, I expected much more from you. You're becoming a trained dog." Losing all my patience, I grabbed him by the collar of his shirt.

In a strength contest, I always had the advantage, making him step back as I pushed him.

"You wouldn't dare throw me into that pool. I have my phone in my pocket, my gun on my belt. Damn it, Valen, I'll stop," my brother pleaded with my mocking smile.

"If I hear one more of your jokes, I'll forget we're twin brothers," I finished with a snarl.

I pulled Santino to my side, my brother about to make one of his jokes when my father intervened.

"Enough, Santino. Sometimes I forget you're both grown men, even with a child, Santino." Tommaso narrowed his eyes at both of us.

"Since when does having a child mean being a buzzkill? Besides, this is a family matter. When it's about the clan, I'm serious... well, sometimes." He directed that gleam in his eye, adjusting the collar of his shirt.

"Let's get moving. Not everyone shares your unfunny humor." I rolled my eyes and continued walking towards the hideout.

"For someone who just came back from a honeymoon, you should be more relaxed. I'm starting to think my nephew isn't on the way." Santino persisted.

"Shut the fuck up, Santino," I said in unison with my father.

"Wow, now I feel like the talking donkey from that Shrek movie little Tommie keeps watching," he mentioned Pietra's son, my sister.

Like me, my father fell silent. Giving Santino more rope only spurs him to talk more.

We passed through the short stone passage, stopping in front of the iron door we called the hideout because it was concealed near the rocks. I entered the code and pushed the door open, descending the underground stairs. The lighting was dim, but the environment was air-conditioned since we had some of our men on watch when we had someone locked up there.

In the center of the light, sitting in the chair, was our prisoner, who looked down at his own feet.

My steps made him raise his eyes towards me, blinking several times as he adjusted to my face.

"You're going to tell us everything you know," I declared in English, knowing he probably understood that language.

But it was of no use; he started speaking in Serbian non-stop, spitting out words. As promised, Santino left him intact.

"Let's start the torture session. Try to get anything out of him," I declared, looking at Santino, who quickly directed the soldiers present to fetch the tools.

My brother ordered what needed to be used, starting with the fingers on a table. The man screamed but said nothing. My hands, in my pockets, were clenched tight, to the point of feeling my nails digging into my palms.

I approached the scene, exhausted from the trip, frustrated by the lack of news about Darko Cosic. The prisoners we captured never revealed anything, which irritated me because it felt like we were going in circles.

I grabbed my gun from my back.

"Stop everything," I ordered, bending down in front of the filthy man. His bloodshot eyes barely seemed to be able to see anything in front of him.

From the smile that formed on his lips, I could tell he was seeing me.

"Kill me, cut off every part of my body, but you'll never find out who our godfather is." Blood leaked from his bloodied mouth, his missing teeth making his speech come out in a rasp, but he spoke

Italian flawlessly, our language, which he hadn't spoken even once until now.

"So you'd rather die than say anything?" I growled, pressing my gun against his head.

"Kill me, and I will witness from hell the grand return of Darko Cosic. He will avenge every clan that killed our men." Knowing he wouldn't say anything more, I pulled the trigger, firing a precise shot to his head.

His body slumped to the side, the chair falling with him. I straightened up, accepting the cloth they handed me to clean my gun before putting it away on my back.

"And that's all. Nothing we didn't already know. Darko is preparing a return, but when? We need to alert In Ergänzung and Los Sombríos. Since no one knows when it will happen, we'll stay prepared," I declared, looking from my father to Santino.

"And what about Bratva?" Santino asked.

"Sergey Petrov doesn't take sides. He's a real pain in the ass. I wouldn't be surprised if he allied with the Serbs just to go against the Cosa Nostra. We maintain good neighborly relations, but we'll never be allies," Tommaso nodded in agreement, as we shared the same thoughts about the Russians.

I let out a long sigh, as it was for nothing. Again, a prisoner with no information—always the same. They preferred death over talking.

"And does Matteo know anything?" Tommaso asked as our men cleaned up the mess.

"Dump the body somewhere, I want everything clean," I ordered, heading for the exit, knowing my father and Santino were following me.

"Matteo got the product they're selling, and it's not the same as the Serbs'," I declared, as we had already obtained drugs being sold by the rival mafia.

"You think it's not them?" Dad asked, curious.

"I believe it could be a small gang out there trying to make easy money, and Matteo is about to reach the source." As we passed through the door, I noticed it was already dark. I hadn't even realized we had been there for hours.

"When it's rookie gangs, we quickly catch those involved because they're stupid enough not to know what they're getting into," I agreed with my father.

Even though Tommaso had retired from the mafia, he was always around when he wasn't traveling with my mother, assisting and giving his opinion. I always listened to him because this clan was once his. Even though I had my own way of leading, Dad had a great perspective on everything.

CHAPTER FORTY-THREE

Yulia

Mrs. Verena joined me at the dinner table. Cinzia was no longer there, as her lovely little girl had a whole evening routine, and she preferred to stay at her own house.

"Do you always dine alone?" I asked curiously as we sat across from each other.

"Well, it's a bit difficult to dine alone when you have a husband and three children. When they were kids, they were always here. This house was always noisy. If it wasn't Pietra yelling at her siblings, it was one of them getting into trouble with each other. We're not a quiet family; we're quite boisterous, you know. When I get together with my siblings, it feels strange because Italians speak loudly, unlike my siblings, who are quiet," she said affectionately.

"Amélia told me you came from the Swiss mafia. Was your marriage, like mine, arranged?" I asked curiously as I prepared my plate.

"Oh, please, I love being called mother-in-law or Verena until we get used to it. I'm always nagging Cinzia, but she loves calling me 'Mrs.' even though I've watched her grow up." — Mrs. Verena's blue eyes sparkled at me. "And yes, my marriage was arranged, and I understand perfectly that I gave my husband a hard time. For that reason, even though I know it's in the blood of these Italians, throughout my children's childhood, I tried to make sure they weren't aggressive towards women."

It seems it didn't work out too well, maybe it really is in the blood, I thought to myself.

"What's the topic of discussion today?" I raised my face as the two men entered the dining room.

"I was just telling my daughter-in-law how my husband was the most affectionate man during our first year of marriage," Verena said, her eyes fixed on her husband, who sat down next to her after giving her a kiss on the top of her blonde head.

"Do we really need to talk about this?" her husband grimaced.

At the end of the table, Valentino sat next to me. He had a serious expression, his eyes fixed on the table as if only his body was present, but his mind was far away.

He didn't even glance in my direction, as if I wasn't there.

"Has Santino gone home?" Verena asked.

"Yes, he said this is the precious time he has with his daughter," Tommaso quickly replied to his wife.

"You should see, dear. Today, Bella learned to say 'grandma.' Her little tongue gets all tangled up. It's the cutest thing." Tommaso gave a small smile to his wife, clearly enjoying the happiness she felt from a small gesture from their granddaughter.

The couple chatted throughout dinner, which made me wonder if I would ever have that kind of relaxed conversation with my husband, if he would sit next to me and smile like that just because of something I said.

Valentino finished eating before any of us.

"I'm going to my office to review some contracts. I don't want to be disturbed." He got up from the table. He didn't even seem like the same man from the honeymoon; in fact, he resembled the man from the first day of our honeymoon.

I was left alone with my father-in-law and mother-in-law.

"Aren't you going to snap your fingers and do that thing you did today when they arrived?" My mother-in-law asked hopefully.

"No." I shrugged. "I was right next to him; there was no way he didn't see me. If he wants to sulk, let him. But I can sulk too."

"Knowing that guy like I do, he's doing this because Santino has been getting on his case, so he's going to want to believe it's all lies." Mr. Tommaso got up from his chair. "I'm going too; I want to go over these contracts with him."

"You know it's not your duty anymore, don't you, dear?" Verena raised her face to her husband.

"I do. I won't be long." He winked and left the dining room.

"At least now I have you." My mother-in-law smiled at me. "Sometimes Tommaso misses being the boss, so he's on Valentino's back. But the two of them never clash; on the contrary, there's no one he respects more than his father."

We both got up from the table, with Verena accompanying me to the living room and then turning to me.

"Dear, you can go to bed if you're tired. You don't need to keep me company. It's still early. We can go to Pietra's house; do you want to come along?"

"Well, I'm not sleepy. I practically slept through the whole trip. I'd like to go," I nodded, feeling Mrs. Verena's hand on mine as we left the house.

"The good thing about living in a condo like this is that we can go out freely on the street," Verena talked non-stop, always bringing up topics, wanting to know about my life.

My mother-in-law was the type of person with whom you could talk endlessly because she was adaptable in conversation.

My sister-in-law's house was the last one on the street. All the lights were on, so there was no need to knock on the door; little Tommie, who was seven, saw his grandmother through the window and ran to open it.

Embraced with Verena, we entered the cozy residence. Unlike the headquarters, which was excessively large, this house had a normal standard compared to the headquarters.

Pietra was super affectionate with me, and as Verena said, they were very boisterous. Her daughter was elegant, but the son let out such screams that I found myself jumping a few times without anyone noticing.

But I didn't judge her because that boy never stopped for a second, until his father appeared, promising to take him to see the new motorcycle he bought, which reminded me of the story Valentino had told me.

When we left Pietra's house, it was already late. I headed to my room, took a shower, and lay down on the bed. Valentino still hadn't returned, which made me even more irritated, as since we returned from the island, he hadn't even spoken to me, as if I didn't exist.

But what made him change so suddenly? Why was he acting like this?

CHAPTER FORTY-FOUR

Yulia

I was lying in bed, possibly because I had slept so much during the flight that I couldn't fall asleep. The bedside lamp was on, and with my eyes closed, I was trying desperately to drift off, until I heard the door open abruptly, causing me to sit up quickly in bed.

With my eyes wide open, I saw my husband walking past it with his phone to his ear. Valentino hung up when he saw me, closing the door behind him.

"Sorry, I forgot you were here..."

"Of course, where else would I be?" I muttered, lying back down on the bed.

I closed my eyes, trying my best to ignore Valentino's presence, the bastard who pretended I didn't exist for the entire dinner. Maybe it was childish of me, but I was right next to him; he could have at least given me a smile, anything!

I heard his footsteps dragging, and I knew he was standing right in front of me.

"What did I do now?" he asked as I felt the bed sink beside me when he sat on the mattress.

I didn't answer him, wanting to get back at him, until I felt my husband's hand gently caress my arm. I quickly moved away, dodging his touch, and sat on the opposite side of the bed from where Valentino was sitting.

"Have I ceased to be invisible to you now? When we're alone, isn't it embarrassing to talk to your wife?" My words came out sharp.

My husband's eyes widened briefly, then he pulled his lip to the side as if contemplating the matter, realizing I was right.

"I had a lot on my mind today..."

"Valentino, your wife was sitting right next to you throughout the dinner, and you didn't even give a mere smile, a wink, nothing! It was as if I didn't exist there." I crossed my arms, noticing his eyes drop to the neckline of my nightgown. "We're talking now, look me in the eyes!"

My husband gave a small smile, the kind that could make any girl weak at the knees. Damn Italian, but I wasn't going to give in.

"Sorry, looking at your body is stronger than me," he muttered, bringing his impeccable green eyes back to mine.

"I swear I try to understand you, but it's hard," I whispered, shrugging my shoulders.

"I messed up. I had a million things on my mind and let myself be swayed by words..."

"From your brother? Because your father said Santino was making fun of you. What did he say?" I asked, already guessing he wouldn't answer.

Valentino fell silent, but not for long, as he soon began to speak:

"He tried to imply that I'm in love when I'm not." At that moment, I wished he hadn't said anything.

It hurt me in a way I didn't expect. I hadn't thought about the word 'love,' about affection, but there was something inside me that longed for that from my husband, and hearing from his mouth that he wasn't in love with me was painful, even though we had been together for only a few days.

Usually, passion was the first to arise, that overwhelming feeling, a crazy emotion that made you just want to be near the person. Love came afterward, when passion was strong and didn't fade away; it prevailed, and love followed.

"Ah..." was all that escaped my lips. I tried not to show any reaction, but it was impossible.

"You're not in love with me, are you? It's not possible to fall in love in such a short time together." My husband squinted at me as if trying to decipher what was going on with me.

"Actually, it is possible. There are people who fall in love quickly," I declared, trying to maintain my composure.

"Well, that's not our case," Valentino said, getting up from the bed.

"Why?" There I was, seeking humiliation.

He was heading toward the suite when he turned around, his eyes meeting mine as he lowered his head.

"Because I'm not in love with you," he said clearly, and I simply closed my eyes in agreement.

"You're right." I opened my eyes, relieved that Valentino had gone to the bathroom, as at that moment, tears threatened to burn my eyes.

I just didn't expect that before entering the bathroom, Valentino would turn and look in my direction, just as a tear fell from my eyes. He stopped, turning back to me.

"What's wrong? Why are you crying?" The Italian walked back toward me.

"You know, during dinner tonight, I envied your parents. I envied their kind of relationship, the smile your father gave your mother just for sharing a silly fact, but simply because it made her happy, he was happy. I feel envious every time I see a couple together, jealous of that complicity, something I know I won't have because you close yourself off whenever someone says they might be in love. Why can't you always be my Valentino? Why do you let yourself be swayed by what others say? Is it impossible that my husband, who appears tender at times, is the same one who is cold to avoid showing he can talk to me..." My voice faltered as I wiped a tear that had fallen from under my eyes.

"So that's it, you're in love with me and want the same from me?" His assertive words felt like a punch to my stomach.

"And so what if I am? What's the big deal? Meanwhile, you're cold enough to feel nothing!" I grabbed a pillow and threw it at him, wishing it were a stone capable of disfiguring that beautiful face.

"What blame do I have for that? Damn it, what do you want me to do?" His words were aggressive.

"I want you to go to hell, to the devil with you, I'm not in love with an asshole like you!" I jumped out of bed, angry and wanting to get far away from him, wanting to cry alone.

But I didn't move; I stayed there, my chest heaving up and down. I knew that if I ran now, he would come after me, so I decided to let him shower first.

"It's impossible for someone to stop being in love so quickly." He crossed his arms as if he hated that I said I wasn't in love.

"There's a chance we could be wrong, just as you said it's impossible to fall in love in such a short time. Maybe it is impossible, because my foolish mind was already forgetting what a tremendous jerk you are," I spat out, noticing him grinding his teeth.

"Good, you got what I wanted..."

"Yes, I realized how idiotic you are. After all, a person can't change," Tears of anger streamed down my face. All I wanted was for him to go into that damn suite and leave me alone to cry in bitterness.

Valentino let out a long sigh, realizing that our argument wasn't going anywhere. He turned and went to the suite. When I heard the shower turn on, I quickly grabbed my robe, left the room, and searched for any place distant, away from him.

CHAPTER FORTY-FIVE

Yulia

Walking through the house's corridors, I noticed a quieter place and entered it, looking around and realizing it was a private room. I moved towards a small lamp, turning it on so I could close the door with the light inside.

Tears were still streaming down my face. I couldn't remember the last time someone made me cry this much.

My eyes were tired, my mind exhausted. I went to the corner of the window, opening the curtain and noticing that it had a wide ledge where I could sit and look through the glass at the distant sea.

How could I have thought living near the sea was a good idea? In theory, it might be, if I weren't living with a crazy husband.

I tried to hold onto the positive aspects of him, but he had a tendency to lose his patience easily.

I hugged my knees, resting my head on them, just wanting a clear answer for myself. Was I demanding too much from someone who couldn't offer anything?

Was I being selfish, spoiled?

He promised in that ridiculous blood pact that he would never leave me, but at the first opportunity, he ignored me. Is that it? Was the pact only meant to prevent him from leaving?

Why did everything have to be so complicated? Why was I so complicated?

I lost track of time; the tears had stopped falling. A yawn escaped my mouth; crying must have made me sleepy.

I was about to get up from the window when I noticed the door open. Mrs. Verena walked in, and I could clearly see my mother-in-law let out a sigh of relief.

"Mother-in-law?" I said, surprised as I got off the window ledge.

"Oh, we finally found you." The woman came toward me, and like me, she was wearing a long robe. She pulled me into her arms and gave me a tight hug.

"H-how come?" I stammered.

"Valentino thought someone might have taken you or that you had run away. He's with our men, looking through the street..."

"Oh, heavens..." I murmured, alarmed. "I just needed distance from him."

"Dear." My mother-in-law held my hand as she stepped back, looking into my eyes. "I know the first days of marriage are tough, but if there's one thing these men wouldn't abandon, it's their wives. He was in a panic when he didn't find you in the room."

"And didn't it occur to him that I might have just been hiding in some room?" I pointed out the obvious.

"We've had a kidnapping in this family, and obviously, Valentino thought the worst." My mother-in-law tried to give me a forced smile.

I should have been concerned about what I had done, but at that moment, all I wanted was to punch that idiot's face. First, he made a whole show of it, and then he acted like a worried husband.

"Well, I'm fine," I whispered with regret. In truth, I felt embarrassed that he had called his parents.

"Come on, let's go downstairs." Verena placed her hand on my waist.

We both left the room together, heading towards the stairs. I preferred to go to my room, but I felt guilty that Valentino had called everyone when I was just in a room.

My eyes widened when I saw Valentino's sister in the room with little Tommie lying on her lap, wearing even a pajama. On another couch sat Cinzia with the little baby in her lap.

We approached them, and they both looked at me with relieved expressions.

"I... I'm so sorry," I stammered again, feeling my voice falter in the face of my shame.

"Dear, it's all right. We're family, and here we protect each other. If something came up that alarmed everyone, action needed to be taken," Pietra said in a calm voice.

"I'll let Santino know so they can return," Cinzia said, grabbing her phone to notify her husband.

"I feel guilty for making you leave your homes," I said, feeling my cheeks flush.

"Sister-in-law, you don't need to feel guilty. What's a marriage beginning without a bit of chaos? At least we have a story to tell," Cinzia said with a mocking tone.

They really didn't mind being pulled from their homes late at night. A movement at the door caught my eye, and I saw my husband passing by. No, it wasn't my husband; it was Santino, as his steps led him towards his wife.

"I've informed Enrico; he's with Valentino, and Dad is also on his way back," Valentino's brother said, looking at me. "Damn, you really scared the hell out of Valen. I've never seen him so flustered."

There was mockery in his tone.

"Santino, watch your language!" Pietra scolded her brother, as there were children present.

"Sorry, sis." He walked around the couch, bending down to take his little daughter from his wife's arms. She was asleep, curled up in her father's embrace.

Mr. Tommaso was the next to return, going to his wife and kissing the top of her head without directing a glance at me.

"This reminds me of the day you ran away from me in Las Vegas," I heard Tommaso say to his wife.

"At least we had a better ending than that," she murmured to him, but since I was close, I heard what she said.

Last to come through the door was my husband, alongside Enrico, Pietra's husband. My eyes immediately met Valentino's, and the distress in his gaze was evident.

His quick steps came towards me, but all I could do at that moment was back away, moving behind my mother-in-law.

"Yulia," Valentino said in a sharp tone.

"Stay away from me," I declared, taking a step back behind Verena.

"What's the problem now?" he asked, releasing a long sigh.

"What's the problem? Are you crazy? Where did you think I could have gone? Why did you call all of them?" I narrowed my eyes, trying to contain my anger.

"I was worried, damn it! What if you had run away?" I stepped out from behind my mother-in-law, pointing my finger at his chest.

"Worried? Where would I go? I'm your damn wife; I know my responsibilities, but I'm not obligated to tolerate your moods. Now, in front of your family, do I exist to you? Or do we need to pretend we don't have a relationship?" I raged as my husband grabbed my fist.

"Yulia..." he murmured, clearly trying to contain his anger, but the problem was, I didn't know how to control mine.

"Go on, Valentino, do what you do best, hit me. Why don't you tell your family that I've asked you to hit me? I must be as crazy as you, crazy!" My eyes grew cloudy as tears began to fall, exhaustion from everything, from always losing my patience so easily.

With force, I felt his hand grip my hair, pulling me to his hard chest, where I clung to his shirt, letting the tears fall.

"Shhh, no one here thinks you're crazy; after all, anyone who does will get a punch from me," he murmured audibly for everyone to hear.

"Well, now that everything is resolved, I'll take my wife and child and leave," I heard Enrico say, and soon after, Santino also left.

I was still clutching Valentino's shirt tightly, trying to feel anger at everything he had done to me, at my past ruined by him, but that Italian always showed me that things were never as simple as they seemed.

With ease, Valentino picked me up in his arms, whispering something to his father, guiding me to our room.

CHAPTER FORTY-SIX

Valentino

D*amn*, I didn't want to admit it, but I was scared, really scared. For the first time in my life, I felt like the ground had been pulled out from under me, thinking the worst, fearing she had run away after our argument.

Yulia was still clutching my chest tightly, and I could feel her nails scratching my skin through my shirt, but that pain was nothing compared to the terror I felt when I thought something might have happened to my wife.

I entered our bedroom and closed the door. The lamp was still on, just as I had left it. I stopped by the bed, where I laid her small body down, my wife opening her eyes. I knelt beside her, as she kept her hand grasping my shirt.

"Don't hate me, *bambina mia*," I whispered, sliding my thumb across her cheek.

"I wish I could hate you, even punch your perfect face," my wife whispered with a choked voice.

"If it makes you feel better, I'll let you hate me for a few seconds. I'll even offer up my face for the occasion." A half-smile appeared on my face.

"Shut up, Italian," her tone was calm. "I hate you for being a jerk, for ruining my last two years of college, for sleeping with those women at my college, for everything you've done in my life, even for existing. I hate you, and I wish I could hate you a little more, but I can't..."

I let her speak, just listening, realizing the mess I had made of her life. I bitterly regretted participating in that orgy, but not for attending college.

"*Ragazza mia*, I'll never have forgiveness for what I did. I was childish and reckless. I regret participating in that act, but I don't regret attending college. I don't regret driving those men away from you, because I wanted to be your first in everything. I'm selfish enough to admit it, because I'm crazy about every part of you," I whispered, still feeling her skin under my thumb.

"That's cowardly of you," she whispered, still not looking away from me.

"I'm a coward when it comes to my wife. When it comes to you, I am everything, just to have you by my side, being touched only by me." Yulia fluttered her black lashes, images of her coming to my mind, her loss of control. "I was so scared..."

My voice died off, making me realize that being without that dramatic woman, who had taken over my life in just a few days, was like being breathless, as if all the air had been taken away.

"You're not scared." Yulia rolled her eyes.

"I'm afraid of losing you, *bambina mia*," I murmured, noticing she fell silent but soon tried to come up with an excuse.

"That's nonsense. We both know we're married and that I might be pregnant with your child..."

"And what if something happens? Accidents happen, kidnappings aren't premeditated. Do you understand? It's not just your issue; it's something in the universe that surrounds us. I promised to protect you, to keep you safe, and I will do that." I lowered my lip, kissing the top of her forehead.

"Valentino?"

"Yes?"

"About our argument this morning, I'm not in love, so you can relax." I remained silent, looking into her eyes, tormenting myself because Yulia said this, as I didn't know I needed it until I heard from her lips that she was in love with me.

"Are you sure?" I whispered, looking for any trace of a cough.

"I don't understand you. I thought you didn't want my love. Hating you is easier than loving you." Her hand released my shirt, and I looked down at her robe, undoing the knot that kept it closed.

"*Bambina*, that's because I'm the fool of us both. You're perfect; I'm the one who complicates everything." I helped Yulia sit up, removing her robe and revealing the generous cleavage of her breasts.

I ran my hand between them, adjusting, just making sure the nearly visible breast was properly covered.

"What are you trying to say?" Her skin tingled at my touch.

"That it's possible to fall in love in a few days," I murmured, making my feelings for that hot Latina explicit in the air.

"Did we fight for nothing? Did we fight so you could stage that circus, so I could lose control in front of all your family, and now you come to say that I was right?" There was my short-tempered wife that I knew.

"Did anyone tell you that marriages were easy? Because if they did, they lied. It's everything but easy." I got up from the bed, unbuttoning my shirt.

"I... I'm still in disbelief. What a jerk. Wasn't it easier to just admit that I was right?" She said, trying to stay angry, but her eyes fixed on the buttons of my shirt.

I removed my shirt, throwing it on the floor, then took off my pants, leaving only my black boxer.

"You know that saying, we need to feel the despair of parting to value what we have. I felt it, felt like the air was missing, the pain was agonizing me. All I needed at that moment was to find the reason to make me breathe." I placed one knee on the bed at a time, lying down beside her.

"What are you trying to say, explicitly, without all these word games?" My wife fixed her eyes on my chest.

"I mean that I'm also falling for you, *bambina mia*," I said directly, taking her hand, wanting her delicate fingers on my chest.

"And don't you think this feeling came too quickly?" She raised her eyebrows in a funny way.

"Are we moving too fast? Screw it, I just want my wife by my side every day…"

"But being in love doesn't mean I trust you one hundred percent. After all, we have a not-so-great past together." Holding her neck with my other hand, seeing Yulia suppress a yawn.

"I'll have a long journey ahead, then…"

"With many bumps and pebbles, because I love making things difficult." My wife laid her head on my chest.

"Sleep well, my butterfly, you're tired. We had a pretty crazy first day back. Will all our married days be like this?" Yulia let out a long sigh.

"I hope not, as I also appreciate calmness," she murmured, hugging my chest and snuggling.

"Sleep well, *bambina*…"

"Sleep well, my Don." I smiled, knowing she did that to provoke me, and I loved it.

Love? Falling in love was one thing, but loving?

Damn, what was happening to me?

It didn't take long for her breathing to become slow; Yulia was already asleep, and I stayed there, stroking her long black hair for many minutes.

I found myself imagining that just a week ago, I thought it would only be a marriage, that she would just be the mother of my heir. But in such a short time, Yulia had taken over me.

That little thing curled up on my chest had me in the palm of her hand. I took on her pain, wanted to be the best for her, and if Yulia asked me for the world, I would do the possible and the impossible to give it to her.

CHAPTER FORTY-SEVEN

Yulia

Sleepily, my eyes started to open, adjusting to the brightness of the room, recognizing my new room—or rather, our room. I turned my face, feeling the arm that was beneath my neck.

I remembered sleeping against my husband's hard chest; it had been a quick sleep. I was so exhausted that I simply conked out.

I raised my hand, my fingers itching to touch that defined chest that was completely exposed to my eyes. I brushed over his warm skin, feeling the rise of his muscles. A shiver ran through my husband's abdomen.

"It feels like a kitten's paw scratching my stomach," he said in a hoarse voice.

"And you know what a cat's paw feels like?"

"No, but it must be something like this." I lifted my face, seeing him with his eyes closed. The hand that had been under my neck moved, pulling me closer to his chest.

In response to his movement, to tease my husband, I ended up straddling him, my legs on either side of his waist. His eyes opened, a glint of mischief in his gaze.

"I could easily get used to this view," my husband said, lifting his hand to grip my waist.

"Well..." I bit my lip, coveting that defined chest, those strong arms. "Do you go to the gym?"

I changed the subject drastically, and Valentino chuckled hoarsely at my shift.

"I do, or do you think I have this build just because of genetics? I wish, but I've always been a gym rat. So now it's easy to maintain. Santino and I have always had my father's push to keep us moving since childhood." His fingers gripped the fabric of my nightgown, pulling it up.

"Should I thank your father for all this?" I teased, trailing my hand over the length of his chest.

"Maybe we should thank my mother too, after all, they both made me." I shook my head, as my husband's playful version made me feel slightly relaxed.

I lowered my face as Valentino's hand moved towards my exposed backside. His finger circled my panties, giving a small tug and tearing them.

"Can we enjoy the perks of being married?" he whispered, bringing his lips close to my neck.

"What would those perks be?" I played dumb, feeling my pussy slightly swollen, craving his touch.

"Morning sex is one of them..." I lowered my pelvis slightly, feeling his penis brush against my intimacy.

"And where do our fights fit in?" I teased, remembering the events of the previous night.

"Leave that for later; there will be many more ahead." My eyes met his, noticing his smile.

"Are you implying that we'll fight again?" I raised an eyebrow.

"And do you believe we won't?" My husband moved his hand to the front of my legs, touching the sensitive spot of my pussy.

"Are there marriages that survive fights?" I asked with a mix of playfulness, closing my eyes as his fingers grazed my moisture.

"If it depends on me, our marriage could even become immortal, so I'll never have this bed just for myself, but for both of us." His hoarse voice made a brief moan escape from my mouth, my head tilting back as I rocked gently on his penis covered by his underwear.

"Titi," I murmured.

"That could be quite a buzzkill if it weren't for your delicious lips." I smiled, opening my eyes to fix them on his.

"I love provoking you, Italian." I bit my lip mischievously.

"You love it, huh?" My husband quickly moved, making me lie on the bed with his body covering mine.

He removed his underwear, becoming completely naked, holding the sides of my nightgown and pulling it off, leaving me naked with him.

"Do you also love being fucked by my cock?" he asked possessively, rubbing his penis against my wet pussy.

"*Yes... oh... yes...*" I bit my lip, not taking my eyes off his intense gaze.

"What else do you love, *bambina*? Without realizing we were stepping into dangerous territory, I let myself get carried away by the moment.

"You, I love you." Valentino stopped, my eyes widened. How did I say that?

Oh God, that was instinctive. I didn't even realize what I had said.

"*Ah... fuck...* I need to fuck you, Yulia Vacchiano," he said, not uttering an "I love you too," but showing complete possessiveness over my words.

His penis penetrated me deeply, my head tilting back, my husband gripping my breasts tightly, our bodies pressed together amidst the frenzy of emotions. My mouth was slightly open, allowing my moans and sighs to escape.

I felt his member sliding through my pussy, receiving it eagerly, wanting to belong to my husband completely.

"*Ragazza mia*" I grunted, thrusting forcefully inside me. "Say it again, say it..."

"Valentino," I murmured his name as if it were madness.

"*Bambina*, say it..." My husband seemed out of control, his breathing ragged, our eyes locked.

This sex felt different, as if there was a need for us to be together.

Raising his hand, he circled it around my neck, I felt his tense back beneath my fingers.

"Yulia Vacchiano, say it, fuck..." he ordered as if I were obliged to say what he wanted.

"I love being a naughty girl." I smiled mischievously, grinding beneath him.

"If you don't say it, you won't get your final pleasure..."

"I can do that with my fingers later." I bit my lip.

"Fuck, little Colombian, just do what I ask for once," he was almost pleading.

"Only if you beg," I whined, as I was at the peak of my pleasure, and Valentino hadn't even noticed.

I took advantage of that moment, surrendering to the wild mix of passion. My husband had no choice; he seemed to be on the edge as well.

"Fuck..." he grunted, making me feel his hot jets inside me.

With one last thrust, he collapsed on top of me. We stayed like that for long seconds, just feeling our breaths, my hand caressing his sweaty back.

"You're not going to say it anymore, are you?" Valentino whispered with his head in the curve of my neck.

"Not until I'm sure about it. Besides, I was the only one who spoke. You stayed quiet, which should be considered humiliating." He got off me, making me feel his liquid trickling down my leg.

He lay down beside me, both of us looking at each other.

"I think we were too hasty. I practically forced you to say it, but now that I know the taste of those words from your lips, I'll do everything I can to hear them again." My husband lifted his finger, touching my lip.

"Good luck then, Italian, because I'm very difficult." Obviously, when it came to him, nothing was too hard—sometimes a bit complicated, but mostly pleasurable.

"I don't give up on what I want..." He got up from the bed, easily picking me up in his arms, which I straddled, hugging his neck. "Let's take a shower and then go down for breakfast."

With a quick kiss, he guided us to the bathroom.

CHAPTER FORTY-EIGHT

Yulia

Valentino was holding my hand as we descended the stairs after our shower, which had been accompanied by yet another morning of sex. It was practically impossible to be next to him naked; it always ended up in sex.

I could admit it was delicious. Was there a possibility of loving him? Certainly, but the fact that I had only said it at that moment left me unsettled.

My heels echoed on the polished floor, the dress a bit above my knee. I heard laughter coming from the dining room, making my cheeks warm. After my performance the previous day, I expected to be noticed.

Valentino didn't seem to care at all. We entered the dining room, and I swallowed hard when I noticed his entire family present.

My husband pulled out the chair next to him, so he sat at the end of the table. In front of me were Mrs. Verena and her husband.

"Is there a special event for everyone to be gathered? Did I miss something?" My husband asked right away.

"We're asking the same thing, since Santino and Cinzia requested this coffee with everyone," Pietra, who was sitting next to me, said.

"I love the coffees at Grandma's house; we could come here every day." Tommie, sitting next to Tommaso, received a wink from his grandfather.

"So small and such a brown-noser," Valentino said, making me realize he had a good relationship with everyone.

"Uncle Valen, are you going to give me a cousin?" Tommie looked with that pleading child's gaze. "Bella is boring and a girl; I want a boy, and my dad said he won't give me a brother."

The little one crossed his arms and pouted.

"When you're older, you can have your own children. I've already done my part for the world; I refuse to have more children," my sister-in-law Pietra grumbled beside me.

"Speaking of children," Cinzia interrupted the mother and child dialogue.

Little Bella was sitting in a high chair next to her mother.

"Cinzia is very emotional about these things." Santino rolled his eyes, receiving an elbow from his wife.

"You're the one who's insensitive." They exchanged looks, and I noticed that, like Valentino and me, they enjoyed exchanging barbs, but not in a negative way, as if they liked to poke fun at each other.

"Well, we already know Cinzia is having another kid. Congratulations, brother, let's hope this time it's a boy," my husband cut through their banter.

The guests gave Valentino disapproving looks. My mouth dropped open at his insensitivity.

"Wow, Valentino, go screw yourself," Cinzia grumbled, grabbing a piece of toast and tossing it at her brother-in-law.

My husband dodged it, laughing.

"You guys keep stalling. Just say it; we're having another kid. Look how practical." My husband rolled his eyes.

"Let's see when it's your turn," Cinzia grumbled.

"He'll be so insensitive he won't even get excited," Santino mocked.

"I doubt that," Tommaso joined the conversation.

"If I know Valentino well, he'll be the kind of dad like Tommaso—sneaks a knife, takes the kid out at night after the mother is asleep to see the hideout." My eyes quickly shifted to my husband.

Valentino gave me a half-smile.

"Don't pay attention to what they're saying. We don't even have a kid yet." He winked, hoping to change the focus of the conversation.

"That is, if his first child isn't a girl. We know my dad never gave me a knife," Pietra said beside me, standing up from her chair.

"My little princess deserved the best, but unfortunately, she fell for this thing." She made a face at her son-in-law.

"Admit that this thing here is your most beloved son-in-law," Enrico teased.

"Of course, he's the only one." Santino laughed amidst the mockery.

Everyone stood up, congratulating Santino and Cinzia on the new pregnancy, both beaming. Cinzia even had tears in her eyes.

"Damn, I hate these pregnancy hormones," Cinzia grumbled, wiping her eyes.

"It'll be nine months of lots of foot massages for you, wife." My husband's twin brought his face close to his wife's hair and kissed her.

I found myself watching the scene. Would Valentino be able to be that kind of husband? Was it too much to ask? Even knowing that both of them had gone through chaos just as Verena had told me the day before, it seemed like Santino did everything for his wife.

My hand was resting on my thigh as I sat down, and I turned my face when I felt Valentino's gentle touch on my finger. He noticed my gaze on his brother.

"You better not stay close to my brother; he does some pretty weird things," Valentino said loudly, making everyone look at us.

"Look, Yulia, he's already dodging massages. Don't let him get away with it; it's a husband's duty to pamper his wife, especially when we're pregnant. We carry their offspring, we go through the hormones and body changes, so don't let this one slip away." Cinzia shot me a mischievous look.

During breakfast, or when the family was gathered, it was as if the mafia didn't exist, just a chaotic family.

"I, I... I'm afraid just thinking about getting pregnant. Even though I know I could get pregnant at any moment... I'm scared," I stammered several times, as I'd never had a maternal image and wasn't sure if I could be a good mother, even though I wanted a little something of mine and Valentino's.

I felt long fingers touching my chin. Naturally, in front of all his family members, Valentino said to me:

"I'm sure you'll be a great mother to our child." His voice was calm and affectionate.

"She'll definitely get plenty of massages," I heard Santino's mocking tone. "I bet that if Yulia snaps her fingers, he'll bow his head."

My eyes met Mrs. Verena's as my husband removed his finger from my chin. She watched the scene with a sigh, as if relieved by what she saw.

"Shut up," Valentino grumbled at his brother. "Before I forget, we have an event to attend tonight. Santino and Cinzia were supposed to go, but it seems pregnancy comes with nausea..."

"And a lot of sleepiness too," Cinzia finished my husband's sentence.

"But tonight? Just like that, at the last minute?" I said, somewhat exasperated with my husband.

"Don't worry, dear, I'll help you, and when we arranged your closet, I saw you have many beautiful dresses in it. It will be a great debut as the Don's wife." I swallowed hard, as being introduced alongside him made me anxious.

The rest of breakfast was calm; they didn't even mention what had happened the night before, which relieved me. It was easy to feel part of their family. It was as if the Vacchianos had embraced me as one of their own, even taking on my troubles and not caring about my brief disappearance.

CHAPTER FORTY-NINE

Yulia

The car stopped in front of a luxurious event, resembling a gala ball, with a red carpet laid out. My husband got out on one side while they opened my door.

I reached out my hand when I saw Valentino's, his fingers covering mine, a small smile on his lips. I stayed by his side, releasing our hands and holding onto his arm, which was bent toward me.

"You're simply the most beautiful woman I've ever had by my side," he whispered in my ear.

"What are you planning to do with that comment, husband?" I whispered back, looking ahead as we walked toward the door.

"Take off that red dress with my teeth by the end of the night..."

"That's going to be a tough task," I declared as we stopped in front of the entrance. They didn't even ask for his name; it was clear they already knew who he was.

"I have all night, *bambina*," he said as we passed through the door and entered the luxurious event.

There were several elegant, tall, slender women accompanied by men. On the golden-toned stage, a projector kept running advertisements for the new hotel they were about to open.

The presence of the Don of Cosa Nostra was essential for business, just as there were rulers and mayors present. Valentino told me that they had connections with all the powerful men in Sicily.

My husband was quickly intercepted by a young man who immediately extended his hand to him.

"My Don." Valentino took his hand and brought it to his forehead, whispering something I didn't understand.

"Carson, good to see you." My husband seemed to know him but didn't introduce him to me.

"My father is waiting for you, let's go." The man made a gesture with his hand, and out of respect for the Don, he didn't look at me.

I felt eyes on us. I knew I looked beautiful, but Valentino next to me was breathtaking. It should be illegal for a man to be that handsome, and worse, to have a twin.

We approached a group of men, some of whom were accompanied by women.

"My Don." A man approached, extending his hand, which Valentino brought to his forehead, whispering the same thing again.

"Lucas Carson, I see you've put effort into this new venture," my husband said.

"It's just as we organized it. Did you like it, Don?"

"Yes, I liked it surprisingly." Valentino looked around. "By the way, this is my wife, Yulia Vacchiano."

He introduced me.

"It's a pleasure, madam." He only nodded without extending his hand, perhaps because he knew Valentino hated people touching what was his. "When I heard that the Don got married, I was doubtful."

"There was no doubt. It was always stated that I had a fiancée; it just hadn't been the right time." A tall young woman approached, touching the man in front of us on the shoulder.

"My Don." The woman smiled at my husband, and at that moment, I felt that the way she called him "my Don" made it clear that she did this at other times, just as Valentino made me address him.

I tightened my grip on my husband's arm.

"Rebecca, I thought you went traveling," he called her by her first name.

"I decided to return early, and imagine my disappointment to find out you married so suddenly." Her blue eyes turned to me, and I narrowed mine.

The whole situation made me uncomfortable, making me look away, noticing many women's gazes on us, questioning me—how many more had he taken to bed? How many more had sat on my tattooed thigh?

All my anger surfaced, my loss of control hitting me like strong gusts of wind.

"Rebecca Carson, this is my wife, Yulia Vacchiano. From now on, she is my only woman, my First Lady, and I expect everyone, without exception, to treat her with respect. And for the men, if I see any of you coveting my wife, I'll rip your damn eyes out. If you ever saw me with another woman, it was before her; now my life is about only one woman."

I lifted my face as he spoke proudly and loudly so that everyone present could hear. Noticing my tense body, Valentino lowered his face, touched my chin, and kissed me gently.

"I didn't want you to go through this," he whispered, only for me to hear.

"Jerk," I murmured, giving that scoundrel a smile.

I lifted my face, seeing several women sighing at the Don of Cosa Nostra's declaration.

"The last public declaration we saw like this was from your father, and we know how devoted he is to your mother," Lucas declared.

Valentino simply nodded, continuing to talk with those men after my husband's possessive outburst and his declaration to everyone, making it clear that he wouldn't sleep with any other woman. However, the words of that woman kept echoing in my mind.

Knowing that it was all about jealousy, because he had a life of debauchery before me, and I was his first woman, it was easy for Valentino. He didn't have to see other men touching me; now, with me, he had to bear the emotional burden of having slept with half of Sicily.

I felt foolish with his declaration, but still jealous.

He was my Don; why did everyone need to keep calling him that? Was it the same with Verena? Did everyone call her husband "my"?

An instrumental band played slow music for couples to dance in the middle of the hall. I looked at it several times, wondering if my husband knew how to dance that kind of waltz.

I stayed by his side the entire time. His conversation was mostly boring, but I remained there, fulfilling my role as his wife.

My lips started to ache from holding back a smile until my husband slowly looked at me.

"You're bored, aren't you?" he whispered.

"Yes." I made a face, speaking the truth.

"Do you know how to dance?" he asked politely, as if he was sure I did.

"Of course." I flashed a smile.

"Then grant me the next dance. I want to touch every part of your body," he murmured close to my ear, making my cheeks flush and my body shiver.

"I thought you'd never ask," I declared softly, biting my lip amid my smile.

"*Bambina*, don't squirm like that in front of everyone. They'll notice you're wet and ready for my cock," he whispered, holding my chin.

"It's hard when you have a charming husband with a roguish smile." I blinked my eyes.

"Yulia Vacchiano, you will still be my undoing," he said, excusing us from the guests and guiding me to the center of the dance floor.

CHAPTER FIFTY

Yulia

Valentino placed his hand on my waist, his fingers firm. The waltz was slow, smooth, a rhythm that made couples glide across the ballroom. My husband knew what he was doing; I was even impressed.

"I'm offended that you thought I didn't know how to dance," his raspy voice close to my ear made my neck tingle.

"But I didn't say anything." I lifted my face, playing dumb.

"You didn't need to say anything; your expression gave you away." Through the open part of my back, I felt his hand sliding over my skin.

"So now you can read my expressions. What does this one mean?" I asked, with a hint of mischief, smiling with a bite on the corner of my lip.

"It means: I want to be fucked by my husband all night long." I swayed my hips, the spot between my legs growing warm.

"Valentino Vacchiano, you're wrong..."

"Wrong? I never get things wrong, but I bet you're wet." We were gliding across the ballroom, my husband guiding me with skill, our bodies pressed together. He danced in a way that made me feel every part of him.

"Husband, I hate to inform you, but I'm *very... very...* dry," I whispered, lying. "*Ah...*"

A hoarse moan escaped my mouth as he nibbled discreetly on my ear.

"Liar, you lie so badly; you're so wet that my cock would slide into your pussy like a glove." At that moment, with our bodies rubbing together, I felt his penis pressing against my stomach.

"We're going to need to switch to another waltz if your little friend doesn't calm down; we can't be out there flaunting your trophy," I grumbled, feeling jealous.

"The only trophy I have is having the most beautiful girl by my side." We looked at each other.

"Saying that, I might even think you're the last romantic left," I teased, raising my hand to touch his neck.

"*Ragazza mia*, I know how to make my wife melt."

"I'm starting to worry that you can do that with every woman," I muttered again.

"Your jealous version turns me on. I can't change my past, but I can make my present different. Little butterfly, you're mine, and I make it a point that everyone knows I'm yours, if that makes you feel better." Our eyes locked at that moment.

"It's hard when I see a woman calling you 'my Don' right in front of me. You're mine, not hers." Valentino broke into a broad smile at my pout.

"Say that again?" he asked, our eyes locked as if we were one in the middle of that dance.

"Mine, only my Don, and I'm too jealous to share you. Well, I make just one exception." I pretended to think.

"And what would that exception be?"

"For our child," I said, making my husband lower his face, taking my lips in a slow kiss, aligning them perfectly.

"You're perfect, Yulia Vacchiano. How could I ever think that a sharp-tongued little thing wouldn't tame me?" he whispered, pulling away.

"Italian, admit that you love me and can't live without me," I said sarcastically, realizing that my moment had gone too far, just as he had forced me to say I loved him, I had done the same.

"*Bambina*, I admit it." He didn't say he loved me in so many words but agreed with what I said.

"Sorry, my joke went too far." I looked away.

"Keep your eyes on me, don't look away. I really don't mind; I can't live without you. How can I have my bed just for myself when I have the chance to wake up every day next to my half meter?" I ran my nails down his neck, keeping my gaze fixed on his.

The word "love" hadn't left his mouth, just as it hadn't left mine. It was as if we were avoiding it, even though our bodies spoke differently. Our connection went far beyond a simple "I love you"; I felt it, felt his torment, just as he felt mine.

"Did you just call me half a meter?" I teased, laughing and raising an eyebrow.

"It's not just half a meter, it's my half a meter." He smiled with a hint of mockery.

"Well, just so you know, that half meter can cause some damage." I ran my hand down his jacket, feeling his firm arms beneath my touch.

"Believe me, I thought you were just another spoiled little girl. But I was wrong. You saw things about me that my family never knew," his tone made me sigh.

"No one knows about that?" I asked, knowing exactly what he was referring to.

"No, and I prefer it stays that way. I wouldn't be able to handle their pity," he murmured, his eyes distant.

"Since when do you do this?" I tried to delve into the topic.

"I don't know. I was a kid. I wanted to earn Santino's trust, to be better than everyone else. I saw my father sitting in that office chair and would think it could be me there. Bearing the name Tommaso is a burden; my father was one of the best Dons the Cosa Nostra ever had, and since then, I've held myself to impossible standards. If I wanted to be like him, I needed to be perfect, and I punished myself every time I failed. It started with a lighter between my legs, burning in places no one could see, until I found that if I kept my nails a bit long, I could punish myself by squeezing my hands. The methods I found, the greater the mistake, the greater the punishment..."

"What was your greatest punishment?" I whispered through my fear.

"Spending an hour in my apartment whipping my back until the wounds opened and the blood trickled down my skin." My eyes filled with tears, but I didn't let them fall, only the image of my husband doing that came to mind.

"And did it help?"

"It always helps. I felt punished; it became my addiction, my flaw. I just can't stop." The music grew softer, indicating it was about to end.

"Promise me something, husband?"

"Yes." He answered without hesitation.

"When you feel the urge to self-harm, you'll tell me, no matter what. You'll tell me, because I want to deal with your pain just as you embraced mine." The music ended slowly, his lips came close to mine, giving a slow kiss.

"*Bambina*, you're perfect just for existing," he deflected, not answering my question.

"Promise, Valentino, and mean it!" I was firm as we pulled away, my arm entwining with his. Valentino lowered his face, his eyes meeting mine.

"Yes, I promise, but I assure you, it's not the nicest thing to see," he seemed scared.

"I know how to be strong." I smiled triumphantly, noticing his eyes lost in my face.

Loving Valentino Vacchiano was turning out to be easier than I expected.

CHAPTER FIFTY-ONE

Yulia

I stepped away from Valentino to go to the bathroom, despite his reluctance to let me leave his side. I needed to check my makeup and perhaps use the powder room.

I stood in front of the mirror, taking my lipstick from my small purse and applying it delicately to my lips. Out of the corner of my eye, I noticed two women entering. As I was in the corner, they didn't see me.

"Did you see the Don's wife?" one of them said.

"She's very beautiful. I wonder if he does with her what he did with all the others he slept with," the other replied.

"Look, if he doesn't, you can be sure he'll cheat. That man is a sex machine..."

"Did you see the way he looks at her? Obviously, that girl doesn't even have to do anything he likes; the man is in love, it's clear between them. I found myself sighing several times watching them dance; there's a connection there, a very passionate one." Well, I liked hearing that.

That meant many had noticed that man was mine, and those days of him being with everyone else were over because now he belonged to me! *Damn, that was a bit possessive.*

Before either of them could say something I didn't want to hear, I intentionally knocked my lipstick onto the sink, and they noticed me through the mirror.

"Good evening, ladies," I said with a forced smile on my lips. "And that was a nice observation of yours; my husband is madly in love with me, his words."

The one who mentioned our connection sighed dreamily, while the other just looked at me.

"I wish you both happiness." She gave me a half-smile that lacked falseness, appearing quite genuine.

"Thank you. We're very happy, you know how it is, early in marriage, everything is wonderful, and just as you said, *my husband* is a machine in bed, but the good thing is I already know how to handle that machine." I winked in a way that made my jealousy and possessiveness clear.

I put my lipstick back in my purse, smiled at the two of them, took my bag, and left the bathroom. Was it now clear that he was my Don? I didn't think I could feel jealousy over that man; it was something even beyond my control.

I was leaving the bathroom when I felt a strong grip on my arm. I turned my face.

"Who are you?" I asked, trying to pull my arm away, looking into those eyes, a light brown, marking those features.

Without saying anything, he pulled me forcefully to the corner of the wall and took a phone from his pocket.

"Let me go! If not, I'll scream." I kept trying to pull away, moving my arm repeatedly.

"Quiet, I'm not going to hurt the Don's whore." I widened my eyes.

"Who do you think you are to call me that?" I looked around, beginning to panic. Where was Valentino?

"I'm no one important, just the person with something essential in my hands, and it's up to you to tell your little hubby to keep quiet."

"What are you talking about? Why don't you go tell him yourself?" I asked with ironic fear.

"I'm not an idiot; I know that man is always armed. What better way to go for his weak spot? We knew your husband would want to take down our gang, so tell him to get that guy in Las Vegas to shut up and stop killing our drug dealers, or this will get out for everyone to see." He pulled out his phone, unlocked it, and played a video showing explicitly my first time recorded.

My eyes widened even more as despair took over me, our naked bodies by the pool, having our first sex, recorded, explicit, with all the details, even my sighs and shudders from the experience.

There it was, laid bare for everyone to see. How did they manage that? The grip on my arm tightened, and the man blocked the phone when I tried to grab it with my other hand, putting it back in his pocket.

"Now, be quiet and go back to your husband. Tell him that if he doesn't leave what is now my territory, this video will be posted for everyone to see. I want the Cosa Nostra out of Las Vegas immediately, or tomorrow night everyone will see how delicious the wife of the Italian mafia boss is." With a victorious smile, he released my arm, leaving me stunned.

Tears began to fall from my eyes, leaving me feeling grounded, the video vividly in my mind. I didn't know who that man was, or where he had gone, only that I was in despair.

"Ah!" I let out a small scream, turning quickly when someone touched my shoulder.

"Yulia, what happened? Why did you take so long to come back? *Damn*, why are you crying, your arm..." My husband began speaking without stopping, as I realized something was wrong.

Without thinking, I clung to his chest, crying while gripping his jacket tightly, sobs escaping from my mouth.

"*Amore mio*, please, tell me what's going on." That was the first time he had called me that, and I couldn't even be happy about it because a catastrophe was about to unfold.

"Please, get me out of here, let's go, just get me out of here." I begged loudly, afraid of having our intimacy exposed for everyone to see.

Without arguing, he nodded, holding onto my shoulder, not saying goodbye to anyone, just ordering his men to be ready immediately. As soon as we left the party hall, the car was waiting for us with the door open. I got in first, and Valentino quickly pulled me into his arms.

"Yulia, tell me what happened, please." I turned my face to his bewildered eyes.

"*I... I...*" I couldn't speak as I was overwhelmed, in shock, the words simply wouldn't come out, fear was all that prevailed.

I, who had always been afraid of relationships, was now about to have my intimacy exposed for everyone to see.

Even though he wanted to know what had happened, my husband noticed my state and, without pressing, just held me against his chest, stroking my hair, wanting desperately to calm me.

CHAPTER FIFTY-TWO

Valentino

Yulia spent the entire drive home clutching my jacket, her sobs audible, her fear evident in every tense part of her body. My wife couldn't speak, and I had no way of pressuring her.

Damn, that silence was driving me crazy, making me lose my mind.

The car stopped in front of the estate. I helped Yulia out of the vehicle. She walked beside me, her hand clasped tightly around mine as if seeking salvation from me.

As we entered the estate, we passed the room where my parents were. They were talking calmly until they looked up and noticed Yulia's red, swollen eyes from crying.

"Oh my God, what happened?" Mom was the first to stand and come towards us.

"I don't know. Something happened to her when she went to the bathroom," I said, guiding my wife to sit on the couch.

"I'll get a glass of water." Verena went to the kitchen while I removed Yulia's heels, trying to make her more comfortable.

Mom quickly returned with the glass, handing it to Yulia's trembling hands. The redness on her arm was still there, driving me even more insane. She needed to say something.

"*Amore mio,* please, your silence is killing me," I pleaded with a sigh.

She turned her face after taking a few sips of water, her eyes filling with tears again as she began to speak.

"They have a video, a video of us, a video of us..." A sob escaped from deep in her throat.

"Video of what?" I asked, stroking her hand as my mother took the glass from Yulia's hand.

"Of our... our first time, everything... everything is in it, all explicit." A white cloud came over my vision.

Shit, what the hell? What kind of video was this? I needed to stay calm to get more information from her, but at that moment, I was nearly getting up to punch something.

Dad stood up from his sofa, coming to stand beside Mom, realizing the seriousness of the situation.

"Who are 'they,' *bambina*? Tell me everything you remember," I begged, as Yulia lowered her face, clutching the fabric of her dress and letting out a long sigh. She began to speak, trying to maintain her composure.

"I was leaving the bathroom when a man grabbed my arm, right here." She showed the redness on her arm, making me furious that someone had done this to my girl. "He said he knew you would try to take down his gang, so he had already anticipated it by recording the video. It's an intimate video of us, a moment that was just ours..."

Yulia wiped under her nose, trying to control herself, resuming her speech after a pause.

"He said that if you don't stop hunting him, if you don't stop killing his men—" that night, Matteo had told me he had killed two men from this gang in a conflict with dealers. "—He said the Cosa Nostra had to leave Las Vegas, otherwise by tomorrow night, our video will be online for everyone to see."

Everyone fell silent, no one said a word. Damn!

How could I not foresee this? How could I have failed so miserably? I needed to think clearly, keep my thoughts in check. I got up from the couch, reaching into my pocket. Yulia noticed my move; she knew that at that moment, my anger was surfacing. Even in her torment, my wife was aware of my condition.

I went back to her, kneeling in front of her, holding both her hands and caressing her fingers.

"Don't do this, it's not your fault," she whispered, shaken.

"I'll take care of this. I'll find out who's behind this video, I'll find the source of this gang. I promised I'd protect you, *mia bambina*, and I will." My voice held a firmness that was almost frightening, even to myself.

"I'm so scared, he was so sure of his words. Valentino, I don't want our video on the internet, I don't want it." She began to cry again. Mom sat beside her, nodding at me, assuring me that she would take care of my wife.

I stood up, looking at my father.

"I need all the men who were on the trip with me. We'll interview each of them, leaving no information unturned. I'll call Santino." I acted quickly, turning back to my wife. "I need to know, Yulia, can you describe the man who intercepted you?"

She lifted her face, tears still streaming down, speaking in a hoarse voice:

"He had black hair, brown eyes... I can draw him, I'll get my sketchbook. I'll have it done for you in less than an hour..."

"What do you mean?" Dad asked, and at that moment, I felt proud of my *bambina*.

"Yulia can draw perfectly," I answered Dad's question.

"I'll go to our room and get my drawing materials." Standing up from the couch, she went towards the stairs with Mom.

I took my phone from my pocket and sent a message to Santino, demanding his urgent presence at the estate.

"Son, are you prepared for the consequences of what might happen? Ready to make the most risky decision since becoming

Don?" Dad asked, already thinking I'd pull our men out of Las Vegas and shut down our casino there.

"I'm the Don, and I have you as an example. We're not pulling our team off the field, and that damned video isn't going online," I growled decisively. "No one messes with my wife and gets away with it. No one invades the Cosa Nostra's territory and comes out victorious. We're the largest Italian mafia, and I'm going to show them they messed with the wrong Don."

I didn't take my eyes off my father. I noticed his eyes shining in my direction, his hand gripping my shoulder.

"There was never any doubt when you became the Don of the Cosa Nostra. I'll be by your side, and we'll show that no one messes with these Italians." Dad squeezed my shoulder.

Even with fear, even with apprehension, I didn't show any weakness because my mafia needed a strong Don. My wife needed me to be her rock.

And I would be.

CHAPTER FIFTY-THREE

Valentino

I watched all the men in the room and scratched my beard.

"I'm going to give one of you the chance to come forward," I declared, keeping my eyes fixed on them, looking for any small reactions, "and in doing so, the consequence for your actions won't be as severe."

No one said a word, causing a long sigh to escape my lips. It was clear that finding out who was behind this wouldn't be easy.

"Enrico and Aldo, I want you to speak with each one of them," I ordered to the former *underboss* and the *consigliere* of the Cosa Nostra.

"Yes, Don," both replied promptly, moving to carry out the task.

Suddenly, a young man, one of the new soldiers, stepped forward. I recognized him as the son of an old line of Cosa Nostra members.

"My Don," he said, swallowing hard. Noticing his desperation, I gestured for Santino to act, to not seize him abruptly but to approach calmly and be ready in case the boy tried to flee or even harm himself. "I ask for mercy for what I've done. I was cowardly; my family has nothing to do with this. They offered me a large sum; my eyes grew wide, and I didn't think—I failed, I was cowardly..."

His voice trailed off as he tried to grab his gun and put it to his head, wanting to kill himself. But Santino was already behind him, knocking the gun from the boy's hand, causing it to fall to the ground. My brother applied an arm lock and tightened his grip on the boy's neck.

"You wanted to be spared, you wanted a quick death. Now you're going to feel every bone in your body break," I growled, clenching my fist in anger. "Take him to the hideout."

Santino nodded and turned, taking the now crying boy with him.

"I want all the Rossis in this house," I ordered one of the *caporegime* present, who moved to gather his *soldiers*. "Now everyone get out of this headquarters and stay on standby in case I need you."

Only my father, Aldo, Enrico, and I remained in the room. Santino would return in a few minutes; my brother would bind the traitor at the hideout and leave our men to watch him.

My phone rang. I looked at Matteo's name on the screen, accepted the call, and put it on speaker so everyone could hear.

"Matteo?" I said impatiently.

"Given what we discussed, I ordered that the nightclub be closed today, making it seem like we're backing down from their demands," my *consigliere* said on the other end of the line.

"And what about the men you said discovered the boss's hideout?" I asked anxiously.

"They're monitoring his house from a distance, observing who comes and goes. I've obtained the complete dossier on Martilho Gutiérez, a Mexican who spent five years in a Mexican prison and was released a year ago. According to what I found, he has no direct conflict with the Cosa Nostra; he just wants our territory."

I remained silent. Even though we knew where Martilho was, it wasn't that simple. We couldn't just barge in. And what if someone else had that damned video?

"Matteo, keep me informed about every step they take. We have until tonight to bring them down." I looked at my watch, seeing that it had just struck midnight, giving us 24 hours to act.

"You know what I don't understand? What guarantee do they have that we'll leave? Something doesn't add up, or they're too stupid to realize we could come back." Matteo's voice held a thoughtful tone.

"Simple. They'll have that video to continue blackmailing me for the rest of my damned life, or they'll release it on the internet for everyone to see. Either way, I'm cornered. If they release the video, it'll be at anyone's mercy. If I give in to their demands, I'm sure they'll keep threatening me." I ran my hand through my hair, almost tearing it out in my frustration.

"Don, have you considered the possibility of letting the video go live, while we're prepared with hackers to take it down once it's up?" My *consigliere* proposed another option.

"No, that hasn't even crossed my mind. In such a short time, people could see it, and I don't want anyone to see it!" I growled in response.

"I have a hacker friend who can handle that. I believe it's a viable solution. I'll keep him on standby in case it's needed."

"You're right. Have him come to the headquarters. If he's someone you trust, send him over," I ordered, knowing Matteo wouldn't send someone if he wasn't trustworthy.

"Yes, I'll send him."

We said our goodbyes, ending the call. I looked up as my mother entered the room, holding a piece of paper.

"Here's the drawing Yulia made. Wow, she draws really well and fast," she said, handing me a drawing with all the characteristics of the man.

My girl was truly perfect in everything she did; what a remarkable memory she had to recall every detail of the man who had terrified her.

Dad came over to see the drawing with me, letting out a whistle.

"It seems you're the encyclopedia, and she's one of those people with a photographic memory." Tommaso was impressed.

Everyone called me the encyclopedia; I had a knack for remembering names and knew almost every member of our clan by heart.

"We'll send this to our detective." I took my phone out, snapping a picture of the paper and sending it to the Cosa Nostra detective, the same one who had discovered everything about Martilho.

I received a message from him promptly: "Checking, Don."

Santino entered the room alone, his eyes meeting mine.

"We'll head to the hideout soon. I'm going to deal with that idiot. Everyone will know what happened to him, and this will serve as a lesson to anyone who thinks they can be a traitor," my father agreed with me.

"What are you talking about?" Mom asked.

"Dear, stay with our daughter-in-law. It's one of those matters you don't like to know about." My father placed his hand on his wife's shoulder, giving her a kiss on the head.

The two had some sort of agreement: when it was a matter that went against something she believed, she simply didn't like to know about it.

"How is Yulia, Mom?" I asked before going to do what needed to be done.

"She just went to take a shower. She's still very shaken, but you can do what needs to be done. I'll take care of her. We need to find a way to resolve this; we've never had anything about our family exposed..."

"And it won't be the last time," I growled, clenching my fists, feeling that damned sense of failure.

I had failed and deserved to be punished, but at that moment, my family, my clan needed me, and I couldn't show my weakness in front of them.

CHAPTER FIFTY-FOUR

Yulia

I felt my mother-in-law's hand gently stroking my hair as she settled beside me on the bed.

Verena had just entered the room; she had come to bring the drawing I made for my husband. I took the opportunity to take a long, relaxing bath, although nothing at that moment could make me feel relaxed.

"Would you like me to dry your hair, dear?" my mother-in-law asked.

"It's not necessary," I whispered. "How are things downstairs?"

"They didn't want to tell me, but judging by their faces, things are still not good," she said, and we fell silent.

Nothing was good; Valentino was racing against time. I knew my husband was doing everything he could to find out who was behind this, but it was something beyond his control, something even he couldn't foresee.

The gentle caresses of my mother-in-law on my hair made my tired eyes close softly, my eyelids slowly shutting, and I surrendered to a deep sleep.

SOMETHING NEXT TO ME vibrated incessantly, irritating me. My eyes opened abruptly to the daylight—had it already dawned?

How long had I been asleep?

Verena was no longer there, but the vibration continued to echo in the room. I turned my body, sitting up in bed, grabbing my phone that wouldn't stop vibrating. The display read "restricted number," but I answered it, holding it to my ear.

"Are you alone?" a robotic voice asked from the other end of the line.

Acting quickly, I got out of bed and walked slowly out of the room.

"Yes, I am," I declared while continuing to walk, keeping my voice calm as if I were standing still.

As I reached the stairs, my eyes guided me to the living room, where I saw my husband coming in with his men. I put my hand over my lips when Valentino made a gesture for me to stay quiet, descending one step at a time.

"Where is your husband?" the man asked again.

At that moment, Valentino was walking towards me, climbing the stairs to meet me.

"A-And... I don't know where my husband is," I stammered in fear.

Valentino stopped beside me, placing his ear next to my phone, as I listened to what the other man was saying.

"Tell the Don he has until midnight to remove his entire mafia from Las Vegas; we will be the new kings of that place, and we don't want any competition. Otherwise, the video of his little whore will be posted online for everyone to see just how hot the Italian mafia's first lady is." A laugh echoed on the other end of the line as the call ended.

Instinctively, I pulled the phone away from my ear, my eyes meeting my husband's.

Valentino said nothing, remaining silent, our eyes locked. I noticed a small drop of blood on the side of his neck. Quickly, I lifted my hand to touch it, afraid it might be his blood, worried that my husband had been hurt.

"Valentino," I whispered, terrified.

"It's not mine, bambina," he murmured, holding my hand and intertwining our fingers.

"Whose is it?"

"The person who recorded our video."

"So they found them?" I asked as we descended the stairs, joining his family and some members of the Cosa Nostra who were present.

"We found the traitor who recorded our video. All he revealed was that he was paid a large sum and that his family had nothing to do with it." My husband pointed to a man and a woman sitting in the corner.

"What did you do with him?" I asked, anxious.

"We killed him, just as we kill all traitors of this clan. Betrayal of our own is unforgivable. His death serves as a warning to anyone who tries to betray the Cosa Nostra," my husband was firm in his decision.

The dead man's father had a stern expression, while the woman's eyes were streaming silent tears.

"I'm truly sorry, Don. I'm grateful for sparing the rest of our family. I'll keep an eye on my other children." The dead man's father stood, making a slight bow to my husband, showing his gratitude.

"They will receive weekly visits so we can monitor your family's behavior. Any slip-ups, and they'll all be killed," Valentino said directly. "Now you may leave."

I remained silent, observing everything around me. They had nothing; the Cosa Nostra had obtained nothing that gave them an advantage.

I couldn't allow them to lose their nightclub in Las Vegas, not because of me, not because of a video of mine. I knew Valentino was doing this to protect me.

"We've called a hacker in case the video ends up on the internet," my husband said when his eyes met mine.

"So we have nothing, do we?"

"We know who's behind all this, we know how to get to him, but if we act without having anything in our favor, our video might end up online anyway." A long sigh escaped his lips.

"Let it fall. You can't remove the Cosa Nostra from Las Vegas; I know how important it is for your business. I can't be selfish. Go after them, and if our video goes online, keep your hacker on alert to take it down..."

"No, Yulia, it might take time; he might not be able to remove it quickly, and in the meantime, people could see it..." My husband held both sides of my face.

"Because of our video, you're putting a valuable part of your clan at risk. No, Valentino, I'm willing to take the risk. Thinking clearly right now, I don't care if my video goes online for everyone to see—I'm yours," I said firmly.

"What you don't understand is that I'm not willing to risk it. I need Las Vegas and you intact for me; no one can see you but me." His hand tightened on my face.

And at that moment, I realized he was pushing himself hard; he wanted more than anything to prove he was perfect enough to save both.

"My Don, right now you need to risk something, and to keep Las Vegas, I'd rather our video go live. I don't care; I am yours. It's just a video. I am yours," I emphasized once again.

"Mia bambina, I can't allow this," he whispered, his fear evident.

"But you have to decide something. Our video needs to go live," my voice was resolute as I held his hands, lowering them.

His face lowered, his lips met mine with firmness, giving a lingering kiss right there in front of everyone.

"Sei perfetta," he murmured, pulling our lips apart.

We both looked at everyone around us.

"She's right about this, son," Tommaso said, Verena's eyes shining towards us. "Even so, we'll do everything possible to prevent this video from going live."

"I'll order Matteo to put the best men in Las Vegas into action. We're going to break into Martilho's house. I want you to keep an eye on everything. If this video goes online, I need you to work to take it down," Valentino ordered, pointing to the hacker who was there.

The man nodded in front of a table full of computers.

I had never seen my husband act so quickly; here he was, the Don of the largest Italian mafia, working to ensure our video didn't go live, even though we needed to be prepared in case it did.

CHAPTER FIFTY-FIVE - BONUS

Matteo

The tousled blonde hair beside me revealed that I had succumbed to temptation, and there was the spoiled girl I swore I wouldn't sleep with again. What the hell was she doing on my sheets? How was Billie Harris, for the second time, sleeping in the same bed as me?

I didn't repeat with women; the last one I did ended up being my girlfriend, and she demanded more than she should have from me, a marriage that was never on the table.

She wanted a marriage, a happy family—something I had been stalling to give, making her believe that at some point, she would get what she always sought. I loved Juliana, but she left me for someone who could offer what I never could: marriage, family, children.

My phone buzzed beside the bed. I picked it up, seeing Valentino's name flashing on the screen. Walking toward the balcony door, I opened it wearing only my underwear, looking down at the city that never sleeps, Las Vegas.

"We're going to act," he said quickly.

"Act?" I ran my hand through my hair, pushing it back.

"I spoke with my wife; she's willing to take the risk. I want you to organize the best men in Las Vegas and break into Martilho's house. Leave only when everyone is dead, including Martilho Gutiérez." The Don spoke with conviction.

"By your tone, I don't need to ask if you're sure," I whispered thoughtfully.

"My friend, just do your best. I don't want my wife's video going anywhere, but I'm going to need to take some risks." I heard his long sigh.

"That was the most sensible choice, Don." I had already given this option to Valentino.

But it seemed that all he needed was his wife's approval. I always knew Valentino wouldn't be an unfaithful husband, despite his claims to the contrary. Knowing the Italian who led that mafia well, seeing the reflection in all the men of that family, the Don would be the next to fall in love. I didn't judge him; I had fallen in love myself and chose to let her go because I could never give her what she wanted.

Ending the call, before going back into the room, I texted Mike to gather everyone at the club. I needed all the Cosa Nostra soldiers, all the *Caporegimes*, without missing a single one.

Mike was the manager of everything there when no high-ranking Cosa Nostra members were present; he was the one in charge.

Entering the room, I saw the curvy woman sit up on the bed, running her hand through her long dark blonde hair. I didn't know much about women's hair color; I just liked the longer ones to grip and pull.

"Stupid, stupid, stupid..." The girl kept repeating, not noticing my presence. "Billie, where have you ended up..."

"I'd be offended if you didn't remember, after all, you weren't even drunk," I cut in, seeing those clear eyes meet mine, her slightly full lips forming an *oh*.

This was the second time we ended up in the same bed. The first time, I didn't even know how it happened. I only saw her at the Cosa Nostra club, I was too drunk after seeing Juliana's engagement photo, and all I wanted was a pussy to drown my sorrows. I just didn't expect that the pussy I chose would be my friend's wife's friend.

And here we were again, the second time, in a sex we both remembered. The first didn't count. Although I knew it was her, I didn't remember the details of her body from that first time. *Did that make this the first time?*

"I thought you had already left." Billie traced the tip of her finger along her mouth, the same finger I had sucked on the night before, those pink nails gliding over my chest.

"I'm leaving now," I declared, finding my pants on the floor and putting them on.

"You remember everything about last night, don't you?"

"Yes," I replied without looking in her direction, pulling on my pants.

"So there's no need to repeat it; we've both satisfied our curiosity." I lifted my eyes as I noticed she was casually walking around the room.

Billie wasn't shy about showing off her body, and damn, she didn't need to be; she was the type of woman who caught my eye. Perfectly proportioned for me to hold in my arms and even turn inside out.

She had that small gem in her navel, her pointed breasts, which she had just adorned with her daring lingerie.

"Where's your panties?" I asked, noticing she was wearing a denim skirt without the bottom piece.

"Do you really think I'd wear a pair of panties that was on a hotel floor, possibly harboring bacteria and risking some disease? I'd rather go without." She shrugged.

"But you're wearing a skirt. If you spread your legs a bit too much, you could show your intimate parts." I wasn't sure why that bothered me.

"What's the big deal? I just showed you a moment ago, and nothing happened." She was nonchalant, putting on her shirt that left her stomach exposed.

Billie put her hair in a bun on top of her head, her eyes lifting to meet mine.

"Well, I'm heading back to New York today. My curiosity is satisfied, and I hope I met your expectations." She picked up her shoe and put it on.

"I'd say the same," I said, watching her eyes travel down my abdomen.

"I've been with better." She gave a slight shrug.

"I'd never claim to be the best," I teased, watching her bite her lip.

"You're right, hairy Italian." The woman winked.

Without even coming over to say goodbye, she headed for the door, grasped the handle, but before leaving, turned back toward me.

"You know, Matteo, you're good in bed, you just need to accept that for the first time in your life, you came like a little boy." She pouted in a self-satisfied manner.

"Really? On what basis are you saying that?"

"Men like you don't let women be on top. I had you, and you came like a kid, which is a shame, knowing we'll never repeat this." Billie didn't wait for my response, opening the door and walking out.

We wouldn't repeat it. I didn't repeat women; that way, I avoided the risk of falling in love.

I let out a long sigh, finishing getting dressed, needing to start Valentino's plan.

CHAPTER FIFTY-SIX

Valentino

I should be there, in control of everything happening in Las Vegas, but instead, I was here, monitoring everything through phone calls, which made me feel useless. How would I know if something went wrong?

I got up from my office chair again, moving towards the window and losing myself in the distant sea. I trusted Matteo; I knew he was doing his best, but I also knew that damned video of my girl was out there.

Damn it, it wasn't even about me. I couldn't care less if my body was exposed for everyone to see. After all, I had shown it to various people before. But with Yulia, it was different; she belonged to me. Only I had seen her naked; only my eyes had seen those curves.

"Son." I turned my face to see my father beside me, his voice low. "You did everything within your power. Don't feel guilty. This was an incident..."

"An incident that means I'll never have sex with my wife outdoors again," I scoffed with a forced smile.

"Far from it. After all, I've done it countless times with your mother. There was no way to predict..."

"There was a way. We need to test all the men in the Cosa Nostra. If that damn failure hadn't been there," I growled, clenching my fists as I felt my father's hand on my shoulder.

"Valentino, don't blame yourself. Damn it, you can't be perfect at everything in this clan." Tommaso squeezed my shoulder tightly.

"I failed, Dad. I failed with the most innocent person in this whole story," I roared, frustrated.

"Have you asked her if she feels you failed her? From my perspective, she made a tremendous decision, standing by your side and agreeing to let the video go public. Yulia maintained the demeanor of a first lady, holding your hand and facing this problem with you."

"She doesn't deserve this. She's sweet, naive, and tormented. She didn't deserve to go through all this. I wasn't a good husband to her," I declared, running my hand through my hair, wanting to pull out the strands in my rage, feeling the whole situation slipping out of my control.

"When the deal was sealed, Ferney Aragón knew all the risks that his sister would face. If anyone is far from being at fault, it's you. On the contrary, I see a Don, a husband, doing everything to keep his wife safe. My son, I'm proud of you..."

"No, Dad, don't be proud, because if that video goes public, I'll never forgive myself," I retorted, feeling like the worst kind of person.

"This will only be the first of many decisions you'll have to make, Valentino. All I can say right now is, stop blaming yourself. You're not perfect; nobody is perfect. Everything that was under your control has been done." He might insist on that topic, but nothing would change my mind that I was to blame.

Damn it!

Dad removed his hand from my shoulder and moved away, joining Santino, who was sitting on the couch, cigarette in his mouth, his thoughts distant.

"If that video ends up on the internet, I don't want anyone in our family to see it. Understood?" I declared to those present.

Everyone nodded. I knew none of them would see it even if I didn't say anything, but at that moment, I wanted to emphasize it.

The door was abruptly opened.

"Son, Matteo is on a call with Carlo," Mom said, breathless.

Carlo was the hacker downstairs. Without a second thought, I ran down the stairs, seeing the man with his phone in hand, talking to someone.

I approached him, noticing that he was on a video call with Matteo. My friend seemed to be sitting behind a computer.

I didn't want to interrupt their conversation, as Matteo must have called Carlo first for an urgent matter. I watched the hacker relay information to my *consigliere*, who was working on those computers.

All this anxiety was making me nervous. I looked around for my wife but couldn't find her anywhere. My eyes met my mother's, and she noticed that my focus was on Yulia, who was missing.

"She just went upstairs; her brother was calling her," Mom answered my unspoken thoughts.

I nodded, knowing that Aragón must already be aware. I requested that this matter not spread; I didn't want our allies to worry. Although Ferney needed to know, since we shared a part of Las Vegas, this damned gang wanted only my part, not the Cartel's.

"Damn it, I did it." My focus shifted to the video as Matteo swore.

"Can someone explain what happened?" I asked, as Matteo turned the device to his face, and only then did I see the blood splattered on his neck.

"We won, Don. Las Vegas is ours, and the video is no longer scheduled." My friend flashed a relieved smile.

"What do you mean?" I asked, needing the details.

"We broke into Martilho's house. He definitely didn't expect it. We started shooting at everyone, and when we got to him, the man clearly didn't know how to use the computer, and we had killed his IT guy. The video was scheduled to be released at 11:59 PM. Martilho tried to upload it earlier but didn't know how, and in his desperation, he started smashing the computers. But as you can see, not everything was destroyed, and we caught him unarmed. It was easier than we expected. We killed everyone; nothing was left. This is Cosa Nostra, damn it!" My friend ran his hand through his messy hair. It was loose; he must have lost his hair tie during the raid.

I relaxed my shoulders, still feeling the tension throughout my body. I didn't feel victorious; it was as if the sense of guilt still dominated me, making me remain inert to everything around me. Many people hugged, jokes were made, Cosa Nostra won, but my mind was distant.

"I need some time," I said loudly for everyone to hear. "I'll be back soon. Ask my wife to stay here; I'll return shortly..."

I declared, leaving the headquarters without waiting for any responses. I headed to the garage, grabbing my helmet and keys, with only one destination in mind: my apartment. I needed to expel this internal pain, and Yulia couldn't know about it. She had been strong enough to face her own torment, unlike me.

CHAPTER FIFTY-SEVEN

Yulia

I descended the stairs after ending my call with Ferney. My brother wanted to know how things were going, and I ended up telling him everything that had happened with Valentino. Of course, my brother was not pleased, but at that moment there was nothing more to be done; my husband was already taking care of everything.

I arrived in the living room to see everyone smiling. That had to be a good sign. I approached my mother-in-law, who turned towards me and gave me a tight hug, which I accepted and returned.

"It's over, Yulia. We did it. It's over," my mother-in-law's relief was palpable.

"Oh, heavens," my tense body became light, and all I wanted at that moment was to embrace my husband and hear him say that I was still only his.

I pulled away from Verena, looking around for Valentino, but the only person I saw was Santino. I knew it was him because he was hugging his wife.

"Where is my husband?" I asked, confused.

"He said he needed to leave, but that he'd be back soon," Verena replied.

"Leave? What do you mean, leave?" I didn't like that at all, though I wasn't sure why.

"We don't know. He just said he needed some time. He was still a bit dazed; it was a big blow for a new Don," she said, and my heart skipped a beat.

"He was dazed?" I tried to convince myself that it was just in my head, but something told me it wasn't.

"Yes, as he always is when things spiral out of his control."

No one in his family knew what my husband did, and I knew exactly where Valentino had gone. All that time, he had been feeling guilty, imperfect, believing he had made mistakes, and I was sure he had gone to hurt himself.

If anyone could give me information, it would be Santino.

I approached him, and my brother-in-law immediately noticed me, his smile fading as he saw my serious expression.

"Where did Valentino go?" I asked directly.

"I don't know. He left on his bike," my brother-in-law looked at me, confused.

"Please, tell me where he goes when he wants to clear his head?"

"I don't know..."

"I know you do. Tell me. He needs me..."

"If he needed you, he wouldn't have gone alone," my brother-in-law raised an eyebrow, obviously too loyal to his brother to reveal anything.

"Damn it! You don't understand. Where is it? The apartment?"

"You know about the apartment?" Santino looked surprised.

"I know more than you think. Hell, Santino, tell me where the damn apartment is if that's where he is. Believe me, your brother needs me. I know what he's going to do, and I need to stop him," I pleaded desperately.

"Just tell her, Santino. Can't you see her desperation?" Cinzia stepped in to support me, practically forcing her husband to speak.

Seeing that he would give me the location, I took out my phone and entered the address into the GPS.

"He went by bike, right?" I asked again, knowing that would give him an advantage.

"Yes..."

"You have a bike too, don't you? Can I borrow it?" Santino looked at me as if questioning my sanity.

"You must be crazy if you think I'm going to do that. My brother would kill me." He widened his eyes.

"I know how to ride a bike; I have a license. Just give me the keys," I insisted, stamping my foot.

"He'll lend it, Yulia," Cinzia declared, pushing her husband.

They both came with me outside, heading towards Santino and Cinzia's house. The bike was there. Fortunately, I was wearing denim shorts and flats; it wouldn't be uncomfortable for me to ride.

We approached the couple's garage, which Santino promptly opened, revealing a large bike.

"Damn, your foot won't even reach the ground." My brother-in-law let out a long sigh.

"If she asked for it, it's because she knows how to handle it. The women in this family are badass." Cinzia walked around the garage, grabbing a key from the key holder.

Then she handed me a helmet as I approached the bike. I didn't know its model, but my foot wouldn't reach the ground, which was a given considering my height—one of the disadvantages of being short.

Spotting the phone mount on the bike, I placed my phone on it, setting the route. I took the helmet from Cinzia and put it on, adjusting it tightly.

"You really know how to ride, don't you? I don't want to end up killing my brother's wife." Santino stood beside me as he put the key in the ignition.

I easily swung one leg over the bike, keeping one foot on the ground and the other on the brake, started it, and heard the engine roar in the garage.

"I know how to ride, brother-in-law, don't worry. I love the adrenaline of biking." I smiled, though I was anxious about why Valentino had disappeared.

"Here, this is the key to his apartment." My brother-in-law handed me the key, having retrieved it from a key holder. "It's the penthouse, his parking spot is 501."

I held the key in my hand, slipping it into the pocket of my shorts. Along with the key was a remote control.

"May Valentino not kill me. At least send a message when you reach the apartment. I'm worried after all this." Santino's gaze remained fixed on me as he spoke.

"I'll make sure that stubborn brother of yours sends something," I replied, gripping the handlebars, noticing Santino's worried expression in the rearview mirror.

I revved the bike, feeling the engine's roar as a quick twist of the throttle sent me speeding out of the complex. I maneuvered rapidly between cars, the wind whipping against my body, my eyes locked on the road and the GPS.

As I neared my destination, I stopped in front of the apartment building's entrance, took the key from my pocket, and used the remote to open the gate.

I entered the underground garage, following the numbers until I spotted a bike parked in the distance. There it was—my husband's bike.

I wasn't sure whether to feel relieved or frightened that it was there. I parked in the spot next to it, knowing the two spots belonged to him since they were both labeled 501.

I dismounted the bike, removed the helmet, and placed it on the handlebars. I let my hair down from the bun, tossing it back, and sighed deeply, practically running toward the elevator.

CHAPTER FIFTY-EIGHT

Yulia

I stopped in front of the door, took the key from my hand, and inserted it into the lock, unlocking the door and opening it.

My steps guided me into the room, my eyes widening when I saw the entire space adapted for sadomasochistic practices. What was supposed to be a room contained a guillotine, with various implements laid out on it.

I closed the door behind me and locked it, moving through the room, searching for my husband but finding him nowhere.

Then a crack echoed, my heart pounding so hard in my chest that I could almost feel it in my hand.

I followed the sound, pushing open the ajar door, and found the most horrifying scene I had ever witnessed in my life.

My husband, with his back to me, a whip in his hand.

"No!" I gasped as I saw him prepare to strike his already bloodied back, the tattoo of a skull visible underneath the blood.

Valentino turned slowly, his eyes meeting mine in the red-lit room.

"What are you doing here?" he murmured, not moving towards me.

His face was marked by guilt. He was gripping the whip so tightly that the knuckles of his fingers were turning white.

"When they said you had left, a tightness gripped my heart, my husband, you made it," I murmured, moving towards him, trying to defuse the situation.

"No, I didn't make it. You were in danger, I put your reputation at risk," he whispered through clenched teeth.

"It wasn't your fault..."

"No, butterfly, don't pity me. I'm awful, I ruined your life. Be angry with me, I'm not good, don't forgive me." My husband shook his head from side to side, his eyes reddening with the tears that were beginning to well up.

"Valentino." His pain was starting to affect my emotions.

My husband extended the whip towards me.

"Hit me, hate me, don't pity me, do to me what I did to you, I don't deserve you, Yulia. You're too perfect for a selfish man like me." I didn't take the whip. "Take it, take it, I beg you, hit me, do to me what I did to you, take away this feeling of pain that consumes me..."

"No, I can't." I bit my lip as a tear rolled down my face.

"Bambina, hit me..." he held my hand, placing the whip there.

I felt the leather in my fingers, the fear of holding it, of feeling it. "I can't..."

"Yes, damn it, you can. I ruined you, remember? I slapped your face, belittled you, fucked women at your college to hurt you, pushed all the men away from you, remember? Your words even said I ruined two years of your life." My husband wanted to throw all the atrocities he had committed back at me.

I gripped the whip tightly, Valentino turned, showing his back, there was my husband, a tormented man, full of his demons, a perfectionist.

"No, Valentino, I can't do this." I knew he was trying to persuade me.

"Go on, Yulia Vacchiano, do what you've always wanted, hit me, know that I fucked many women before we married, all of them sitting on your face tattooed on my leg." He was trying to hurt me, and he was succeeding.

"No..." I murmured, biting my lip, knowing he was hitting the point that hurt me most—the way he reduced me to nothing.

"Yes, you can... remember all the harm I did to you, remember how hateful I was to you, I didn't want you, I only married for my mafia, hate me, Yulia..."

I gripped it tightly, raising it up. His words made me change my mind, a momentary rage surging in my mind. The tattoo of my face, several women on it, I closed my eyes tightly and struck him on the skin, the crack echoing through the room.

My eyes opened; it seemed that my lash wasn't enough because Valentino screamed for more.

I began to lash his back repeatedly, tears burning my eyes, feeling dirty, weak, and cowardly for doing this to him. I could hear his moans of pain.

"I can't... I can't do this anymore." I let the whip fall to the ground, watching Valentino's bloodied back.

My hands trembled, feeling his pain within me.

My husband turned around, our eyes meeting, noticing that tears were also streaming down his cheek.

"I don't deserve you, Yulia. I don't deserve a perfect wife like you, I don't deserve your kindness, your innocence. I'm sorry, I'm not perfect." His body fell to his knees in front of me, his hand going to his eyes, hiding the sobs that escaped his mouth.

Without a second thought, I knelt in front of him, taking his hands in mine.

"My husband," I whispered gently, lowering his hand and holding his face on both sides. "I'm not perfect either, and that's okay..."

"No, mia bambina, you are perfect, small, delicate, kind, with the most beautiful eyes I have ever seen. I don't deserve a woman like you." I brought my face closer to his, pressing our foreheads together.

"My stubborn Italian, you helped me heal my torment, turned my past into chaos, but as I said, it's in the past..."

"Don't say the word 'forgive,' I don't deserve it." He was adamant in his denial.

"Valentino Vacchiano, I love you, damn it!!!" I declared through gritted teeth.

"No, I don't..."

"Stop, enough. Look into my eyes. I hated you, hated you for two years, hated you for making me delete photos from my Instagram when we didn't even know each other yet, hated you for being involved in that thing at my college, hated you for tattooing my face on your leg, hated you in the early hours of our marriage. But deep down, I couldn't help but love you. Your heart is big, wanting to embrace the world, to protect everyone around you, even when it's a hard task. I'm here for you, to help you just as you helped me. We are one, we are a couple, you are my husband, and I am your wife. Let me take care of you." My voice trailed off as his lips pressed against mine.

"I'm too selfish, I don't deserve your love, but I want it anyway. I promise with everything that exists inside me that I will make you the most loved woman of all. And if I ever made mistakes, I will make amends every day of your existence, Yulia Vacchiano, my first lady, made and perfect for this cruel world." Our tears mingled in that kiss.

Valentino moved his feet, and I sat on them, my hands trailing up his neck, feeling his tongue touch mine. His fear was replaced by desire, a burning desire that consumed us from within, the desire of passion, of surrender.

CHAPTER FIFTY-NINE

Valentino

My hands craved her skin, needing to feel the softness, the lightness of having this sweet woman under my touch.

Holding her waist, lifting my wife's shirt, feeling her like a dream. It was too dirty for her, but I was selfish enough never to let her go.

I felt her fingers sliding down my back, closing my eyes as her small hand brushed over the cuts from the leather whip, her touch like that of an angel, numbing me.

"Titi," her hoarse voice called me, and I opened my eyes to meet the vastness of her dark eyes, my Latina wife. "Make me yours..."

"Forever?" I murmured, something we both already knew.

"Sempre" I watched, mesmerized, as her lips moved toward mine.

I felt the softness touching mine, my lips parting slightly as hers fit against them, a brief gasp escaping from my wife's mouth, our tongues touching, gliding over each other.

I held the hem of her shirt, lifting it and briefly releasing our lips as I removed the fabric and let it fall to the floor, pulling my wife close to me, our bare chests touching.

Without releasing my lips from hers, I unfastened her shorts. My wife slowly lifted, pulling them down along with her panties, standing naked before me, so flawlessly beautiful, perfect.

Yulia knelt in front of me, not even realizing that I was still in my pants. She held her button, managing to remove the fabric without my help, leaving us both completely naked.

Her black hair falling over her shoulders, long and contrasting with her beauty. I ran my hands along both sides of her face, pulling it close to mine, feeling her cunt brush against my cock.

"I love you, Yulia Vacchiano, fuck, how I love you," I declared, not taking my eyes off hers. "Damn, I don't deserve someone as perfect as you, but I'm a fucking selfish brat who will never let my woman be far from me. I promise on my life, you will always be the only one in my arms, the only one who touched my heart. I crave your touches, I need your smiles, and even if I have to prove for the rest of my life that you will be my only woman..."

My voice trailed off as she ground her ass against my hard cock.

"My Italian?" My wife bit the corner of her lip.

"Yours, only yours," I whispered, panting as her pussy descended over my hard cock.

"Then tell me, who is the only one who can do this?" she said, lowering my hand to her ass, feeling it grind as she sat on my cock.

"Only you, fuck... you know how to grind so well..." My eyes briefly closed, knowing I would have this for the rest of my life.

"From where this comes, more can come." There was a Yulia I didn't know, wicked and bold.

"Is this a tease?" Her movements were slow, languorous, and torturous.

"Far from it, my Don. It's just for my husband to be aware that this cock has an owner, this abdomen has an owner, this whole body has an owner. I'm jealous, Italian, very jealous. What's mine is only mine." Her eyes didn't stray from mine, reflecting my wife's possessiveness.

"We'll be quite a toxic couple then, because what's mine is only mine... and you're mine, all these curves, only mine." I lowered my eyes to her perky breasts, fuck, what a gorgeous woman.

"If that's toxic, then I'm very toxic." Yulia held onto my knee, spreading her legs.

I looked down, fixating on the sight of my cock sliding in and out of her pussy, how she enveloped it, her walls embracing it, the image of perfection, my pussy. I touched her folds with my fingers, stimulating her clit, causing her to moan loudly, grinding uncontrollably on my cock.

It was impossible not to moan, watching her surrendered expression, my little Latina giving herself completely, giving me everything. I pulled her body close again, lifting us from the floor, without removing her from my lap, heading toward a BDSM table, sitting her on it.

"Spread your legs over the edge of the table, open them wide, because I'm going to fuck you deep. If you're not pregnant yet, you will be now," I growled.

"Please, my Don, just fuck me the way you know how." There I glimpsed that I was a fucking lucky maniac. Yulia knew how to be wicked when we were alone, and it drove me crazy with desire.

"Then repeat, who is your master?" The head of my cock brushing against her wet pussy.

"Oh, Valentino Vacchiano, the master of my whole body, my soul, my heart. He has me..." Her voice trailed off as I pressed deep into her pussy.

I continued to fuck her hard, thrusting roughly inside her, our eyes locked on each other, her hand grazing my back.

"Oh... Titi..." My wife bit her lip hard.

"Scream, little butterfly, scream loudly. I want your screams, no one can hear you from here. Give me your screams, your moans, give me all of you," I pleaded, laying her back, lifting her legs, feeling them pass over my chest, her feet level with my eyes.

My eyes were on hers, my mouth slightly open. Yulia stopped suppressing her moans, starting to scream loudly as I fucked her hard. When I came to the apartment, I didn't expect her to be there. I didn't think I deserved the love of that woman, but I couldn't see myself away from her.

I never thought it was possible to love someone so quickly. Maybe my heart had already loved her; we just confirmed what we both knew when she came to our side. It was impossible not to fall for that sweet woman, for her determination, always pursuing what she believed in, my first lady, my wife, the woman who had my heart beating heavily in the palm of her hand.

"Titi, I... I..." A scream escaped her lips as she moaned loudly, surrendering to the act.

With her walls tightening around my cock, I came, spilling inside her, wanting a damn child with her, wanting a mini-version of us.

"I love you, I love you, I love you forever, mia bambina." Lowering her leg, pulling her into my lap, seeing her hand covered in blood slide over my chest.

I knew that blood was mine.

"It seems like sex involving blood is becoming a habit of ours." My little wife smiled lazily.

"Come, let's take a shower." Our lips met in a lazy kiss as we headed to the bathroom.

CHAPTER SIXTY

Yulia

"Turn around," I asked my husband, holding the washcloth in my hand.

He did, revealing his tattooed back, covered in bruises. My heart tightened; it hurt to see how he punished himself. It pained me to see him like this.

I began to glide the soft washcloth over his skin, removing the dried blood stains. My husband said nothing, allowing me to clean him. After finishing, I placed the washcloth on the rack, holding his waist and embracing him from behind, resting my head against his skin.

"Titi," I whispered.

"Speak, mia bambina," he murmured, running his fingers over my hand resting on his abdomen.

"I want to be more than just your wife." My husband turned around, the shower water now falling on his back.

"And you are, butterfly." His long fingers traced my face.

"It's not just about that. I want you to tell me everything. I don't want to have to guess like today. For God's sake, I feel broken inside knowing you do these things to yourself. You helped me heal my torments; let me be your cure, Valentino Vacchiano. Tell me when you feel like you're not being perfect. I need to know; I don't want my husband hurting himself." He lowered his face, his lips touching my forehead.

"I promise I'll tell you when it happens. I promise I'll try to be strong for you, for our future child who will be on the way soon." He smiled amidst the kiss, his hand sliding down to hold my thigh, lifting me into his lap. "I love you, my perfection in the form of a woman..."

"I love you, my Don." I felt his penis harden again, brushing against my pussy.

"Fuck, I need to fuck this sweet pussy again," he groaned with the familiar roughness in his voice.

"Don't think, just fuck me, my mafioso." I bit my lip, giving a little grind, knowing how to drive him to his limit. For God's sake, it was becoming incredibly delicious being married to Valentino Vacchiano.

I WAS STANDING IN FRONT of the mirror, brushing my damp hair when I saw my husband enter the room through the reflection.

"Did you say anything to Santino?" he asked suspiciously.

"Well, I asked for the address of this apartment, and since he didn't want to tell me, I started making a fuss, saying that you needed me." I bit the tip of my lip, setting the brush on the counter and turning to face him.

"You really said that, and he believed you?"

"No, of course not. Your brother is very loyal to you, but I had Cinzia's help, who practically forced her husband to tell me." I shrugged. "Why?"

"I just saw several messages from him asking how I'm doing and apologizing for letting you use his motorcycle to get here. Damn,

Yulia, I'm trying to control myself from freaking out about you coming here on my brother's bike."

"Which shouldn't be news to you, you know I can ride, I mentioned that, remember?" My husband stopped in front of me, holding my waist as he lifted me onto the sink counter, bringing our faces close together.

"Our bikes are huge, Yulia. If you fall, it's going to be a nasty crash." He was clearly worried as he held both sides of my face.

"I'm fine, and I'm a really good rider, by the way. Don't you trust me?" I pouted innocently.

"You can take that pout off your lips, you're going back on my bike, with me!" His expression hardened.

"No." I shrugged my shoulders.

"No?" He narrowed his eyes at my single word.

"I'll return the bike and still get to the headquarters before you," I said proudly, holding onto both sides of his shirt and pulling him closer. "Are you ready to lose to your wife?"

"That's obviously not what I'm afraid of. What I'm afraid of is that you don't know these streets well, and what if you fall?"

"Scaredy-cat." I smiled at my words.

"Scaredy-cat?" Valentino let out a loud laugh.

"I bet my ass I'll win." I moved my face closer to his, running my tongue over my husband's lips.

"Now I'm starting to think about it, but still, I don't want to risk it. We're talking about your life here." I rolled my eyes.

"I'll call you a scaredy-cat again, and you'll never have access to my forbidden place. It will be eternally off-limits." I wrapped my legs around his waist.

"So that's what you're going to do? Bet your ass on a competition you know I'll win?" His green eyes were focused on mine.

"Maybe I'm curious to know what it's like to be taken from behind." A mischievous smile appeared on my lips.

"Do you know what I love most about you?"

"What, my Don?"

"The fact that you're always up for anything. Damn, I don't deserve you, Yulia Vacchiano. You're perfect in every possible way." This time, it was him who licked his lips, running his tongue over mine.

"Yes, husband, you don't deserve me. I'm too good for any man, but I love you too much to know you'll always return that love. I trust you when you say you'll take care of me forever. I'm pretty spoiled, huh..."

"I'll make it my mission to spoil this little Latina of mine for the rest of my life, to take care of and protect her from all harm. You have me, Yulia, you have my heart, you are the air I need to breathe. I don't know how I lived all these years without that sly smile of yours." We kissed slowly, our lips touching, our tongues grazing.

"I still want to bet," I whispered amidst the kiss.

"Alright, we'll bet, but know that I won't hold back when it comes to fucking your ass..."

"Oh... have everything, just not pity," I murmured provocatively.

"Let's go before I claim my part of the bet right now." My husband picked me up in his arms and carried us outside.

I HELD THE HELMET IN my hand, placing my phone in the GPS holder, saving the headquarters address.

"Ready to eat dust?" He still looked at me with concern.

"I'm not comfortable with this," he whispered, putting on his helmet.

"Husband, look at this." I sat on the bike, holding with only one foot on the ground, purposely sticking out my ass, noting the smile on his lips.

"Yulia Vacchiano, that ass is only mine!"

"As you said, let others look." I started the bike, ready before he was, and took off ahead of him.

I quickly saw him mount his bike, following me.

A laugh escaped my lips. Obviously, I knew he wasn't going to overtake me, but he would have an advantage, just to keep an eye on me and still win.

CHAPTER SIXTY-ONE

Yulia

I gradually slowed down the bike, finding my husband with his parked in front of the headquarters, next to the sidewalk, his hand resting on the helmet that was propped up on his leg. I stopped Santino's bike next to his, removing my helmet as my hair fell down my back. My eyes lifted to meet his, finding my husband's easy smile, that same mocking smile.

"The result we both expected." He shrugged in a smug manner.

"This was just our first competition. Let me perfect my skills on these streets, and I'll make you eat dust." I dismounted the bike, stepping down one foot at a time.

Turning my eyes back to my husband, who was scanning my body, coveting my curves.

"Did you find something, husband?" I asked, stopping in front of him, raising my hand as I ran my nail across his neck.

"Just enjoying the easiest bet I've ever won..."

"Hey!" I started to squirm as his hand cupped my ass. "Someone might see us; we're in front of the headquarters!"

I was startled, taking a step back, my eyes meeting his.

"Yulia Vacchiano, you're mine. What's the big deal?" His tone had that usual nonchalance.

"And just because of that, you think you can go around squeezing my ass in front of everyone?" I asked, frowning.

"Isn't that something I can do with my girl?"

"Let's set a limit: no groping in public." I raised my hand as he dismounted his bike, leaving his helmet on the seat.

Catching me off guard, he pulled me by the waist, making my body collide with his.

"Is this an order?" He lowered his face towards mine, our eyes meeting amidst the tension.

"Would it be if I said it was?" I raised an eyebrow.

"Definitely not." With the hand holding my waist, he lifted me slightly, placing my feet on his shoes.

"I feel embarrassed. What if your mother sees us?" I felt my cheeks warm.

"Worried about my mother?" His expression became comical at the grimace he made.

"Yes, Verena is an amazing woman, always calm, the cornerstone of your family. How can I be a mafia first lady like she was?" I pouted.

"That's because you won't be. Just as my mother was a great mafia first lady in her way, you'll be the new first lady in your own way. Don't be hard on yourself, my butterfly; you're only small in stature because inside, your heart is gigantic. I'm sure you'll be a wonderful first lady." His lips brushed mine, giving me a slow, gentle kiss.

I felt his tongue graze mine before we pulled away when someone cleared their throat beside us. I turned my face, finding my husband's twin there.

"Now we're having displays on the sidewalk of the headquarters?" Santino had that same mocking smile as my husband.

"Go to hell," Valentino replied, holding my hand and pulling me along, but he quickly slowed down when he noticed I couldn't keep up with his long strides.

"You didn't respond to my message." Santino came to my side.

"That's because I'm deciding how I'm going to punch you for letting my wife use your bike," Valentino grumbled as we entered the headquarters.

"Well, I had no choice." We entered the room where all the Vacchianos were present.

"No choice? Seriously, Santino, is that the best excuse you have? Do you want my bike, Cinzia? After all, your husband thought it was supernatural to hand over his keys to my wife!" My husband turned to look at his brother.

"Actually, I don't want it. I hate those bikes, and if it were up to me, my husband could sell his," Cinzia responded with a small smile.

"Enough, Valentino!" I was firm in my words. "It was me who asked for it, I was the one who wanted to borrow his bike. Don't try to put me in a glass bubble as if nothing could ever happen to me. I wanted his bike, and if you keep being overly protective, I'll make sure to take it again!"

I crossed my arms, making both twins look in my direction.

"Try to see how far your luck will go," Valentino growled.

"Luck? Since the day I was promised to an arrogant mafioso like you, I realized I had everything but luck," I retorted.

"Funny, because that's not how it seemed..."

"Oh! But you're not going to come at me with that nonsense. — I shook my head at the topic that seemed to want to intrude. — You are indeed arrogant, pompous, know-it-all, possessive, controlling, but that doesn't mean I love you any less because, unfortunately, no one is perfect, and I need to learn to deal with your irritating temper sometimes... What is it? Why are you smiling? Wipe that silly smile off your face."

My husband had a wide smile on his face, as if I were the only person present. I took a step back when he took one towards me, puzzled by his movement.

"Did you just tell everyone that you love me?" Valentino asked in his calm manner.

"And why not?" I frowned in confusion.

"I don't know, it's just strange." My husband shrugged.

"You two are strange," Cinzia interjected. "Strangely cute, but still strange."

I turned my face towards my sister-in-law, only to be caught by Valentino's arms during my brief moment of distraction.

"That's because I love you too, *mia ragazza,* made and shaped to be mine," he said in front of everyone. I heard my mother-in-law's sigh as my husband touched his lips to mine. "I'm not ashamed to show everyone how much I love you, my, only my *bambina.*"

My husband gave me a long kiss, releasing me when his brother cracked a joke:

"And here we have Valentino Vacchiano, the same man who said he'd never fall in love with anyone. In less than ten days of marriage, this same man finds himself eating his words, worse than any other man in the mafia. It's so cute to see him make mistakes, Mr. Perfect," I shuddered at that word.

But Valentino's reaction was the complete opposite of what I expected. Laughing heartily, he said:

"In that case, I'm proud to make mistakes."

CHAPTER SIXTY-TWO

Valentino

I pulled out my wife's chair so she could sit beside me, with all my family present—my parents, siblings, and in-laws.

After the intense day I had, with my beloved coming to meet me, the confrontation with Martilho, and our victory, everything turned out well in the end. Being here with them, having my wife safe and out of danger, was a relief.

The death of this gang served to show everyone what the new Don of the Cosa Nostra was capable of. They thought that, because I had only been in command for a few years, I would be easily shaken. Perhaps my greatest support had been Yulia, who put herself to the test for me. She proved to be loyal to her new clan, a new member in this crazy Italian family.

"Before we start eating, I have something to say," I said seriously, looking at everyone in front of me.

From my look, it was clear that I wasn't joking and that this wasn't just another conversation.

Since the moment I took my bike and headed back to the headquarters, I had been thinking about this topic—about how Yulia appeared today, stopping me from going further into that madness, begging me to open up to her. Perhaps gathering my family on a subject I had never discussed with them could help me avoid these self-destructive actions.

"I'm going to start talking, and I want all of you to remain silent and not interrupt me," I continued, meeting Yulia's eyes.

I extended my hand to her, asking her to stand and come to my side. Having this small woman by my side gives me the strength to address a topic that brings out all my demons.

Yulia stood by my side, and I placed my hand on her shoulder, drawing her close to me, feeling her hand rest on my back and then on my waist.

"For years I hid something. What I'm about to say is not your fault, nor is it your fault, Mom. Knowing the two people who saw me grow up, I know you'll blame yourselves, but it's me. I built walls around myself, I saw myself as a man who, in my eyes, was the strongest I had ever known. For many years of my life, perfectionism was part of my days. I needed to be perfect, I needed to be like my father. Being the Don of the Cosa Nostra was in my blood. I grew up knowing it was what I wanted, and from a young age, I began to demand perfection from myself. I still feel like I need to be perfect. After all, how can I live up to Tommaso Vacchiano if not by being perfect?" A forced smile appeared on my lips as tears gathered in my eyes. I prolonged the topic, having spoken too much to now drop the bombshell. "Only one person has seen me at my most vulnerable, *and damn,* we had been together for less than two days, Yulia made me realize how selfish I was being with myself. This woman manages to sense all my weaknesses, in a way I can't explain. She knows, she knows when I'm about to falter, and that's why she came after me today."

I stopped speaking as I lowered my face, meeting those intense black eyes, her emotional expression, a tear rolling down my wife's cheek, prompting me to lift my free hand to wipe it away, continuing to speak:

"I self-harm," I said abruptly, hearing the shock from some when an "oh" escaped their mouths. My eyes met my father's, who narrowed his eyes. My mother struggled to hold back tears. "When I realized I wasn't doing things right, I started punishing myself for my mistakes, demanding perfection from myself..."

"Oh, my son," Mom sniffled, breaking down into tears she tried to hold back.

"No! Don't feel guilty. This is my issue. I decided to share this with you because today Yulia asked me to call on her whenever I felt incapable, weak, or imperfect. Everything is a process, and I know there will be times when I'll want to falter, but I'm fully aware that if I want to be a good father to my future child, I need to face my worst demons."

"What did you do today? After all, you succeeded. Why did you do this to yourself?" My father pulled Mom into his arms, comforting her shoulder.

"I was weak for putting Yulia in danger. What kind of husband am I for doing this to the woman I should protect?" I didn't want to mention what I did, as I still felt the sting of the lashes on my back.

"What did you do, Valentino? I want to know what my son did under my nose for all these years, and I was never able to see it." Dad had his teeth clenched as he spoke.

"That's beside the point..."

"Valentino Vacchiano, this is a father *to* son matter, I need to know," he was firm, letting out a sigh through my mouth.

I turned, and Yulia stepped aside, my wife closing her eyes tightly. I pulled my shirt out of my pants, lifting it to reveal the various cuts.

"Damn, these aren't superficial cuts," Dad growled, standing up from his chair and walking towards me.

I turned around again, lowering my shirt. At that moment, all the women were crying, and my brother, like Dad, stood up from his chair.

"How, how was it? How did you do it?" Tommaso grabbed both sides of my face like he did when we were kids. "Don't avoid the question, damn it, speak!"

"Lighter between the legs, where no one could see, lashes on my back, superficial cuts on my waist, nails dug into the palm of my hand," I whispered as if I didn't want to talk.

In front of me, I saw Tommaso let a tear roll down his cheek.

"How did I never see this? You're my son, I always thought I knew you better than anyone, damn it!!!" Moving my hands, I pulled him into a hug, feeling his grip on my neck to avoid touching my back.

"Dad, it's not your fault. I was the one putting pressure on myself..."

"Son, I'm far from being the best for this clan. I'm imperfect, I've made so many mistakes in my life. Don't think I'm perfect; the only wonderful things I've had in my life are your mother, my children, and now my grandchildren." His voice was close to my ear.

We slowly pulled away from each other. Tommaso's eyes were red from tears, just like mine.

"Promise your old man that when your wife isn't around, you'll run to any member of this family if you feel like doing something to yourself? We are a family, and here, everyone stands together hand in hand." My father didn't take his eyes off mine.

"I promise..."

"Valen, I swear on everything sacred that I'll break your face if I find out you've done this again." I turned my face and saw my twin brother crying beside me. "Damn, you're my other half. How did I let this slip?"

Pulling me by the shoulder, Santino hugged me.

"I'm sorry..."

"Don't apologize. We're blood of the same blood, sharing the same placenta, so I'll always be here for you," my brother declared close to my ear, pulling away as I saw my sister Pietra approaching.

"You know that as the older sister, I have the right to scold you, right? Come on, little brother, even though having Vacchiano blood is crazy, you don't need to take it so literally." Pietra tried to sound casual, but her tears caught her off guard as she let out a sob in the midst of the hug. "Brother, I'll always be the older and more annoying sister, but I'll never close my shoulder to a hug from you. I want to help you. Please, promise me you won't do this again?"

I patted Pietra's back, pulling away from her and wiping her tears away.

"I promise, my sister." I kissed her forehead, seeing her husband, my uncle Enrico, appear beside her.

"Damn, kid, you're crazy. The door to our home will always be open. I'm your godfather, your second father. My love for you grew from the moment Tommaso said he would be a father. Just don't do this again; I'll drop everything I'm doing to help you if necessary." Enrico approached, kissing my forehead as a sign of respect.

"Thank you, Uncle," I said, feeling the support from everyone.

My sister and her husband stepped back, and I noticed my mother still crying on Dad's chest. I approached her, running my hand on her back, watching her lift her blue eyes to mine. Even though they were red and swollen, she was still beautiful.

"Mom..."

"My son, my little son." Verena released herself from Dad's embrace and threw herself into mine.

"Mom, please," I murmured, feeling my chest tighten with her visible pain.

"How did I never see this? You're my son; it was my duty to protect you..."

"Verena, stop and look at me!" My voice was firm but not reprimanding. Mom lifted her eyes, and I raised my hand to wipe her tears. "You were the best mother anyone could have. If I hid this, it was because I felt like a failure and didn't want you to see it. You will never be to blame for this. You were the first woman I loved, you will always be my love, the woman for whom I would kill and die. But of course, you are no longer the only one; now, your place has been taken..."

"But for a good cause, I relinquish my place." Mom smiled through her tears.

"I love you, Verena. If I know what love is, it's because of you. Perfect, the best mother we three could have. Don't blame yourself for this. I promise that from now on, I'll tell you everything."

"Do you really promise?" She pouted, tears starting to stop falling.

"Yes, I promise." I ran my hand through her blonde hair, pushing it back.

"I love you, my son." Dad came closer as she said this.

"Now let's sit down and celebrate this victory because if he opened up and seeks to improve, it's a victory," Dad declared, holding my shoulder with pride evident in his eyes.

They both stepped back, and I finally locked eyes with my little Latina. She was wiping her tears, trying to smile. I approached her, pulling my little one into my arms and whispering in her ear:

"I will never be worthy of the wonderful woman I have as my wife, but I will make you remember every day of our lives how loved you are by me, how important you are to me. I love you, *mia bambina*. Thank you for making me realize what I never noticed, how much I needed to say this out loud and lift a burden from my shoulders..."

"My Don, don't thank me. After all, we're a couple, one. I will always be here for you." She pulled away, brushing her hand against my beard. "I love you, and I'm proud of you, husband."

"Everything for you, my butterfly." I joined our lips in a lingering kiss.

I didn't regret telling them that. It felt like lifting a weight off my shoulders. Yulia made me open up to my family, shaping us all without any of us even realizing how important we were to each other.

CHAPTER SIXTY-THREE - BONUS

Verena

I felt the glide of fingers through my hair, turning my face to see my son. I knew it was Santino because the difference between his hug and my other son's was that San always slid his finger, while Valentino would just rest his hand on my shoulder or wrap his arms around my waist, unlike Santino who always did it the same way, in the same place.

"How are you, Mom?" he asked, lifting his hand to tuck my hair behind my ear.

"Strangely better. I think this was a huge shock for me," I spoke the truth; I don't hide anything from my children.

"You know we're all going to help him, right? Don't be too hard on yourself, my beautiful." I smiled at those green eyes.

Santino was always the easiest, despite having a fiery temper, a true Vacchiando from head to toe. He never hid anything from us, unlike Valentino, who was often reserved. Even though he was playful, he would retreat into his shell when we broached more personal topics.

We entered the living room, and my son went over to his wife. Cinzia was holding little Bella while talking to Valentino and Yulia. She was the only one who hadn't managed to hug Valentino in his moment of vulnerability because she was with their daughter, who was there with them at that moment.

I spotted my husband, Tommaso, sitting on the sofa with a glass of whiskey in hand. I knew he was feeling the same sense of guilt as I was.

I approached him, sitting beside him and crossing my legs. I smiled as I noticed little Tommie coming over, our eldest grandchild. Easily, my husband settled him on his lap, holding him by the back while looking down at the little one.

"Grandpa, my mommy doesn't know, but I have a girlfriend." Tommie whispered, making me turn my face toward him.

"My dear, but you're only seven years old," I said calmly.

"But Grandma, she said she's my girlfriend, and I just accepted. What do boyfriends and girlfriends do?" my grandson asked with innocence.

"Things that kids don't need to be doing right now. Tell that girl you're happy to be her friend but not her boyfriend. You're too young for that." I ran my hand through his dark brown hair.

"And what if she doesn't want to be my friend anymore? I really like Francesca. She's beautiful, with blue eyes and blonde hair, just like you, Grandma." I widened my eyes, looking up and seeing my husband stifling a laugh.

"Sweetheart, if she does that, it's because she doesn't like you. Be serious. Enjoy your childhood." I was more serious this time.

"Being a kid is boring." Tommie crossed his little arms, glaring with those intense Ferrari green eyes, and jumped off his grandfather's lap, heading outside, probably to play on the swing we had in the backyard.

"Why did the grumpy old man run off, Mom?" Pietra asked.

"Don't say anything, Verena," Tommaso whispered to me.

"But I'm going to say something. This shouldn't be hidden from a mother. He's too young. Stop coddling your grandson, Tommaso." Being a mother in the midst of the mafia was already difficult enough, especially when there were people to cover up the antics of these children. "Do you know any child named Francesca?"

"Yes, last week I was called to school because she bit Tommie so hard on the arm that it left a mark. He keeps complaining that she's a bossy little brat and that he can't stand her." Pietra frowned in surprise, a characteristic she inherited from her father.

"Looks like he likes a feisty girl," my husband mocked.

"What are you talking about?" Enrico interjected.

"Tommie said this Francesca is his girlfriend and that he didn't want to tell her they weren't dating anymore because she would get upset, and he likes her a lot," Tommaso replied.

Of course, my twins burst into laughter at this craziness, and Enrico made a rather unpleasant face.

"Damn, my son is only seven years old. Do I need to teach him at seven that this is not how we treat a woman, letting her climb all over him?"

"Coming from the fifty-year-old who let a teenager climb all over him." Santino would not miss this chance to tease.

"But I can say I lived my life, not at seven years old. Damn, the kid is seven. We need to change his school, get Francesca out of his life. Can you imagine my son, a Ferrari, crying over a girl?" Enrico looked at his wife in horror.

"I agree with Enrico. Either change his school or make him understand that he shouldn't be dating. He needs to be a player first before committing." I nudged my husband.

"Great example you are," I retorted.

"Anyway, I'll talk to the teacher. If that doesn't work, I'll change Tommie's shift. He's too young for this," Pietra concluded wisely.

The topic shifted focus. I rested my head on my husband's chest, smelling the mix of cigar and his cologne that had become a part of my life for thirty years.

My husband, the man who was always by my side, calming me, caressing me, making each year our love grew even stronger.

Looking at my children, all settled with their spouses. The one who worried me the most was now loyal to his wife. My fear was always visible with Valentino and Yulia's marriage. I often saw myself in her, fearing that Valentino might do to her what his father did to me, but that didn't happen. She reached him, that woman made my son open up, and I would always be grateful to my daughter-in-law for that.

I could lay my head down every night on my pillow, knowing that Valentino had a great woman by his side. Their love was evident in the way they looked at each other. Everything happened so quickly; I admit I didn't expect it to be so fast, but I thanked God that it was.

"Shall we go to bed?" Tommaso asked when Santino and Cinzia headed to their home.

I nodded, saying goodbye to Yulia and Valentino who stayed there, once again thanking my daughter-in-law during our embrace for what she did for my son, accepting that girl as my new daughter.

I intertwined my fingers with Tommaso's, following him to our bedroom.

"What do you want tonight, my queen?" he asked, opening the door to our room.

"Just your big, strong hand on my body, making me feel yours, just like you know how to," I requested as the door closed. Turning my body toward him, Tommaso easily slipped his hand onto my backside, lifting me up.

"Your wish is my command." I lost myself in his dark eyes.

My husband, the same man I married thirty years ago, the one to whom I gave my heart, the man who knew he moved worlds for me and our family.

"I love you, my crazy Italian." My lips met his, feeling his hand caressing my backside as he lifted my dress.

"I will always love you, my little suicide. Let me take care of my wife tonight, show her how perfect she is, and that none of this was her fault."

"I feel guilty..." I turned my face away from his as he laid me on the bed.

"Don't feel that way, my dear. You'll never be to blame for this. You're the best mother our children could have." His fingers stroked my face.

"Make me forget all this madness, love me, love me just the way you know how," I pleaded, running my hand along his neck, opening my legs and seeing his large body fitting between them.

"Yes, my queen, whatever you ask, I will do..." His face lowered, fitting into the curve of my neck, my eyes closing as I felt the brush of his beard against my skin.

And there I lost myself, in the strong, protective arms of my mafioso.

CHAPTER SIXTY-FOUR

Yulia

We were alone in the living room; everyone else had left. I turned my face towards my husband, Valentino lifted his hand, touching my face.

"Is this the moment I claim my share of the bet?" he asked with a sly half-smile, intertwining his finger with mine and subtly pulling me onto his lap, where I sat with my legs on either side.

"Valentino, what if someone comes in here?" I asked, alarmed.

"No one will come in; it's just you and me. I've always wanted to get a little intimate with my wife in the living room of the mansion." He smiled, lifting me onto his lap, laying me on the sofa with his body covering mine.

"You're crazy, Italian." I clutched his shirt as his finger slid inside my dress, grazing the lace of my panties.

"A completely crazy man in love," he murmured with a sigh as he moved my panties aside, his fingers slick with my arousal.

"My Don." I bit my lip as he moved his kisses down from between my breasts to my thighs.

"I'm going to suck on your little pussy here and fuck your ass in our room..."

"Oh... we might get caught." The fear of being discovered overwhelmed me, but his desire to pleasure me there made me want to take the risk. "Go on, Italian, suck me already."

His soft laughter echoed in the room as he pulled my panties off, tearing them. My dress rode up to my waist, held between my thighs, his face buried in my legs, his tongue exploring me. Unable to contain my moans, I let one escape, moving against his tongue. It was impossible to stay still; his beard brushed against my sensitive skin as his finger penetrated me.

Shivers coursed through my body, I felt at the peak of pleasure as Valentino licked me up and down, drawing many sighs from my lips.

"Titi... I... I..." My words faltered as I bit my lip, letting go on his lips.

My husband sucked me for long seconds until he lifted himself, sliding over my body and pressing our lips together in an urgent kiss.

Our teeth clashed as his hand squeezed my backside, lifting me up effortlessly with me in his lap, my taste in his mouth. The urgent kiss slowed down, his lips pulling my tongue forcefully, swallowing my moans in the process.

"So fucking delicious." His hoarse and sensual tone started to excite me again.

"Valentino," I whimpered, tilting my head back as we climbed the stairs towards our room.

We continued with our slow kisses, his hand splayed on my backside. Entering our room, the door closed behind us as he set me down on the floor, holding the hem of my dress, lifting it over my head.

I was already without panties, and the dress I wore had no bra, leaving me completely naked for him.

"Your turn," I whispered, unbuttoning his shirt.

One by one, until the last button, I brought my mouth close, leaving kisses on his chest as I unbuttoned his pants, kneeling in front of him, pulling down his pants and then his underwear.

"What does an obedient wife do in this case, my Don?" I bit my lip provocatively.

"She definitely takes my cock deep down her throat." I held his hard member, veins bulging, so hard that it touched the tip of his stomach.

"What do you mean?" I moved my mouth awkwardly, trying to keep the seduction as I attempted it for the first time, taking his cock into my mouth.

"Oh, fuck! That's it, you almost seem obedient..." My husband held my hair, gathering it into a ponytail, pushing his cock deep into my throat.

His cock began to slide in and out of my mouth, his hand gripping my hair tightly. I clenched my fingers on his thigh, letting my saliva drip onto the floor with each of his thrusts, my eyes filling with tears from the gagging.

"I want to come on your face, I want to see my cum sliding over your delicate skin, I want to see you shining with my cum." I lifted my eyes as he began to thrust more roughly into my mouth.

My tongue brushed over his hard skin until a roar escaped his mouth, and his warm, shiny jets coated my face.

"Stick your tongue out and keep your eyes open." I did as he instructed, feeling bold and excited.

I noticed the mafioso becoming even more possessive as he came on my face, his liquid dripping all over me.

Valentino helped me up, removing his shoes and then his pants, becoming completely naked.

"I'm going to eat your little ass now, as we bet..."

"Wouldn't miss this, would I?" I mocked, heading towards the bed.

"Get on all fours and stick that sexy ass up for your husband."

"Ow!" I let out a squeak as Valentino smacked my buttock.

I got onto the bed, sticking my ass up and positioning myself on all fours, feeling his cock touch my skin. His fingers explored my pussy, as if gathering my arousal and using it to lubricate my ass.

"Stimulate yourself, butterfly, use your fingers on your pussy," he said, and I complied, sliding my fingers into my folds.

I felt my husband press his cock against my ass, squeezing hard as though tearing me apart. His cock entered me, and I bit my lip.

"Don't stop touching yourself, Yulia!" he ordered with a strained voice.

His fingers covered mine, continuing the stimulation himself. Without stopping, his cock filled me completely, and I focused on the pleasure from my pussy.

Returning to stimulate myself, Valentino, standing, held my buttocks tightly. Strangely, I began to enjoy that pain, that combination of pain and pleasure from being taken there.

"Fuck!" Valentino roared, thrusting hard into my ass, the echo of our bodies filling the room.

Moans escaped my lips, my eyes open, my head turned sideways, watching my husband through the mirror. The way he squeezed my ass, how he fucked me hard and fast, I felt hot and at the peak of my pleasure.

His face turned as he noticed me watching him through the mirror.

"Do you see how you're the most delicious woman? Do you see how much I love fucking your little ass? Damn, ragazza! I'm completely crazy about you... crazy." I bit my lip, moaning loudly, feeling my walls tighten around my fingers, coming again as I was taken from behind.

Valentino roared, thrusting one last time inside me, releasing himself there.

Our sweaty bodies collided on the bed. Feeling his weight on top of me, I slowly turned to see him lying beside me.

"I think we need another shower..." I whispered, feeling exhausted.

"You're tired, aren't you, mia bambina?"

"You forgot to add a clause to our marriage contract: having the stamina to handle a sex-crazed husband." I smiled, raising my hand to touch his sweaty face. "Can I just sleep like this? Would it be that unhygienic?"

I murmured, feeling tired.

"Come on, butterfly, I'll bathe you and then put you to sleep. After all, you deserve it."

Without saying another word, he gently picked me up in his arms, and I rested my head on his sweaty shoulder as we entered the suite.

CHAPTER SIXTY-FIVE

Yulia

A Few Days Later...

I descended the stairs of the mansion and saw Cinzia, my mother-in-law, and Pietra in the living room. I entered the room, still feeling that lingering nausea; I must have eaten something that didn't agree with me the day before.

"What's wrong, dear?" Verena asked, her eyes fixed on me.

"Oh, nothing." I shrugged. "Did Valentino say where he was going? I usually see him leaving the room, but for the past two days, I've been so sleepy I haven't even seen him leave."

"He didn't leave, I mean, he didn't leave the mansion; he's at the hideout with one of the clan's debtors." I sat next to Cinzia, watching the little baby holding onto the coffee table to lift herself up.

"Now no one can hold this little one back." I smiled as she stumbled towards me.

"Someone needs to remind this little girl that she's only one year old," her mother said with a tone of affection.

"Colu... colu..." she said, tugging at my dress with her high-pitched voice.

I looked at her mother, not understanding what the little girl had said.

"She wants to be held," Cinzia explained.

"Oh..."

"But you don't have to, Yulia; she'll take advantage of it." The baby's mother must have known her little troublemaker.

"I don't mind; after all, I love babies." I picked up the little girl with dark brown hair and green eyes, she was the spitting image of her father.

Bella grabbed my hair with her tiny fingers, wanting to play with it, but in her clumsy act, she ended up pulling it.

I raised my eyes as I saw the men walking through the door: Valentino, Santino, and Matteo, who had returned from his trip the day after Valentino's confession to all his family. Matteo never mentioned my friend; it was as if she had never existed for him.

But my focus was different; it was on him, my Italian. It was easy to distinguish him from Santino; my brother-in-law didn't look at me the same way Valentino did, with that glint in his eyes and the mischievous half-smile.

My smile faded from my face as he approached, and the same nausea from this morning resurfaced. I turned my face away, noticing Cinzia next to me, lowering myself and handing Bella over to her.

"Are you okay, Yulia? You look like a ghost, so pale," Cinzia said as she took her daughter.

"That smell, the same smell that made me nauseous this morning," I replied, turning to bump into my husband, realizing that it was his perfume making me ill, the same scent that had lingered in our room this morning.

"Mia bambina, what's happening?" Valentino asked, concerned, holding both sides of my face.

"Your smell is making me sick," I complained, holding my hand over my nose to block it out.

"My smell?" My husband stepped back, still looking confused. "But it's the same smell as always; I haven't changed anything."

"Yes, but your perfume is making me nauseous. Please take a shower, Valentino," I begged, stepping away from him.

"Take a shower? Are you calling me smelly?" He raised an eyebrow in a comical way.

"No, Italian, I'm just saying that this perfume is making me sick."

"This conversation between you two is quite strange," my mother-in-law interjected as I saw Valentino's brother struggling not to laugh. "Are you pregnant, dear?"

"No!" I said with such conviction that I soon found myself thinking. "I mean, I don't know. Can it happen that quickly? Doesn't it take months?"

I looked at my mother-in-law.

"It depends; when was your last period?" she asked.

"I don't know; I don't have a regular cycle, but it was before the wedding, I believe about ten days before." I found myself pondering the issue.

"If it was about ten days before the wedding, let's use that as a basis. How many days have you been married?"

"Twenty-five days," Valentino answered.

"Twenty-five days plus the ten you mentioned makes thirty-five days. A cycle is around twenty-one days, so you're late. Yes, dear, this could be a symptom of pregnancy." My mother-in-law caught me by surprise; my eyes widened as I met Valentino's gaze, who wanted to walk towards me.

"No! You and that perfume stay away from me." I blocked his steps.

"So my wife might be pregnant, and I can't touch her?" he spoke in that authoritative manner.

"You can, my love, but first take a shower and get rid of that perfume." I pointed to his suit jacket.

"Look on the bright side, brother, it could be worse; she could have gotten sick of you, but it's just your perfume," Santino mocked, causing my husband to roll his eyes.

"Let's do this: Valentino will take a shower, and I'll get one of the pregnancy tests I have at home. I went a little crazy during my last pregnancy and bought several; I still have some at home." Cinzia volunteered, getting up from the sofa and handing her daughter to her husband.

I LEFT OUR SUITE, AND Valentino was sitting on our bed, freshly bathed and dressed in new dress pants and a button-up shirt, his damp hair and eyes meeting mine.

"Did you throw the perfume away?" I asked, still holding the pregnancy test in my hand, which I hadn't looked at yet out of fear.

"Yes, butterfly, I would never keep something that harms you, especially if you're carrying one of my bambini."

I moved closer to him, sitting on his lap with one leg on each side of his waist.

"Are you ready?" I asked, biting my lip in anticipation of the test.

"I was born ready to be the father of our children." Our eyes lowered as I placed the test there.

Tears began to fall down my face, a spontaneous smile spreading across my lips as I saw the positive sign.

"We're going to have a baby," I whispered in awe, as I hadn't expected this news that day.

My husband turned me around, laying me on the bed, his body covering mine.

"I'm going to be a father." The excitement was clear in the glowing look in his eyes.

"Oh, heavens, I've always dreamed of being a mother." His lips touched mine, starting a slow kiss, his hand lifting my dress and revealing my panties, but his focus was elsewhere.

Running his hand over my flat belly, Valentino kissed my abdomen.

"I promise to protect you from all the evil in this world, my child, I promise to love you unconditionally until my last breath," he whispered, making me burst into more tears.

Valentino proved to be what I least expected; perhaps when I married him, I had the thought that he was a big jerk, which wasn't entirely untrue. It might have been due to his family background. But my husband is the best husband I could have hoped for.

But that was obvious; we still had a whole life ahead of us, and this pregnancy was just the beginning of everything we would go through together. But one thing I was sure of: Valentino Vacchiano was my Don, my mafioso, my husband, my man, and I was far too jealous of him, just as he was of me. And God, how I loved this possessive and controlling Italian.

Valentino chose me when he decided to become the Don of the Cosa Nostra, and my heart chose him when his touched mine.

EPILOGUE ONE

Valentino

A Few Months Later...

Next to my wife's bed, on the hospital crib, were our two children. Yulia kept her eyes closed; it was a struggle to get her to sleep.

It was a scheduled delivery due to the twin pregnancy. The obstetrician had been monitoring all the appointments, preparing for an early arrival if necessary. That's what happened, but despite the injections my wife received to speed up their lung development, both came out healthy, even if they arrived earlier than expected.

I positioned myself next to the crib, wearing a blue robe, admiring the small bundle with a lot of black hair. The boy had so much hair that some strands even fell across his forehead.

I lifted my hand, running the tip of my finger over his cheek. We had already decided on their names: Raffaele Vacchiano, the future Don of the Cosa Nostra, my son, my successor, my heir.

"Do you want a cloth? He's drooling," I turned my face to meet my wife's beautiful eyes; her voice was weak and sleepy.

"Have you told her that our children are the most beautiful little creatures?" I declared proudly, feeling honored to be the father of that boy.

"Even if he looks like me?" My wife had that proud smile.

"You're saying that because he has your dark hair, but let me tell you something, he has my nose..."

"He has the nose of a baby Titi," she teased affectionately.

My eyes shifted to the other crib on the other side of the bed, that pink blanket, knowing that there lay the future headache of my life. Every man has a punishment, and mine would be that, being the father of a daughter.

I moved to the other side of my wife's bed, focusing on that little pink bundle.

"Can I buy a chastity belt for her? Is she our daughter or my mother's?" I asked jokingly, as our little Verena had a lot of blonde hair just like my mother's.

"I don't think even your mother's children looked as much like her as this granddaughter does," my wife whispered, smiling at our baby girl.

"Raffaele might have a baby's nose, but our Verena has her grandmother's nose, small and pointed, even the shape of her mouth, living up to her name, eh, daughter," I concluded with pride.

"That means we both know we're going to have problems, because if your mother is already beautiful, just imagine this little one..."

"Did you have to remind me of that now?" I grimaced, unwilling to accept that one day my daughter would need to find a boyfriend, a husband...

"Husband, I'm afraid. I'm informing you," Yulia said with a teasing smile.

"I didn't make you suffer, did I? I don't need to be scolded for my mistakes, right?"

"Do you want me to remind you of the past two years?" I took a step toward her, lifting my hand to run it through her black hair.

"You can throw it in my face, after all, I deserve it. You gave me a world, while I messed up two years of your life. But I confess there's one thing I don't regret, something you already know, because if it weren't for that, I wouldn't have you all to myself..."

"Crazy Italian," my wife interrupted me.

"Crazy in love with the most beautiful woman," I murmured, lowering my face to kiss her forehead.

"Not now, okay? I'm exhausted, with deep dark circles under my eyes..."

"Beautiful, Yulia Vacchiano, you're stunning, even more perfect after bringing our two reasons for living into the world. There's no way not to become a madly in love man. I love you, I love every detail of you, I love your post-partum version, and I'm sure I'll love the mother of our children. My face close to hers was taking in all her details.

"Our children... our... mine and yours..." she smiled, blinking those black lashes.

"Two little things that came from our love." I caressed her face, touching her lips.

A knock on the door made me pull away from her. I looked up and saw my mother and father passing through the entrance.

No one knew the names of our children yet, just as Yulia and I decided to keep the mystery from them.

"Where are Grandma's grandkids?" My mother came proudly toward the baby's crib, followed by my father.

They both smiled when they saw our daughter. I stayed by my wife's side, holding her fingers, my hand intertwined with her tiny hand.

"At least I can say that someone looks like me." Mom sniffled, taking the tissue my father handed her, wiping her tears. "Thank you, dear. Look at this, Tommie, she looks just like me, my granddaughter looks just like her grandma."

Verena wouldn't stop crying, needing constant attention to wipe her tears.

"Someone had to take after the Swiss blood," Dad said mockingly. "But can we end the mystery now? We want to know the names of our grandchildren."

"What do you think, dear?" I looked at my wife, who, with a smile, nodded. "This is our Verena. I swear we had chosen this name before she came with this look, maybe she was thinking, why not come to torment my father and have the beauty of my grandmother..."

"Are you serious?" Mom couldn't help but throw herself into my arms, crying copiously in her joy.

"Yes, why not name my daughter after my mother who has always been by my side." I stroked her blonde hair.

Mom pulled away, looking at my wife, going to her and hugging Yulia, who was also crying with emotion at that moment.

"It seems like little Raffaele doesn't like the attention being given to his sister," I said, seeing my son starting to fuss in his crib.

"Raffaele?" Dad asked, looking surprised.

"Yes, why?"

"A name with presence for a new Don, I like it. Raffaele Vacchiano, the future of the Cosa Nostra." Tommaso's eyes sparkled as he looked at my son, who was fussing impatiently.

My eyes focused on that scene, my family, my wife, my newborn children, knowing that this was exactly what I wanted for my life: a wife I loved and healthy children.

Damn, I was one lucky bastard, even though I didn't deserve everything Yulia gave me, everything she represented in my life, I was selfish enough to never leave her, to make her remember every day how much I loved her, how important she was to me.

I was Valentino Vacchiano, and she was my First Lady, the woman chosen to be mine, who stole my heart with her sweet nature. I loved her with everything inside me.

And now I loved her even more for giving me the chance to be a father.

EPILOGUE TWO

Yulia

Four Years Later...

"Valentino Vacchiano knows I hate surprises," I complained with that blindfold over my eyes, my husband's hand on my waist guiding me out of the house.

"I'm sure you're going to love this one." His voice close to my ear made me shiver.

My feet dragging on the ground, I realized we were outside, stopping to walk and turning around, knowing that at that moment he was making me face him, removing the blindfold from my eyes, blinking several times to adjust to the daylight.

"Are you ready?" he asked with that half-smile, mischievous.

"Depends." I bit the corner of my lip nervously.

My husband turned me around, and leaning against the sidewalk, I saw a motorcycle, my mouth opening in an admiring "oh." The motorcycle was white with some pink details.

"It's beautiful," I whispered in awe, walking towards it.

I could hear my husband's footsteps behind me, my fingers itching to touch it, stopping beside it and sliding my hand over it.

"If it's not mine, we're going to have a big problem," I declared as I felt Valentino's hand wrap around my waist.

"It's yours, my butterfly. Now you can stop borrowing one of my big bikes. Although I'm still scared, at least this one isn't as powerful as his." I turned in his arms.

His green eyes met mine, touching the back of my husband's neck, I pulled his head close to mine, our lips meeting.

"I loved the surprise, my Don," I murmured, biting his lip.

"Does this mean *tie me up in your apartment, my Don*?" He pressed my body against his.

"You know I love it when you tie me up, don't you?" I whispered, just the memory of those scenes making me wet.

If there was one thing I loved, it was our getaways to my husband's BDSM apartment, where we let all our sadomasochistic instincts take over, surrendering to him as he surrendered to me.

I was never one to shy away from new experiences, and when Valentino began to introduce me further into that world, I felt drawn to it, becoming his submissive when we were there, trying every type of position, and oh God, I loved it all. I loved being his submissive in that apartment; it was as if when we went through the door, we were different people, the Don and the submissive, and afterward, when we left, we were the couple, where submission had no place, as my free-spirited mouth never allowed such a thing.

"Wow," we turned our faces seeing our Raffa running towards us. "What a cool bike, Mommy..."

His little fingers immediately started touching the paint, his black eyes shining with delight.

"How about taking a ride with your mother, my son?" Valentino released my waist and grabbed the pink helmet from the bike seat.

"I'm going to get my helmet," the little one said, running off to the garage where his helmet was kept.

"As if he would ever say no," I teased affectionately.

"He may look like you, but he's a born Vacchiano." My husband positioned himself in front of me, placing the helmet on my head.

Years could pass, and he wouldn't lose that exaggerated protective essence. I stepped out of my heels, standing barefoot, watching my four-year-old son already with his helmet on. Raffaele was as adventurous as his father; we didn't take long rides when he was with us, as he had his small bike, which we used on a terrain designed for him to ride on.

I got on the bike first, Valentino placed him sitting in front of me, and I started the bike, hearing the roar echo.

"Go, Mommy, accelerate." The little one tapped my arm subtly, urging me to go faster.

That was so like him; Raffa was electric, always impulsive, never straying from his father. I accelerated the bike, but not too quickly, as I was cautious with my son, just taking a short ride and stopping in front of our house.

"Is that all?" Raffaele complained, getting off the bike, removing his helmet, and running back to the garage.

I took off my helmet, looking at my husband.

"Definitely, that boy is a born Vacchiano," I teased affectionately.

"Anyone who disagrees is crazy." My husband helped me off the bike.

"I loved the surprise, my Italian." I hugged him around the waist.

"Later, you and I will take a ride. We both know where it's headed." Biting my lower lip, we stepped away.

His hand intertwined with mine as we reentered the house, hearing the sweet, delightful laughter of our daughter, walking into the living room where I found her next to her grandmother. The two Verenas were inseparable, and they had even confused people into thinking they were mother and daughter.

"Mommy, look how pretty the doll is that Grandma and I did her hair," my daughter said, lifting her blue eyes towards me and showing the doll.

"It's beautiful, my love." I moved closer to them.

Verena was the grandmother in every detail, even in patience, in the loving way she viewed everything, always delicate, observant, a little crystal, which made her father even more protective.

"Grandma, shall we show our doll to Bella and Giulia?" she asked about the cousins, daughters of Santino and Cinzia.

"Yes, my dear." The grandmother got up from the sofa, brushing her dress, a movement mirrored by her granddaughter, both doing the same with their dresses. "By the way, beautiful bike, my daughter-in-law, although I think it's a bit crazy."

"Motorcycles are dangerous, Mommy." My daughter made a funny face.

I took a step towards her, pulling her into my arms, holding my little one in my lap.

"I'm much more relieved that you think so." I kissed her forehead.

"Where's Raffa?" my mother-in-law asked.

"I saw him running to Pietra's house," my husband replied.

Inside the gated community, being a safe place, we always let them run freely.

"He'll probably bother cousin Tommie," Verena said, knowing how much of a terror her grandson could be.

"Are we going to Aunt Cinzia's house, Mommy?" my daughter asked.

"Mommy will be right there, okay?" I smiled, winking.

She nodded, getting off my lap, grabbing her doll from the sofa, giving her little hand to her grandmother. I turned my eyes to my husband, who was watching our daughter.

"Is there a way to pause time? Can I make her stop growing? I'm so screwed; she's too good for this world." Valentino grumbled, making me smile.

"Husband, calm down, she's only four years old..."

"That's enough time for everyone to notice she'll be a copy of her grandmother and want to take advantage of her," he complained, making me walk towards him.

There were a few instances where Valentino slipped, times when I caught him gripping his hand hard enough to hurt himself. At first, it wasn't easy, but he was strong, always asking for help when he felt he couldn't manage. It had been about a year since he last self-harmed or had any crises; it was a long process, but we overcame it.

"No one will take advantage of our girl; what she has the most are men to protect her— you, her grandfather, her brother. Have you seen Raffa defending his sister?"

"He loves her openly, protects her as if she were me and Santino, but in a different version," he teased, pulling me by the waist. "Luckily, we're not at risk of having more children. Can you imagine me as the father of another girl? I'd go crazy; I don't know how Santino manages it."

"Or how he thinks he manages, right? Because Cinzia almost goes crazy with your brother's excessive protection." I shook my head.

"I need to go to the office; after all, Matteo called me from his family trip and said he sent me an email." He rolled his eyes.

"That man doesn't know the meaning of vacation, does he?" I smiled, remembering the *consigliere* of the Cosa Nostra.

Valentino gave me a gentle kiss on the lips, turned, and headed towards the stairs.

I watched him for a long time, recalling all our moments together, the times he was jealous when we went to parties and someone looked at me by chance, or the times he loved me all night long, his large hands on my body, the way only he knew how to love me.

Valentino had every chance of becoming an arrogant husband over time, but his heart opened up to me, and it was impossible not to give myself completely to him.

If there was one thing our marriage could never be called, it was monotonous. We fit together, we completed each other, sometimes even argued, because who was I trying to fool, no marriage was perfect, but I loved my Don, my mafioso.

THE END.

EPILOGUE THREE - BONUS

Tommaso

I entered the dining room, seeing my son pulling out a chair in the center of the table and making a gesture for me to go to him.

"That seat is your father's today." Valentino, who always had the imposing presence of a Don, shook his head for me to sit in that spot.

"No, it ceased to be mine when you became the Don." I shook my head as well, feeling an arm around my waist.

"No, Daddy, today that seat belongs to the man who raised us." I turned my face to see my eldest, my daughter, that little rascal I saw running around the house.

She was a married woman, mother to a boy. Obviously, it wasn't the marriage I had hoped for her; in fact, I had never hoped for any marriage for Pietra. My little girl should have remained my little girl forever. But she married, and I know Enrico was the best for her. I could never have expected anything different for Pietra. Enrico loved my daughter like no other man could and endured all her pampering, because my girl was raised to have the best.

"You know this is just another date, right?" I grumbled as my daughter guided me to the center of the table.

"It's 67 years, Daddy. Not every year you reach this age with such grandeur," Santino, with his usual mocking tone, appeared next to his brother.

"Of course, because next year I'll be 68." I rolled my eyes as I sat down in the chair.

"Precisely why we need to celebrate every year as if it were the last." Pietra bent down, looking into my eyes, those beautiful green orbs, my little girl, she would always be my little girl.

"Which reminds me that this year your husband turns 65." I caressed her delicate cheek.

"With the bearing of a 40-year-old." Pietra never cared about Enrico's age; on the contrary, the way she loved him went far beyond age.

"One day, maybe he'll overcome the fact that I'm more loved by his daughter than he is." Enrico appeared next to his wife, holding her hand, leading her to her seat at the table, pulling out the chair for her to sit.

"You're her second love; I'll always be the first." I shrugged, competing with the man who practically grew up with me.

At that moment, we were interrupted by my other girls, Bella, Giulia, and Verena, my three granddaughters. I never imagined that one day I would have the house so dominated by women.

Bella had grace, Giulia was the little whirlwind, and Verena had the shyness and delicacy of her grandmother. Even if we wanted to, we couldn't compare our children with my wife in terms of appearance and behavior.

I thought having a daughter, seeing her married, would end my worries, but now I had three granddaughters, and all three were incredibly beautiful. Damn, I was so screwed.

The girls came towards me. I stood to the side, receiving a hug from Giulia first. That little whirlwind wouldn't let anyone go before her.

"Congratulations, *nonno*," she gave me a tight hug, her little hands resting on the back of my neck. Giulia had heavy hands and knew how to give hugs tighter than any of my other grandchildren.

She pulled away, followed by her sister, who hugged me. Bella was the tallest of the girls, almost two years older than the other two.

She resembled her father a lot, with green eyes, dark brown hair, and the tanned skin of the Vacchianos. In contrast, her sister looked a lot like Cinzia, short, with blonde hair, blue eyes, an oval face, and that always contagious smile.

Bella hugged me, her arm brushing gently against my neck.

"Congratulations, *nonno*," Bella's voice was graceful as she stepped away from my side.

Lastly, the little copy of my wife. It was strange to look at that little thing and not see my wife.

"*Nonno.*" Verena took a delicate step towards me. "Congratulations..."

She extended a drawing, which I took, seeing that it depicted all of us. She inherited her mother's talent; at four years old, she drew very well for her age.

"Come here, *mia bambina.*" I extended my arm. Unlike her cousins, she took it, showing her shyness even with relatives, just as my Verena was when she married me.

Although she always had a sharp tongue, she was always delicate and shy.

I hugged the little one, tucking the drawing into my shirt pocket, watching as the three girls took their seats at the table.

My grandsons burst into the dining room.

"Raffaele, how many times have I told you not to run in here?" Yulia scolded her son.

"Sorry, Mom." Without looking at her, he flashed a mischievous smile at me.

My grandson, the future Don of the largest Italian mafia, came towards me, throwing himself into my arms.

"Congratulations, *nonno.*" His mouth came close to my ear. "Can we celebrate in the hideout?"

He whispered, directing those bright black eyes at me, just as his father's were in childhood. This Vacchiano was the same, but unlike the pressure put on Valentino, I didn't want that for him. But of course, I wouldn't miss taking him on our secret adventures.

I winked at him in agreement; it was our secret, mine, his, and Tommie's. After all, what kind of grandfather would I be if I didn't spoil my grandchildren?

My last grandchild hugged me. Tommaso, the blend of the Ferraris and the Vacchianos, was perfect. Tommie had made it clear several times that he would follow in the mafia's footsteps, just like Raffaele, the pride of the Cosa Nostra.

The table was complete. My whole family gathered, my children with their spouses, my grandchildren playing together and laughing.

If there could be a greater fulfillment than this, I was unaware of it. My family, whom I always thought I wouldn't have, had the complete package. Yet something was missing, her, the woman who made all this possible.

My eyes turned toward the entrance of the dining room, seeing my little thing, the love of my life. It had been over 34 years in a marriage that had everything to go wrong.

Verena was my sunshine, the first thought of my days, my wife. She would always be the only woman who touched my heart and shaped me to be better for my family.

Standing in front of me, I rose from my chair, running my hand through her blonde hair, pushing it back.

"Thank you for making me a better man, thank you for never giving up on me even though I was a bit arrogant, thank you for making all this possible." I lowered my face, pressing my lips to hers.

"Husband." Her delicate voice filled my senses. "I love you, my crazy Italian..."

We turned to look at our children, our daughters-in-law and son-in-law, the best grandchildren anyone could have.

I loved each of them and couldn't imagine a life different from the presence of each one of those who were there.

I, Tommaso Vacchiano, who once had nothing, *today had everything.*

Did you love *Bound by Shadows*? Then you should read *Fate's Gamble* by Amara Holt!

Fate's Gamble: A Mafia Romance

When **Matteo**, the brooding **consigliere** of the Italian mafia, takes a spontaneous trip to **Las Vegas**, he's not looking for love. Haunted by a **traumatic past**, Matteo has sworn off family and commitment. But fate has other plans. In the city of lights and endless possibilities, he crosses paths with **Billie**, a spirited woman who embodies everything he never knew he needed.

One **chance encounter**. One unforgettable night. And one surprise that changes everything—a **baby**.

As Matteo and Billie are thrust together by **destiny**, they must navigate a world filled with **dangerous secrets**, powerful enemies, and unexpected alliances. In a game where hearts and lives are on the line, Matteo will have to confront the **demons** of his past if he wants a chance at a future he never thought possible.

But in the high-stakes world of **love** and loyalty, will Matteo's fears be stronger than the growing bond between them? Or will Billie be the one to break through his hardened exterior and show him that sometimes, taking a **gamble** on love is the only way to win?

Fate's Gamble is a thrilling, **emotionally charged** romance that will keep you hooked from the first page to the last. Perfect for fans of mafia romance, forbidden love, and unexpected twists, this book is a must-read for anyone who believes in the power of **destiny**.

About the Author

Amara Holt is a storyteller whose novels immerse readers in a whirlwind of suspense, action, romance and adventure. With a keen eye for detail and a talent for crafting intricate plots, Amara captivates her audience with every twist and turn. Her compelling characters and atmospheric settings transport readers to thrilling worlds where danger lurks around every corner.